Mission Improbable:

Vietnam

A Blanche Murninghan Mystery

Mission Improbable:

Vietnam

A Blanche Murninghan Mystery

Nancy Nau Sullivan

Light Messages
Durham, NC

Published 2022, by Light Messages
www.lightmessages.com
Durham, NC 27713 USA
SAN: 920-9298

Paperback ISBN: 978-1-61153-428-3
Ebook ISBN: 978-1-61153-429-0
Library of Congress Control Number: 2022933235

For the soldiers

"The way is not in the sky.
The way is in the heart."
—The Buddha

Prologue

1969

HE WAS DEEP ASLEEP under the cover of his poncho. The ground was hard and damp, but he'd fallen into dreamland easily—into a Fourth of July picnic at a park on the coast of Florida. The red and white fireworks burst over the turquoise Gulf; his high school buddies were swilling beer they'd persuaded an older sibling to buy for them. Another explosion lit up the dark blue sky, and he smashed the can in his fist. The crackle of metal on metal felt good. It was a great night to be alive.

The next explosion woke him up. He was not back in the world. He was in Vietnam, awakened from a holiday, and he was paralyzed with fear. Now he could hear shouting and feet stomping past his hootch. The metal on metal was the grinding of his teeth. The popping of unfriendly fire from AK-47s shot off around him. Then tubing. *Mortars.* He had four seconds before the mortar landed. But where? The sound of fire was coming from all directions.

He peeked out from under the poncho. The inky Vietnam night was the blackest he'd ever seen, except for the red and white flashes of weaponry. The pungent smell of gunpowder, like burnt steak, a metallic odor, assailed him.

Boots pounded, the sergeant running. Yelling. "You pick up rifles. Double time. Now."

And go where?

He grabbed his rifle and shoved his feet into his boots. Wearing only boxers, he crept out into the night.

Keep a low profile, the lieutenant had said.

How low can I go?

Dark figures scurried among the humps of canvas. They wore khaki shorts. Not American issue. They moved slowly and wildly. Viet Cong. *Inside the perimeter!*

He hit the dirt and held his M-16 level with his head. His hands were shaking, but he kept the rifle steady. He got off several rounds. Hoped one hit Charlie. He recoiled at the thought he'd aimed at one of their own. Too late. His eyes burned, but he began to adjust to the darkness in the light of the flares.

He belly-crawled backward, away from the VC. They seemed to move in teams of threes or sixes. There had to be dozens of them! His legs twitched and scrabbled over the dirt. He needed to get back to his poncho. And back home, the sooner, the better. He was beyond afraid, sweating with fright.

The lieutenant ran by, his boots stirring up the hilltop. The fine red cloud rose in bursts of dry fog. It clogged the sinuses and filtered the ambient light. He shouted from a few feet away. "You locked and loaded, Mac?"

It was hard to talk, the words stuck in his throat: *Oh, sure, of course. What the hell?*

"Sir, yes, sir!" He held up his rifle. His insides constricted.

The lieutenant was cool. *Was he smiling?* He aimed his rifle at the small khaki-clad VC running toward them.

And the rifle jammed.

The lieutenant held up the useless thing. He reversed the weapon and rammed it into the attacker's torso as his legs skittered for advantage. The VC grunted. A strangled cry. His AK-47 rose above his head, and he fell. The lieutenant turned away, determination hunching his shoulders. He was still clutching the M-16 close to his chest when the soldier slowly rose up like a ghost. The glare illuminated the blade of a knife.

"Lieutenant!" A shot blasted a hole in the middle of the enemy soldier as he lunged at the officer. The lieutenant looked around for the source of the gunfire that had saved him. He grinned maniacally, his face rimmed in sweat and fear and dirt in the firelight.

It was over.

The sergeant stomped past them, announcing the end of it. "All secure."

The dust clouds were still rising. Men staggered by, and the half-dead moaned in the early morning.

The lieutenant clapped the shooter on the back, the peace medallion catching the light. "Good work, soldier."

The soldier's rifle was still hot and poised. He watched the lieutenant lope away. Relief slowly loosened his arms and legs, untightening his stomach. He looked around for the latrine. But he couldn't move. He saw a faint white line in the eastern sky. Another f-ing day.

All secure.

One

2003

THE GIRL WAS WATCHING from a corner at the Peel 'n Eat pier. The wind off the Gulf blew the long black hair across her face, but Blanche could see that stare perfectly well. It was unnerving and steady. Almost a challenge.

"Hey!" Blanche called out, but the girl pulled back and was gone. Blanche shrugged. She yanked the fishing pole at the stubborn sheepshead circling the pilings. Wiggled the line. Nothing. She squinted across the pier toward the concession. Nothing there either. Blanche was beginning to feel like that fish, her mind zigzagging off to nowhere after no one.

The late afternoon was hot, the blue water taking on the milky hue of low-hanging clouds, and her beer was losing its frost. She gulped the last of it. For a dollar, there wasn't a better draft bargain in Florida. But she wasn't here to drink beer, or fish, really. She'd crept away from daily duties to think without interruption.

But there was that girl again with those almond-shaped eyes. She looked Blanche's way, now hesitantly, her gaze zipping off when caught. Blanche checked herself all over. Nothing unusual, just Blanche in cut-offs and a T-shirt, swilling beer, sweating. The humid frenzy of curls stuck to the back of her neck. She wished the girl would get on with it. Say *something*.

What the heck? Where'd she go now?

Blanche was about to pack up and go home. She glanced once more into the deep. Gray stripes swished by in the dark water. The fish was back. It nibbled and flipped its tail and took off. "*Damn!*"

"Sorry 'bout that!" The girl, like a sylph, was at Blanche's ear.

Blanche was startled, annoyed, and the fishing pole wobbled in her grasp and clattered onto the deck.

"Jean McMahon." The girl offered her hand, but when Blanche hesitated, she tucked it away awkwardly.

"Blanche Murninghan." Blanche realized this Jean was not a girl but probably more like her: a person in her early 30s. She was tall and thin with silvery skin. Her features open and warm. And those eyes. She looked right through Blanche with a down-to-earth directness. Now Blanche was not annoyed, and she didn't hesitate to open up.

"Been after that fish all afternoon." Blanche grinned and picked up the fishing pole. "Guess it doesn't matter."

"The one that got away." Wistful, her movements unhurried, Jean sat down next to Blanche

and settled her shoulder bag in her lap.

"How did you know?" *Can this Jean McMahon read my mind?*

"I *don't* know." Jean curled her long hair over her ears. "Why? Did someone get away?"

Blanche drew a breath and clamped her mouth shut, but it was no use. *Open yer mouth and tell all ya know.* Blanche could hear Gran saying it, but the words never sank in. Blanche had no filter. It's how she earned her nickname: "Bang." Right off the hip. Out with it before she even thought about it.

She turned to Jean. "I shot my Mexican boyfriend."

"Oh, my. I'm sorry." Jean drew back, but she didn't seem put off; rather, she smiled sympathetically.

"I was *not* trying to get rid of him. It was an accident! He's all right, I think. But I haven't heard from him in a week." Blanche stared out at the Gulf. *Why am I blabbing about this? 'Cause, that's what I do.*

"That's awful. I'm really sorry to bother you." Jean made no move to get up and go away, but Blanche was all right with it.

"It was a terrible misunderstanding." Blanche was glum, and suddenly weary, thinking of the whole mess. "But that's another story."

Jean inclined her head, clearly eager for the details.

"I'm glad you came along," Blanche said. "I'm obsessing over it, and I need to stop. I miss him. A lot. He's coming here on a fellowship, but now he has to wait a year." Two pelicans hovered and dove into a wave. The long silver path of sunlight on the water signaled the end of the afternoon.

Jean nodded and crossed her long legs. "That's awful. I mean, about shooting him, and all. But I'm glad he's all right." A sandal twitched at the end of her toe, and she stole a look at Blanche. "You'll see him someday. Won't you?"

"I hope so." Blanche sighed and jiggled her empty cup. It was definitely the cocktail hour. *Somewhere.* "Want a beer?"

"Sure..."

Jean made a move, but Blanche leapt up and headed toward the Peel 'n Eat concession. If there was one thing she was quick about, it was quenching her thirst. She came back with two Bud Lights.

They sat in companionable silence, the cool evening approaching, still and calm—except for the birds and their final squawking and dipping for the day. The inevitable parade of bedraggled beachgoers retreated past the pier to their houses for a shower, dinner, and the news.

Jean's gaze fixed on the Gulf. Her eyebrows, like perfect black wings, drew down while Blanche's thoughts wandered. She loved this hour when the heat of the afternoon slipped away. She didn't mind sharing it with this girl. Something intriguing was going on here.

"You didn't come here to fish." Blanche perched herself on the edge of the bench, careful with the sloshing plastic cup.

"No. I did not." Jean's tone was flat and sad. "I came out to see you. I've been looking for you, and I found you."

"You could have called."

"Nope, couldn't call. I needed to see you face to face."

"Well, here I am. You found me." It couldn't have been that difficult. She was usually at the newspaper arguing with Clint Wilkinson–her boss and editor at the *Island Times*–or walking the beach in front of her cabin on Tuna Street. Or throwing back a tequila or two with her friend, Liza, or eating, eating, eating with her cousin Haasi, who lately had taken to sailing and was now on her way to Aruba. "It's not like I'm hiding. I'm pretty much a creature of habit. Or rut."

Jean laughed and sipped her beer. "Habit? Rut? I'd say the last year or so has been unusual. Even memorable. Kidnapping? Solving murders? Exposing mummies in Mexico City?"

"You know all that?" Blanche couldn't conceal her amazement even if she tried, which she usually didn't.

"There *are* newspapers. You work for one," said Jean.

"Yeah, but the *Island Times*?"

"Word gets out."

Blanche was aware of that. The adventures of Blanche had gotten around, for better and for worse. "It's been a trip. Especially lately." She looked out across the water. "Wish Emilio could come up from Mexico."

"He'll be here, but that'll be a while. Right? You do have some time now?"

"Yup."

"You're not tied up with some new adventure?"

"I've got time. Nothing much going on." She raised her eyebrows. "How about *you*?" Blanche leaned off the bench and gave the fishing pole a good yank, but the sheepshead had moved on. For good, it seemed. She tucked the pole under the bench. She had other fish to fry with this girl who had appeared out of nowhere and wanted to be her new best friend.

"I've got quite a lot going on."

"Like?"

For an answer, Jean nodded. "That's why I'm here. You're kind of famous. Locally. For your, er, detective skills, mostly."

"Famous? Detective skills? That's hilarious."

"Yeah, well, you have a reputation for grabbing hold of something and not letting go."

"There's that. But so do lots of people."

"I need your help." Now she had a new urgency in her tone.

"Really? Why?"

"My dad's gone. He died recently." Her lips trembled, and she took a deep breath. "I need to find my mother."

"I'm so sorry, Jean." Blanche touched Jean's arm, gently. "Is your mom lost?"

"Not exactly."

"Have you checked with the police?"

"That wouldn't do much good."

There was that hesitancy again, the quiet before the drop. The pause that was not refreshing. Blanche could feel it like the weather had changed. She studied Jean's expression.

"She isn't here, Blanche." Jean unclenched her fingers, and her voice rose. "She's in Vietnam, somewhere, and I don't know where. I need your help finding her. In Vietnam."

Two

Let it Rip

BLANCHE STOOD IN FRONT of the open closet door and stared up at the box on the top shelf. She'd never touched it, but she knew that one day she would, and that day had come. Jean had ripped something open inside Blanche, a small compartment of love and worry and curiosity that had remained closed and hidden deep. Until now.

Vietnam!

The word itself had always made her stop what she was doing and fight off a sharp little stab of pain. It wasn't a constant pain. No one had talked much about Vietnam in all the years she grew up on Santa Maria Island. Vietnam was far away, and she had little knowledge of her connection to this Southeast Asian country on the other side of the world, except that her father had been killed there, and he never knew her. Didn't even know she'd been born. The pain of that alone was always there, just waiting for a poke.

She didn't move from the open closet door. Her body was leaden, the weight of memory holding her in place. The last time the box was taken down from that shelf, Gran was alive and caring for Blanche in place of the mother she'd lost in a car accident.

Blanche had found Gran one morning, sitting on the floor rooting through piles of papers and photos, arranging them neatly around her, and crying. Blanche was six, maybe seven. The sun slanted through the screen, lighting Gran's cloud of white hair and her teary cheeks.

She looked up then and saw Blanche standing there with a pail and shovel, still in her pajamas, just out of bed and ready for the beach. She dropped her beach toys with a clatter and ran to her grandmother, smoothed the hair, hugged her. "Gran, why are you crying." It wasn't a question, but insistence, tinged with the incredulity of a child who had never seen such a thing.

"I'm not." She wiped her face with the back of her hand. "It's just this humidity."

She held a photo of a young man in a white T-shirt, a large gun in his hand. Blanche peered at it. He was smiling, standing in front of a palm tree, with handsome, broad shoulders. "Who's that? Why's he got a gun like that? Do you know him?" Blanche snuggled closer. *For protection? Understanding?* Her grandmother hastily put the papers back into the box. She left the photo until last, finally placing it on top.

"Someday you'll know. Not today. Now, get your swimsuit on, and let's go dig coquinas."

The diversion was set, the photo packed away. Blanche loved nothing better than going to the beach with her grandmother, digging down at the water's edge for the wiggling coquinas, each no bigger than a fingernail. She brought up handfuls, arranged them according to color, memorized the marbleized pastel shells, and returned them to the Gulf. Once she and Gran had made coquina soup, but it was a cooking failure. Coquinas were better left to the Shell World to enjoy the warm water and white sand. Blanche remembered that morning, jumping up and down with her grandmother in the waves, and just for a flickering moment, she remembered seeing the photo for the first time, a memory long buried and now flaring into life.

Blanche ran her fingers over the rim of the box. She'd known what was in it, but even with Gran gone, she still had not been able to take it down.

Then Jean showed up.

She'd stirred up those hidden questions in Blanche like bitter little seeds that never sprouted, until now. Questions about her father, killed in a rice paddy a couple of months before Blanche was born. Curiosity did not waste one minute. Blanche was never good at hiding things away. It was true what Jean said: When Blanche got hold of something, she couldn't let go.

Jean was coming back, and she wanted Blanche's help. Blanche was leery, and hopeful, all at once. A search was a search. *Never know what will turn up. Not until I dig.*

She needed to tell Jean about her father. When the time was right.

Blanche carried the box to the dining area and set it on the round table. The windows to the porch were open, the wind was light, the pines barely whistling. The Gulf was flat and blue. Her world was waiting.

She couldn't wait a minute longer.

The photo was on top, just where Gran had placed it more than twenty-five years before. Blanche put her fingers on the shiny black and white surface, willing the young man to come alive in her mind. White T-shirt, great smile. A black curl on his forehead. Blanche held the photo up next to her face at the wall mirror, and that numb little spot in her heart woke up. The resemblance was striking.

She turned the picture over: "Sp/4 Thomas X. Fox, cleaning M-16, ready for patrol. April, '70." Her father. She'd once heard her cousin Jack say Thomas Fox had had some college behind him, attended Recondo training in Vietnam, and then had gone from private to specialist quickly.

Thomas Fox was the image of a happy young man, someone confident and fit, and most likely, disbelieving that he would be dead in a month.

She set the photo of him—smiling at her—upright against the potted geranium.

She dug through the papers and letters in the box. *Gran knew I'd be here someday.* Blanche felt the unmistakable, unshakeable spirit of her grandmother, as she often did.

Carefully, she lifted out the documents. Her father in Advanced Infantry Training. Her mother Rose's birth certificate. Her death certificate in 1975 following the car crash. A picture of Rose in shorts holding a speck of a baby, a tiny face and black hair like her mother—*Blanche!* Another photo, a copy of the one framed on the mantel, of Rose. Gran would look at Rose and then at Blanche, and the sadness would go away.

She pulled more papers out of the box.

Letters.

My wonderful Rose,

I just got back from patrol. I'm beat, but I couldn't wait to get a pen and write you 'cause that's all we have now ... the jungle, hours to cut through less than a mile. The heat and humidity smother us during the day; the rains drown us at night...

Rosie,

You should see my dinner, chocolate, all white on the edges, menthol cigarettes, and field rations, prepped flat for easy carry. I put the bag next to my body to heat it up, add water ... the chow's not bad. No, it's bad, and I miss you real bad...

My Rose,

When I get back to the states, I'm gonna scoop you up, and we are going to RUN to the courthouse...

My sweet Rose,

How is that little belly of yours, that rosebud ... I miss you so much...

The last was dated May 2, 1970, just days before he was killed.

The paper was crisp with age, despite the tropical humidity. Some of the bundles were tied in black ribbons. Blanche stacked all of her father's letters separately. The words of her father and the places and people he knew. There were no letters from her mother. Her mother, who'd read these words and probably cried and laughed over them. Blanche closed her eyes and rewound time, picked up a bundle, and held it tightly, squeezing every ghost she could from the well-traveled pages.

At the bottom of the box was an envelope with distinct, florid cursive. Not like the rest. It was addressed to Rose Murninghan. The name on the return address: Margaret Ryan Fox.

Blanche's hand trembled while she opened the envelope, unfolding the letter written on heavy white stationery. It was dated May 17, 1970:

Dear Rose,

We haven't met, so you haven't heard the terrible news until now that I write to you. The young lieutenant and the priest just left hours ago, here to tell me Tommy was killed last week during a reconnaissance patrol north of Saigon. That is all the news they will give me now. They have not recovered his body. There are only witnesses to his cruel death. He was on a mission in the jungle with several other young soldiers. Three were killed. Mortars, grenades,

AK machine guns. What could be so important that one human would annihilate another with such things? It's unspeakable, and it is hard for me to hold on.

My heart is broken, no, shattered until it is no more. But your heart, your dear heart, will be broken, too, so I tell you in hopes you can remember him and the good moments you had together. That's all we can do now. I know they did not notify you, but Tommy sent your address, and he told me about you, how he longed to get back here and be with you again. He asked me some time ago to keep in touch with you, and, sadly, I have not done that. I am very ill. And now I am so deeply saddened I can hardly hold this pen … but please know that I am thinking of you and praying for you, and I would dearly love to see you. I needed to write this, to let you know, and, especially, I needed to tell you how very much he loved you. That will never go away. It lives on. He'll always love you, no matter where he is…

Did Rose ever meet Margaret, Blanche's other "grandmother?" Did she ever know about Blanche? There was never any talk of Margaret and little about Thomas in all the years, and this fed her emptiness. She held the letter against her cheek. It smelled of cedar from its hiding place in the closet. Like the pine trees outside the porch that began to rustle in a swift breeze. A parrot cawed loudly; the gulls swooped in off the beach.

July 10, 1970. Blanche arrived two months after her father's death. He never even knew she was born.

Three

Down Life's Path

"I AM *BUI DOI*," SAID JEAN. "Dust of life."

Blanche looked at Jean, quizzically. They were back at the Peel 'n Eat, drinking beer, with a view of the windy white-capped Gulf of Mexico. Blanche's curiosity simmered. She hardly knew a thing about this Jean McMahon and Vietnam or her dad.

It was all a mystery, and Jean was charging down that path. Gran didn't talk about Vietnam or Thomas Fox. That time rarely came up, and Blanche always got the feeling she was being protected from something. Protected from ugly accidents that had caused great hurt and harm? If Thomas Fox's name were mentioned, Gran's smile would cloud up. Her answer was usually a hug for Blanche and deflection. A word about Rose, who was killed so young, too. That was it. On they went "down life's path," as Gran called it. "Don't look back." For her grandmother, looking back was nothing but pain, and she'd done all she could to spare Blanche.

Blanche had some knowledge of her parents, but not much. She might have been Blanche Fox; she was always Blanche Murninghan. She grew up looking forward, not looking back. The succession of events never presented much of a choice. But this. Here was a real choice—the chance to dig beyond her love for Gran and Rose, back to her father.

Jean had shown up for a reason. There was this compelling business about Jean's mother. And what about Blanche's father?

Blanche gulped her draft. "What do you mean? 'Dust of life,' Jean? Tell me."

"I'm half Vietnamese. My father, Henry James McMahon, was an American soldier."

"Well, here we are. Daughters of the auld sod. My dad was *Mac a'tSionnaigh*."

"Huh?"

"Old Gaelic, son of the fox," said Blanche. "What part of Ireland's McMahon?"

"County Clare."

"Fox and Murninghan—Cork and Monaghan here. Limerick, maybe."

Jean pushed the sunglasses up over her coiled black hair and studied Blanche. "We could be sisters."

"Probably a county or two apart, but, sure." Blanche raised her plastic cup. "*Slainte*. To your health."

"To ours."

She should go on this journey with Jean. Shouldn't she? Blanche wanted answers, and she'd take it on, slowly, but how would she ever do *that*? Probably impossible, given her proclivity to meet life with a bang. For now, she'd try to keep what little she knew about her father close to her. The thought of him was buried deep inside—and somewhere in a place so foreign and unknown to her that sometimes it wrung her out just to think about it. It was her mystery to embrace, and at last, unravel at her own pace.

"And there's something else we have in common," said Jean. "We both lost our fathers to that war, each in our own way. But still…"

Blanche could not hide her surprise. "What's that? How did you know? I didn't say anything about my father. Except that he's Irish."

The wind picked up and drove the ripples across the water and out under the pier. "I think it was in the newspaper," Jean said quickly. "You know. When you became a local celebrity. Routing crooked developers and drug pushers." Blanche searched Jean's eyes for more, but she turned her head.

"I don't remember," Blanche murmured. She was ever reticent to bring up her father, but reticence of any sort was rare for Bang. Jean's remark sparked more questions. Had that line of information about her past been published? She couldn't imagine she'd volunteered it, but now she wasn't certain. Blanche's haphazard filing system of newspaper clippings was decidedly unorganized. She'd have to check this out in the morgue at the *Island Times*. Spend some time riffling through envelopes of ragged, yellow clippings.

Blanche stared into the large plastic cup. She drained it, got up rather woodenly, and went inside the concession stand. She came back with two refills. She handed one to Jean and sat down on the deck, her legs hanging over the side of the pier.

"So." Blanche took a sip and settled herself. Actually, steeled herself, ready to fire away. "Back to Vietnam."

"Yes, our parents," said Jean. "Your dad."

"My father." The word felt distant and unfamiliar, but she loved saying it. "I wish I knew more about him."

"You will."

Blanche turned sharply. "And how do you know that?"

"Because. I just do. Someday you'll know more."

"When? Jean, don't leave it like that."

"Like what? I don't mean to be sketchy, Blanche. I want us to be in this together if you're willing. We'll go on this search. For our parents. For their sake, and ours."

Blanche considered this proposal. "You do have a point. In a way, they're all lost."

It was the wrong thing to say. Jean ran a hand across her forehead, dug her palms into her eyes. "I don't know. I guess you're right. But we'll never find out anything more unless we look."

"Fair enough," Blanche said quietly. "We're both looking for answers." She took a sip, a screech of gulls zooming over the pier. "Tell me about your mother and father."

"I'm proud of them, I love them, but they've left me half and half. Divided between Tampa and Vietnam. My dad's gone, and my mother, Tam Li, is missing. She made a hard decision to give me up, but she did it for the best. I have to believe that. In Vietnam, it would have been a difficult life for me as a child of the enemy. A 'child of dust.'"

"And back then...."

"Brutal. At least, that's what Dad said. When the Communists took over, the country starved. I don't know how many were imprisoned. A million left almost immediately. Who knows how many more tried and failed? Some turned against those who had any vestige of the bourgeoisie—and that's where my mother comes in as a property owner. As if things could have gotten any worse, they had to do that. Turn against one another. My mother was afraid for me. It's why she sent me away to live with my father." Jean's tone was desperate but emphatic. "She saved me. And she was brave to do it. Could you do it? Could you send your only child away, thinking you'd never see her again?"

Blanche slumped over her beer. "How would I know, Jean? It sounds ... terrible, impossible." She'd lost her mother. Not in the same way, but, still, she was gone. "Like you say, your mother did a brave thing. Out of love, people do all kinds of things."

"Yeah, love. Odd, isn't it."

"Takes all forms." Blanche sensed a kinship tightening between them as they talked of their parents in the shadow of Vietnam. "Tell me more about this 'dust.'"

"I should probably start at the beginning...."

Hank and Tam Li met during a moon festival in Hoi An. He was on leave from the Army near Saigon. He'd flown to Danang and gone to the Lotus Hotel in the old town. Her family owned the hotel. Tam Li was sitting at the registration desk, going through a stack of receipts. She smiled at Hank when he walked into the lobby.

"It was a sort of 'electric' meeting, Hank would say, like he sizzled from head to foot just looking at her." Jean laughed. "I love that part of their story. Can you imagine? At a time of war, when everything can go away in an instant? My father said it made everything they did so much more alive because they could be dead before they knew it.

"My mom and dad walked along the river." Jean's eyes lit up. "I want to go there... Where they sat at a table under a longan tree and ate rice wrapped in banana leaves. He told me how beautiful she was and how terrified of the war. He'd tried to reassure her that the war was winding down. That's what they were saying, but it was a lie. It dragged on until my father was wounded and airlifted out of there. They only had a couple of years together."

"Hardly anything," said Blanche. *Like Tom and Rose.*

"But enough for us to come along."

"Jean! You and I were born about the same time. Me, July 1970."

"December here."

They clunked beers. "Do you have pictures? I'd love to see pictures," said Blanche.

"I've got some. They were happy and smiling. I like to think of them like that."

"I hope you find her someday," said Blanche, her voice trailing off. *Maybe we'll both find her.* The possibility of the two reuniting after all these years was appealing. She thought of her own mother, alone, waiting on an island in Florida, and getting the terrible news about Thomas Fox. A mother should be with her daughter, if possible.

The view across the Gulf expanded as the sun came out of the clouds. But it was short-lived.

"It was bad," Jean said. "Not all of it, but most of it. They were together, our parents. And now here we are."

"Yep." Blanche squared her shoulders. "What was your dad's job in the army?"

"Patrols. He re-upped to stay on, so he could be with her. But he took an awful chance. He could have stayed in the rear, but he wasn't the type to sit around. He wanted to go out with the guys, sometimes six soldiers for five days."

"My dad did the same! Could they have known each other? Wouldn't that be crazy?"

Jean's expression was flat. "Blanche, there were half a million troops involved by 1970. But it is possible." Then she stopped. "Even likely."

"Yep. Look at us, sitting here together, almost thirty years later." The sun baked the pier. The heat, the memories, and the curiosity gave her an out-of-body feeling. "Do you know more about their jobs? Were they recon?"

"Listen to you, talking like an old Army hack." Jean grinned. "Yeah, they must've been. Dad said the guys in the infantry didn't like recon. They were the ones who came across the enemy and then called for contact. That meant engagement. He said he wasn't afraid; he said it didn't matter. Being afraid was a luxury, and it was dangerous to waste any energy on it. Besides, they had little energy.

"He had nightmares about those patrols, about hand-to-hand combat, being covered in mud and grease. Calling in the gunships and artillery and dragging his friends out of firefights. It haunted him, and I could see him going away, little by little, before my eyes. Even after all the therapy." Jean frowned. "Maybe my mother knew all that, and that's why she stayed away. She couldn't face the reminders. I don't know, Blanche. He hoped she'd join us. But she didn't, and he was troubled. Right to the end."

"But your mother, Jean? Why..."

"She couldn't leave her family."

"Not even later? After the war ... and everything?" Blanche stopped. Jean's lips were trembling.

"I've always thought there's more to it. But we never knew anything." Jean's eyes implored, drawing Blanche into the tangle of it. "All I know for sure is it's cultural, or at least, that's what dad said. She had an extended family, old relatives who needed her. They had the business to run. She could *not* leave; she wouldn't. After I was born, my dad was wounded and airlifted out of the country. He tried to get me and my mother out of Vietnam, but she wouldn't go.

"Then, she relented. She had no choice. She let me go. I left in Operation Babylift, April of 1975. Arrived in San Francisco with papers sewn into my clothes, my birth certificate, the name of my father, a letter from my mother... I was four. I wore a bonnet. My dad hadn't seen me since I was an infant."

"Wow. Do you remember any of it?"

"Not much. But I still have the bonnet."

"And you have the letter from your mother? There you go."

Jean shook her head as she watched the dark water slap against the pilings. "She wrote it more than twenty-five years ago. No information about where she went. Only that the family needed to move around. At one point, they were in a small village near Saigon. I guess that's something. It's a short letter about how much she loved me and that I would be safe and well growing up in the US with my father, Hank McMahon. That's it. That's about all she ever wrote." She lifted her hands, palms up.

"Can't imagine what she went through. The fear and discomfort, the decisions," said Blanche. "But letters. You never got others?"

"A couple, but they were postmarked Ho Chi Minh City. That's Saigon. He tried to trace them, but nothing. He thinks someone else posted them for her. I don't know. They were brief, a long time ago."

"Seems like those letters would be stepping stones, right to here." Blanche braced her arms on the pier.

"Nope. All dead ends. I'm just catching up, but I haven't been able to find out anything. I've made calls, done some research."

Blanche didn't want to say it. She *tried* not to say it. "Jean, I just don't see how… With all the devastation, the people moving around during the war… How do you suppose you'll ever find her?"

Jean tensed, her mouth shut tight, but then she opened up. "I don't know, Blanche. I don't want to think like that, and I can't help it. Most days, I feel hopeless. I need another set of eyes. I need determination. I need you."

"I don't know whether to be flattered or what. I'm just a person, kind of a Rottweiler at heart…."

"There you go. You need to go with me. Please."

Blanche smiled, her best and brightest. She looked Jean in the eye. "You're making it pretty hard to say no."

They silently drank their beers and stared at the manatees nibbling lettuce thrown to them off the pier. It seemed nearly decided. Blanche was on the verge of tumbling forward with this crazy idea, and she couldn't help herself.

"Dad worked on a plan to find her. I helped him in the end. He was sick, but he really put his heart into it. It's a good plan," Jean said. "You'll see."

Blanche wished they had something more solid than this scant history of her parents. There were too many questions. She and Jean had ties—the war, their mothers gone. Somewhere in that miserable picture, there had to be answers. She took another tack. "I just read letters from my dad to my mother. He was killed in 1970, two months before I was born."

"That's so sad." Jean was sympathetic—and affectionate. And not surprised. "What did he say? Did he give any details about his life over there?"

"Not much. He missed my mother, ate chocolate for dinner. They were going to get married when he got back."

"Yes," she said. That vacant stare again.

Blanche tilted her head. "I still can't believe the coincidence of this."

"Nothing is a coincidence, Blanche."

Blanche drained her beer, upended the cup on the pier, and held it there. "How are you doing, Jean? Your dad's been gone a month?"

"A little more than that. I'm coming around. Now that I have this mission of sorts. With a comrade in arms." She gave Blanche a friendly poke. "Hate to drag you away. I see you're doing well. Nice peaceful life here. It's so beautiful."

Blanche nodded. Santa Maria Island. It sustained her. Developers and drug dealers could come and go, but the sand, sky, and birds remained. That, and her family and friends: Gran's old friend, Cap, her cousins, Jack and Haasi, and Liza. "Yeah, this place is pretty great, isn't it?"

Blanche waited for Jean to say more, but she didn't. She fixed her attention on the clouds puffed up into giant columns on the horizon. "Let's figure this out," said Jean. "Together. We have a lot in common, besides being half Irish."

"We do."

"Your father died there. My father died here, mostly from the war. And my mother? I don't know where she is, and I want to find her." She turned to Blanche. "With your help."

"Why not?" Blanche fiddled with the plastic beer cup. Deep, deep reservations about this whole adventure jumbled her brain.

Jean's urgency did not let up. "We're both children of Vietnam. We are their children." She was a "child of dust," but to Blanche, who knew so little about Vietnamese culture, the term seemed strange and unfortunate. Jean's father was devoted to her, and he longed for Tam Li, the love of his life. There was a lot of love there, and "dust" didn't seem to fit. She gave Jean—a statuesque woman with flawless skin and gleaming hair—a doubtful look.

Blanche began to see her way clear. "We are that, their children. No denyin' it." Blanche set the beer cup down with a deliberate tap. "We should do this."

Four

Up in the Air

BLANCHE AND JEAN WERE ABOUT MIDWAY into the twenty-four-hour trip from Tampa to Ho Chi Minh City (formerly Saigon), with two stops along the way. The sixteen-hour flight from Atlanta to Seoul was the longest. Blanche peeked out the window at the vast blue sky and clouds scudding past at 38,000 feet. She was one meal, one movie, and one nap down. She couldn't believe what she was doing, but she was doing it. It had only been weeks since the two of them sat at the Peel 'n Eat, drinking beer and telling stories.

Jean was asleep in the seat next to her. The girl had been persuasive. Her father, in his dying days, had urged her to make the trip, and he did not want her to go alone. Blanche still thought it odd that Jean had singled her out, but Jean had made a dogged plea for her to go. She'd made the case. Blanche was something of a "detective," and the two Florida girls did have fathers who were tied to the war. In the end, Blanche could not resist the hunt, and Jean laid it out:

Hank McMahon had made thorough arrangements for guides and drivers and left a fat bank account with instructions for procuring visas and flights. He'd done most of this in the waning months of his life—unbeknownst to Jean until he surprised her.

He'd walked her through the steps to return and look for her mother. He handed her the documents she'd arrived with when she was four years old—and then he teared up remembering the call from the State Department back in 1975 informing him that his daughter had arrived! Her first memory was of the palm trees that ringed the swimming pool in their backyard, the park swings, the kids at school who were shy at first but then played nicely. She grew up in the loving care of her father, who never married and gave his daughter his name and all of himself. All those years, he'd held out hope that Tam Li would contact him, but she rarely did. Most of the letters he wrote came back. The hotel where he'd met her had closed up after the war; the family apparently scattered.

Blanche reached under the front seat for her bag and her fingers wrapped around her own trove of documents. She had no idea what she was going to do with it, but she carried it anyway— Margaret Fox's letter and a copy of her father's death certificate, some more photos, some Army papers. Blanche had found all of it in the box; Margaret had sent copies to Rose. Blanche also carried her own birth certificate. She sighed and patted her bag. She would never let go of the papers. They were all she had of Thomas Xavier Fox, blown to bits for all she knew, on or about May 10, 1970.

Thuy met them at the airport entrance after a relatively swift, painless customs procedure. She was tidy and wore a flat-brimmed straw hat and a plaid shirt. Her smile was warm but business-like, her movements quick. "Miss Jean, Miss Blanche. Welcome to Vietnam." The brim of her hat tipped forward slightly. "Please, your baggage." She hustled the two bags through the door and out to the waiting car like they were boxes of cereal.

Blanche shook herself, trying to rid her head of the stupor of too many hours cooped up. She was nearly dizzy from the new smells and confusion.

"You have the reservations? Appointments?" Jean followed close behind Thuy as the guide riffled through a pack of paper.

"Oh, yes, sister. We do it. You will get rest now, and tomorrow I will give you rundown. We will begin visit to Saigon." An accent on the last syllable, hard and emphatic, Sai-GON.

"Funny she doesn't call it Ho Chi Minh City," murmured Blanche.

Jean shrugged. "It's not an unusual reference in the South. They have their way...."

"Now, how do you know so much?" Blanche laughed.

"I don't know anything." Jean's tone grounded Blanche. "I've got a lot to learn."

"*We've* got a lot to learn."

They climbed into the backseat of the Toyota, Thuy into the driver's seat. Her straight little neck, that hat perched just so. Thuy reminded them that they were in a Communist country. She outlined the vagaries of steering clear of authority, keeping their heads down, and relying on her to take the lead. She handily veered into the throng of motorbikes. No one seemed to stop for lights or signs. The vehicles streamed around them, and somehow, no one got run over. At least not that Blanche could see.

Ho Chi Minh City was an outdoor city that bore its history in plain sight; the walls of buildings were pocked and blackened with the dirt of war and the fumes of motorbikes. The sidewalks overflowed with people eating, drinking, cooking, and selling fruit and other wares. Children ran naked; people wore loose-fitting tunics and trousers, their faces staunch and serious in the organized chaos—a tidy, busy city with the occasional hills of garbage.

The unfamiliar mix of sewage and noodles, steamed buns, and mildew wafted into the open window of the Toyota. Blanche could only guess the source of those smells as they sped down the wide street, past the signs, the carts of vendors on the curbs, and the flood of working people. Even as tired as she was, she felt energized; the industry buzzed around her.

She shook Jean's arm. "Can you believe it?" Jean's answer was a dazed expression.

Outside the hotel, Jean and Thuy bowed to each other.

"Thank you," said Jean. "*Cam un.*"

"Jean, I think you just said 'eggplant' or 'cod,'" Blanche whispered. She had been studying Vietnamese, but she hadn't gotten far. The language was confusing, tonal in nature; the letters depended on the accents for meaning, and then there was the influence of French and Portuguese, among others. *Hoa* could mean flower or a suit in a card game. *Ba*, an older woman or the number three.

Thuy held on to her hat, laughing. "No, no, I understand. *Nom Viet* language, very difficult. *Cam un* mean 'thank you.' I get it." Her eyes lit up. "Now, bye, bye, sisters. Tomorrow we begin search for mother. You rest well."

"*Tam biet*," said Blanche with a little bow.

Jean nudged Blanche as they entered the hotel. "Aren't you the one? What's that mean?"

"Goodbye. But don't ask me to say hello."

"*Xin chao*," said Jean. "Blanche, where did you study Vietnamese? Help me. I don't want to be throwing cod and eggplant around."

"I tried to pick up some words and phrases, but I think I'll stop now." The look on her face said no such thing.

They met their bags at the reservations desk. The lobby of the Caravelle Hotel was an expanse of white marble and modern design with a patina of French colonial in the archways and faded velvet armchairs scattered about. Old World elegance running to catch up. Blanche thought of Michael Caine, who'd once sat here drinking tea during the filming of *The Quiet American*.

The journalist in her was delighted. The bar had been a favorite of reporters and photographers who covered the war. Walter Cronkite, Peter Arnett, and Liz Trotta drank here after enduring the "Five O'clock Follies," the press conferences that announced "enemy dead" and "structures destroyed." They were folly for a tendency among the military to twist the truth.

"Blanche, what are you doing? You look a million miles away," said Jean.

"Just thinking."

"Maybe you need a nap," said Jean. They followed their bags to the elevator.

"Really?" The idea was slightly alarming to Blanche. "Don't think I could sleep. The place gives me a buzz."

"Well, then, let's make it official."

They went up to the rooftop bar. Blanche had a hard time relating the past with the vista before her. Thirty years later, the war seemed long gone. The restored French architecture and the gleaming modern buildings contrasted with the horrendous devastation she'd seen on film: the faces of the desperate during the Tet of '68, the scores of young men fighting on both sides, the crumbling walls and awful sounds of gunfire. She stared at the new skyline of lights and listened to the peep-peep of motorbikes, the whistles of the traffic cops, and the hum of activity in the street below. The traffic fumes seemed light today.

Blanche and Jean chose a table on the open terrace. "I feel kinda dopey," murmured Jean.

"Not sneezy or grumpy?"

"Very funny," said Jean.

Blanche pulled her chair up. Skyscrapers poked through the haze, and the sun lowered behind the tops of older buildings.

Maybe her father had stood here—maybe near here—looking at the same skyline. Holding a cold beer, anxious, and as hallucinatory as she was right now. They had that in common, the strange and out-of-time experience of being in Vietnam.

Jean ordered a kumquat-cinnamon cocktail, Blanche a lychee-raspberry-mint mojito.

"This will probably kill me," said Jean.

"Well, I hope not. That would be some obit. 'Young woman dies of Saigon view and kumquat-cinnamon cocktail.'" The drinks arrived with spicy nuts on the side. Blanche dunked the mint leaves and lifted her glass in a toast. "How 'bout we celebrate."

"Someday."

"With my great 'detective skills'?" She was feeling giddy, and this strange pink cocktail was adding to it.

They clinked glasses. "Thanks for coming, Blanche. Dropping everything and flying here."

"It's not like I had a packed agenda. I couldn't be happier that we're in it together."

"It was Dad's dream, and now I'm living it. We're *both* living it."

"Funny, but I feel like, after all, this is something I was meant to do." The cool drink at her fingertips and the hot air on her face played with her head.

Jean sobered. "Yes, you're definitely meant to be here."

Blanche let that sink in. *More of this evasive, serious stuff...* "Jean, sometimes I feel like you're holding back."

"*Moi?*" Her laugh was tinny, forced.

"Yes, you." For one, Blanche had checked the *Island Times* clips that detailed some of her adventures. Maybe her cursory investigation was not thorough enough, but she didn't find anything about her father, or his war record, or Vietnam in those articles. *So how does Jean know so much?*

"It's nothing, Blanche. I'm just edgy. We made it! Together." Jean twisted in her chair, averting her eyes, and she took a large sip of the cocktail. "We've got a lot to see, a lot to do."

Blanche's radar zipped into gear, but she blamed the blip partly on sleep deprivation. She would file her doubt away and look at it later. She drank her cocktail and let the alcohol do its magic.

"We do," she said, eyeing Jean. "It's kind of crazy. I think I told you—Clint, at the newspaper, warned me." Blanche sat up straight and tucked in her chin, suddenly becoming the gruff old newspaper editor. "He says, 'Blanche, now don't get yourself involved in one of your goldarn mysteries over there. Just get the business done and get back here. In one piece.' He wants me to write something for the paper, but he didn't say what."

"For the *Island Times*?"

"Yeah, and by the way." Blanche stopped, bit her tongue, and then gave up. "I checked the newspaper files and didn't find mention of my dad in there." Bang Murninghan didn't hold it for long, given the opportunity.

"You sure? Maybe it was in the *Gazette* I read something...."

"Or maybe it wasn't in the newspaper at all?" They'd only been in Vietnam hours. Now, here was a whiff of doubt about this trip.

"Oh, no, I'm sure it was publicized." Jean fiercely stirred her tall, orangey drink. "I think you should write *this* story: 'Local Girl Finds Mom Wandering Southeast Asia.'" The straw had disintegrated into a pulpy mess.

"I hope I get to write that." Blanche tried to hide her suspicion, but it kept popping up. "She's out there." *And so is my dad. Out there. Part of Vietnam.* "Something else, Jean. I want to be honest. I had Clint check your dad's background—and yours. You understand, don't you?"

"We should be honest." Jean pushed away the dregs of her cocktail, almost knocking over the glass. "Just what did you find out?"

Blanche's tone was gentle now. "All the best stuff. Your dad was a salesman for Allen Bradley, sold automation equipment, and was clearly successful. You, a graduate of the University of Florida with a degree in chemistry. You've been working in a lab in Tampa…."

"Well, you're writing the book on me. I understand. The idea of showing up and pushing this whole adventure is pretty kooky."

"Ya think? But I couldn't resist … getting to know you better. Getting to know *all* of it better. We do have certain things in common."

"I can't say it enough. I'm just so glad you're here."

"Like I said, I am glad to be here."

Jean slumped forward, fatigue bearing down on her. "I have this awful feeling we're not going to find my mother."

"Don't talk like that, Jean." Blanche's gaze skipped over the tops of the buildings of a new Vietnam. She had these bouts of exhilaration, and she would use them to keep both their spirits up. "It'll be great. Look, at least you decided to do something about it instead of sitting around Tampa, thinking and wishing. Your dad would be happy to know you went through with it."

"Yeah, both our dads would." Jean reached for Blanche. "I know you're thinking about your dad. How could you not?"

"You read my mind." *Let's be positive, Blanche.*

Jean drew circles on the marble tabletop with her cocktail glass. "Tomorrow, we start." She took one last sip of the drink and grimaced. "Kinda heavy on the lychee, but interesting. Yours?"

"Kinda sour."

They both looked over the beer list: Tiger, Corona, Saigon, Heineken, San Miguel, Carlsberg. Blanche slapped the drink menu onto the tabletop. "Which country would you like?"

"They're all good, but I guess I'll take Vietnam."

"I'll drink to that."

Five

Getting Started

THE BED WAS HEAVENLY, especially after being curled like a shrimp into that airplane seat for a day. Blanche wanted to sink into the crisp linen under the down-filled duvet and not come up for a good long time. She went off to dreamland and slept the sleep of the dead—until the sound of Jean's singing woke her up the following morning.

Blanche groggily opened her eyes and had no idea where she was. The room was all white except for the large bowl of dragon fruit and oranges. Then she remembered…Vietnam, the Caravelle. The song came from the bathroom, an oyster-tiled platform in the corner of the suite. Voluminous, white silk curtains hung from floor to ceiling, closing off the area where Jean was splashing around and loudly singing about her mother's voice and someone calling in the night.

Blanche sat up and stretched, then plopped back on the pillow. *No waves outside my window today, just the soft thrum of traffic in Southeast Asia. And this song of Vietnam.* She called out to Jean. "That's lovely. What is it?"

The voice behind the curtain stopped. "Phuong Thao, a Vietnamese singer. She's also a child of dust."

Blanche rearranged herself on half a dozen pillows and snuggled in. "Jean, I don't think you're dusty. You're kind of gleamy and shiny."

Jean appeared in a terry robe, a towel around her head. "That's nice, but I can't deny it. Over here, I'm a particle they could do without. The same is said of children of the French and the Vietnamese women. They don't like the foreign influence."

"It'd be nice if everyone liked each other." Blanche sat up and patted the duvet.

"Yes, well, that's unlikely to happen any time soon."

"You're doing your part. Spreading your cheery music."

Jean flopped into a chair. She toweled her hair vigorously. "Blanche, you're still dreaming."

She frowned and balled up the towel in her lap.

"What's the matter? Life's good." But that dread popped up again, the possible disappointment of not finding Jean's mom. The thought always lingered in the unsaid. To believe Tam Li was out there and to search and leave with nothing? Blanche found it hard to accept it. She wouldn't for Jean's peace of mind and hers.

"You know. I'm afraid…."

"Don't go there," said Blanche. "This morning, we start. It is morning, isn't it?" The shades were drawn, the perfumed scent of bath salts threatening to lull Blanche back to sleep. She wanted another hour, but they had work to do. She threw off the duvet and found her slippers.

"It's around seven. We slept almost twelve hours." Jean pulled back the curtain and shook out her wet hair. She began to pull a comb through it slowly. "You feel good?"

"Like a princess." She hugged the duvet.

"I ordered coffee. Egg coffee. You're gonna love it!"

"Egg coffee? I hope that's eggs *and* coffee."

"Not quite. You'll see!"

The egg coffee arrived on a linen-covered tray. It was caffeine heaven with a foamy, custard flavor floating on top of hot espresso. Blanche had never drunk her morning fix with a spoon. It was almost like dessert for breakfast.

"Only in Vietnam is coffee quite like this, Dad used to say. *Ca phe trung*. It was invented in Hanoi out of sweetened condensed milk and egg yolks. He tried to make it at home, then he'd shake his head," said Jean. "The memory of it would send him straight back here."

"I guess you do have to be here." Blanche finished it off. Better than cappuccino. She tried to imagine configuring the espresso, milk, and egg that went into it but gave up.

"We're here!" Jean put down her cup and began rummaging in her suitcase. "They have a buffet downstairs, and it's not to be missed. Thuy's going to pick us up at nine."

The breakfast buffet was a banquet that extended for a block, with stations for eggs and omelets, poached fish, and pork with crackling skin. Shrimp rolls and cakes and rice dumplings. Spring rolls and dipping sauces with chili and lime. A table with dozens of French baguettes, dark breads, and rolls. An entire honeycomb and jams, cheeses, and fruit like she'd never seen—red and green and yellow rambutans and jackfruit, mangos and papaya, tangerines, and kumquats. Blanche read the little signs posted in silver holders.

Jean picked up a lotus cake—a palm-size square with sweetmeat stuffing. She seemed to forget the omelet she was balancing with a plate of fruit. "Dad called this a 'moon' cake, the treat my parents used to share! Let's try one."

"Let's try everything," said Blanche. "We need energy. But after all this, I'll probably need a nap."

Thuy was in the lobby, wearing sturdy sneakers, her straw hat flat on her head. She was having an animated chat with the doorman. She turned to Blanche and Jean. "Good morning. *Ong co khoe khong.*"

"*Khoe, cam on,*" said Blanche.

Jean raised her eyebrows. "What?"

"We are all very well today, thank you," said Blanche.

"Oh, yes. *Cam un,*" said Jean. "Ready to go, Thuy."

"We will go to the place of your birth now."

Thuy bounded out the door, smiling, but Jean wobbled like someone had knocked her a good one. "The maternity ward?" Her voice drifted to a whisper. "You have the appointment?"

Blanche squeezed her hand, and they climbed into the back seat of the Toyota. "Let's do this," Blanche said brightly. In her heart, hope sprang up, and she was determined to nurture it.

Thuy weaved through the city. People bustled along with steadfast purpose, avoiding collision. The car slipped into the endless stream of bikes and mini vehicles until it lurched to a stop in front of a stucco building with green shutters on a shady street. The Tu Do Maternity Hospital had formerly been the administrative offices, in turn, of the French bureaucracy, the Japanese, and the Americans.

"This is it," said Jean, gathering her map and bag, as well as her reserve. "A maternity hospital run by the Sisters of the Holy Cross. My first home."

"Lovely," said Blanche. It was quiet and sun-dappled, the pedestrians strolling here instead of hurrying along in the commercial way.

Thuy maneuvered into a space against the wall. The car was on the sidewalk, but it didn't seem to matter. Vehicles crowded the spot. A man in uniform packed the bikes together, making inches of room. Blanche looped arms with Jean and coaxed her along. A weathered sign swung over the entrance. "It's exciting. Going 'home' again?"

"You know what they say. But I guess I'm going to do it."

Thuy pushed a buzzer, and the carved door under an arch opened. A small woman dressed in a loose black shirt and trousers greeted them. Thuy spoke to her in a manner both guttural and snappy, which intrigued Blanche. Once in a while, she could pick out some English or French, but now she didn't have any idea what they were saying. They talked seriously and at length. Finally, it boiled down to this: "Sister Mary Joseph is expecting you."

Thuy stood aside as they entered the cool, dim lobby—empty except for a threadbare runner and one bench. A high window let in a beam of light. No sound apart from the clicking of rosary beads. A nun hurried toward them, her vestments sailing about her. She could not have been five feet tall, and her face under the white wimple was brown as a nut. When Thuy introduced them, Sister Joseph smiled, and the lines disappeared.

"Oh, *mon Dieu.*" Her dark blue eyes sparkled as she peered at Jean. Tall, thin, and graceful, she was at least three inches taller than Sister Joseph. "It is like seeing Tam Li once again!"

Blanche was still holding onto Jean's arm. She felt her stiffen. "Oh, you know my mother," said Jean.

The nun reached out with both hands. Smooth, long fingers. A gold band. "I cannot forget her. I am looking into her face now."

Jean choked a little as she stared at the nun. "I hope you can help."

"What can I do?"

"I have to find her. My friend, Blanche, has been so kind to come with me. And Thuy."

The nun blessed herself. "Oh, *ma chere,* I pray. But, you know, you're asking for the moon." Jean was visibly deflated, but Sister Joseph took her hand and walked ahead, her thick heels clunking the tile. She pointed toward an open doorway. "Let's sit and talk. I have time before prayers."

Thuy hung back. "I will return later. After you have conference." And she was gone.

The parlor was sparsely furnished with high, white stucco walls. It was institutional and welcoming at once, with red velvet curtains at the French doors. A courtyard beyond was empty except for a couple of tables, chairs, and the canopy of a huge tamarind tree in the center of the garden. The open windows let in a breeze and it wasn't unpleasant in the room, although the temperature outside was in the high 80s.

Jean sat straight on the stern-looking couch covered in vinyl, and Blanche took a seat next to her. A fan creaked overhead. A low table was set with tea and cups. Sister Joseph poured the steaming tea, dropped a lump of sugar in each cup, and handed them around. The gesture lent some gentle relief.

Blanche exhaled; she'd been holding it in. She hoped the news would be good, although that business about "asking for the moon" didn't sound encouraging.

"Your mother." Sister Joseph sipped the tea, her eyes crinkled. "She came here thirty years ago. Her family was distressed by her condition. But she was happy."

Jean relaxed. "Happy?"

"Your mother looked forward to your birth." Sister Joseph brightened at the memory. "I hope you find her. My misgivings come out of living through the war, but I do remember how happy she was. She was strong, a survivor."

Jean leaned forward. "Do you have any idea where she went? Where any of the family might be?"

"Oh, my dear, I'm afraid not."

Blanche dodged a wave of disappointment. She would not give in. "Sister Joseph, did you ever meet Jean's father?"

"No, I did not. But Tam Li talked about him. I believe he was in the field, or perhaps wounded and gone by then. I don't know."

The nun's gaze was benevolent, empathetic. "I will tell you this: she loved him very much."

"She did? How do you know that?" Jean asked.

"She had his picture. He called her and wrote to her, I believe, but he wasn't able to come here."

"My father told me he was in the field when I was born," said Jean. "But how did my mother end up coming to you?"

"It was prearranged. She came the day before you were born. You were together here for nine days. For the time of lying in." The nun patted Jean's hand. "Dear one. So grown and lovely. Now, you tell me. How did *you* come here after all these years?"

"My father sent me. He had records of my birth letters from my mother. And memories."

"I wish I had better news," said Sister Joseph. She added another cube of sugar to her tea, her movements calm and measured. The tamarind whistled; a window slammed shut.

"Tell me. Anything about her," said Jean.

"I'm sure you have traits of your father, but I hardly see them," said Sister Joseph, sitting back, the teacup nestled in her hands. "Your mother was a pearl. Red lips, an oval face, long hair. Just like you. The first time I saw her, her hair was coiled on top of her head and tied with velvet. She was very near delivery. So large for someone so tiny but tall. Now I see how tall you are!" She chuckled. "But the family. Your mother came from a generous family, a long line of Catholics. They were known to help the poor, and they helped us. We were glad to welcome her." She clapped the teacup onto the saucer; her eyebrows shot up. "Now. You might look there."

"Where?" asked Blanche.

"Why, the local charities. We don't have a trace. I don't think … but yes, that's a start. One or more might be able to help."

Blanche was furiously taking notes. "Thank you," said Jean softly. She lifted the teacup. "You said my mother came here? Prearranged? What do you mean by that, Sister?"

"Your mother's teacher contacted us. Your mother confided in her, and it was she who made the arrangements. Tam Li's family were good people, but I must say, not supportive of her love for the American soldier." The nun seemed to size up Jean's reaction. "Many called the Americans invaders...."

"Yes, I know. He tried to be accepted, but it was no use. He was understanding, even when he wrote letters and made phone calls. He wanted her to come to Florida, but she wouldn't leave her family."

"That is the way." The nun glanced out the window. Sister Joseph's eyes, at once kind and sad, reflected the decades of worry and change. "You must understand, it was a confusing time for all of us. Saigon was ravaged; the streets were filthy and muddy most of the year. People were desperate. It was difficult to sort our lives. To trust anyone."

"My mother was fortunate to have you," said Jean. "Is the teacher who sent my mother here still in Saigon?"

"Madame Ngu is dead. Many have died of starvation, neglect, the camps, suicide." She recited this terrible litany calmly, not shying from Jean's tense expression.

"And those who knew the old teacher?"

"Gone, most everyone. But I knew her. There were very few like her, the ones who had the wherewithal to help and did." Sister Joseph shook her head. She flattened her hands on her lap. "I often wonder where all the children went after we brought them into this world. And I wondered what happened to you."

"Sister, there is no way to repay you," said Jean. "You've done so much for so many of us."

"You find your mother. That is payment enough." She smoothed Jean's clenched hands.

Blanche leaned forward. "And there are no records?"

"You know that history. Documents were shredded when the North took over. We could not show affiliation to the Americans or the South, or there would have been consequences. There was trouble anyway."

Blanche sat back, murmuring to herself. "I'm thinking she may have moved south, but the search keeps opening wider the more I think about it."

"Blanche, keep thinking." Two hard little lines of distress appeared between Jean's eyebrows.

"Perhaps you should look in the Ben Tre area," said the nun. "Many landowners and professionals moved into the Delta. If they didn't escape down the river and into the sea, they stayed in the villages and set up businesses. And it could not have been easy. Communist sympathizers infiltrated down there, even before the Americans came. It was a hotbed." The nun tapped her chin. "But there is always commerce. I believe your grandfather was a lender and landowner, and your mother worked alongside him. She was extremely bright. They may have gone somewhere to start over again." She rambled, but that was all right with Blanche; her suggestion offered more avenues to consider.

Blanche kept quiet and listened and wrote down the nun's comments, but then she looked up. "Do you have any idea which villages or towns besides Ben Tre? Other connections? You did mention charity."

"I can't offer the name of another place, but as for charity, I would start with the Catholic church," she said. "Your mother was Catholic—in a Buddhist country. But Catholicism has a long history in Vietnam, dating from the sixteenth-century Portuguese explorers. It's a strange marriage. The Catholics, and the Lutherans, have orphanages and refugees throughout Vietnam. I can give you some names. How much time do you have?"

The search was leading them deeper into the history and culture—into a land of complications with endless questions. Blanche was firm. "We have as much time as it will take."

"Yes," Jean said, her eyes brimming with gratitude.

"Ah, the young. Energetic and hopeful. Thank God for that!" She took Blanche's hands, her fingers cool and smooth. "You, Miss Blanche. How wonderful to travel with Miss Jean. I am sorry that your connection to Vietnam is a sad one."

"So, you know," said Blanche.

"Yes, Thuy gave me background before your visit," she said. "I hope you have been able to recover. Personally. You and your family." This stung. Blanche had little family and those she had held little knowledge. They didn't talk about the loss.

"It's a long way back to finding the soul," said Sister Joseph.

"Finding the soul?"

"Each one is different, of course," she said. "But here in Vietnam, especially in the villages, the fathers traditionally pass the land to the son. This custom was lost during the trouble. So many returned to their homes and fields, and there was nothing there. No person, no house, nothing. But now they are taking it back."

"The fathers," said Blanche. "I guess I have something in common with this place, at least in spirit. My father is here. Somewhere. They were never able to recover him."

The nun's dark blue eyes were reassuring. "You have ties here," said the nun. "Your father is surely at peace. I can tell you that, with all God's grace."

Six

Looking Outside

BLANCHE CONSIDERED Sister Mary Joseph's words. *Yes, my father is at peace, but he's lost. He's dead. His bones are part of one of those shining rice paddies outside Saigon.* She knew this, and painful as it was to think about, she tried to accept it. It helped that Blanche saw the efforts to mend the broken history all around her. It was inspiring, and she wasn't sure why. It had to do with burying the dead and raising the living.

Yet, she fought the sadness. Blanche wanted to think he was watching her. Sister Joseph's faith and her words brought him that much closer. It made him seem more real. He wouldn't be forgotten, not as long as Blanche lived.

Sister Joseph hurried off to prayers after telling Blanche and Jean that they would be in her intentions. She'd keep an ear out and ask around and search the records that remained, but she didn't think it would be much help in locating Tam Li.

Blanche and Jean stood in the lobby waiting for Thuy. "Well, how does it feel to be back?" Blanche asked, somewhat tentatively.

Jean tried to smile. "To think I was here, and my mother was holding me...."

"That's a lovely thought," said Blanche quietly. "Even though you don't remember. It did happen, Jean. And you know she loved you very much."

"Thanks, Blanche." Jean hugged her.

"And think about what Sister Joseph said. She may be right. It's possible your mother went off to start another business. A new beginning!"

Jean did not look convinced. She frowned. "I'm trying to remember ... there's nothing specific in any letter about where she could have gone. She hardly ever mentioned the hotel business or any business."

Blanche preferred to look at this as a clean slate—maybe wiped a bit too clean, but promising. "She's out there, Jean. We'll find her."

Thuy pulled the car around, and they hopped in. As she plunged into traffic, Jean drooped down in the back seat. Blanche was determined to dispel the disappointment.

"What next?" Blanche leaned over the seat toward Thuy. She grinned into the rearview mirror.

"I have list. Jean, your father contact agency and outline many things, but we adapt as we go," said Thuy. Her hands gripped the wheel, the hat bobbing as she careened past vehicles with drivers who had no concept of lanes. They drove around colonial-style buildings with classical arches, pink and yellow with touches of gold. Pots of flowers lined the colonnades, and stately palm trees divided the wide boulevard.

Blanche settled back, happy with the diversion. "What are these buildings, Thuy?" Blanche pointed here and there, poking Jean gently. Jean perked up.

"Notre Dame Cathedral. Post Office. Opera house. Famous hotel where the Americans stay in Saigon during the war against Viet Cong." She had a forceful way of speech, putting heavy accent on the last syllables. It was "Sai-GON. Viet CONG."

"It's so grand, so European," murmured Jean.

"Yes, but distinctively … Saigon," said Blanche.

"We'll go to the embassy next?" Jean wore a strained look.

"Yes, we have appointment, but not until tomorrow." Thuy skillfully threaded her way into a web of narrow streets, passing along the river and the scenes of bustling street life.

They stopped at a restaurant wedged between two narrow three-story buildings. Blanche wasn't particularly hungry, but she wanted to try everything now that a whiff of something spicy and pungent, garlicky, and grilled hit her nose. Inside the restaurant, the walls were turquoise and red and yellow with pictures of Vietnamese in conical hats, the *nom la*, and women in the traditional *ao dai*, the tight tunic dresses slit on the sides and worn over cigarette pants. The large dining room was crowded, charged with talk and laughter, and it quelled the notion of a sordid Communist society. Everywhere she looked, Blanche saw the ponderous evolution of the *doi moi* of 1986, a sort of peace between capitalism and communism that had introduced economic reforms and limited commerce. Saigon was evidently growing slowly under the burden of bureaucracy, but it was growing all the same. Blanche ordered one of those excellent beers—and some broken rice. Jean picked *pho* (rice noodles) and duck curry. Thuy, fried rice.

Jean and Blanche related Sister Joseph's story. Thuy's head bobbed at each point, the hat trembling, her chopsticks flying over the mound of rice and shredded seafood.

"What do you think, Thuy?" Jean sounded a bit frazzled, having skipped ahead twelve hours into this decidedly unfamiliar world. Blanche felt the same but was determined not to show it.

"Miss Jean, it is a journey, and you are making it. This is worth a look, this business that mother went farther south. Many business owners and landowners escaped to begin again."

"Any chance we can get into the consulate today? To follow up?" Blanche wanted to tick off some of the leads.

"No. But I call around to charities tonight. To start the process," said Thuy. "We will all look. If you find mother, that is good; if you do not, she will be with you. The mother is part of the child forever."

"I have to do all I can."

"And you are," said Blanche.

Traffic flooded past the window of the bistro. The sun cooked the river, but Saigon seemed oblivious to discomfort. The country sped from its past. Still, there was another time when rockets dropped from the sky, buildings crumbled in devastation. People screamed and ran for their lives. How many mothers had been separated from their children in those years? In so many ways, they were lucky to be on this journey, searching for Jean's mother. If they were successful, it would be rare. Blanche didn't want to think like that, but she did.

"Where were you, Thuy? How did you survive it?" Blanche measured her words. *It must have been terrible here—while I was in diapers, sitting in the white sand with the waves and birds.*

"I was young, not yet ten. There were nine of us, and we lived in the cave of my uncle. For many years, we lived in cave. We scratched for rice, we fished before the sun came up, we hunted the longan and banana in the wild places and along the river. It was a hard time but not an unhappy time. The war ended. We went to school. We make repairs and live on." It was difficult to gauge her feelings; Thuy was so calm and steady, a small rock of a woman.

"And you went to university?" Blanche was incredulous. Her main issue in securing a college education had been wrestling the paperwork to get a student loan.

"Yes, many study tourism in the university, and English. We adapt. My family is safe and busy," she said, one finger tapping out each word on the tabletop. "Our future now is the world. All people welcome here." There was something rote in her smile, something held back. But what?

—◦◦◦—

Back at the hotel, Blanche went off to soak in the bath and let the first full day of Vietnam sink in. The complimentary bath salts helped, as did the little pillow on the back of the tub. Five star, not like the plumbing in her beachfront cabin. She closed her eyes and breathed. The humid cloud of luxury did the job—until she began to fixate on Sister Joseph's rather tepid news. With not much solid from the nun and the report that most everyone was dead, the day had been disheartening. It had started with promise and fizzled from there. Blanche wracked her brain for ways to get back on track. She lit a candle and set it on the rim of the tub, staring into the flame. *Think, Blanche.*

She considered a side trip to Ben Tre. *Might as well jump off the end of the world...*

Before they did that, however, they had the embassy appointment coming up. With the news from Sister Joseph that records were destroyed, Blanche didn't have much hope, but they'd try. They also needed more information about local charities. Blanche's train of thought worked like she was pursuing one of her news stories; she would make sure one lead led to another.

Blanche wrapped herself in terry cloth and went back into the room—where she found Jean face down on the bed, sobbing. She hadn't even taken her shoulder bag off.

Blanche crept to the side of the bed and patted Jean's back. "What is it, girl? Tell me." But in her head, she knew.

"Oh, Blanche." Jean sat up suddenly. Her arm shot out toward the window. "This place. Millions and *millions* of people out there. It's impossible, a dream." She threw herself face down again and muffled a scream. Disturbing. Blanche sighed. She went to the window. A throng of pedestrians and bikers crowded the street below. True. There were millions of people out there, and how would they ever find Tam Li?

"Now, come on." Blanche thrust her fists into the pockets of her robe. "Jean, this is not the impossible dream." She threw her arms out. "Honor and justice will live."

Jean hiccupped. Her tear-stained face wore the ghost of a smile. "Blanche, Don Quijote, you're not."

"The Don was happy in his own little world. We have to make our world, Jean."

Jean sat cross-legged, wiping her cheeks. "You're right. I'm sorry for blubbering."

"Uh, no. Get it out, and be done with it. Good to let down a bit." *But not too much.*

Blanche turned in search of the minibar. A bit of numbing was in order. "Must be some booze here somewhere," she announced. The mini-fridge was camouflaged under a desk. Inside was a veritable United Nations of liquor: Scotch and Irish whiskey, Russian vodka, Cuban rum, Mexican tequila. She grabbed a couple of bottles. "How about Cuba?"

She handed Jean a rum and unscrewed a Jameson's for herself. Jean flopped back against the pillows and blew her nose. "Cuba's good," she said.

They dispensed with glasses and drank out of the bottles. "It's frustrating, but we've just started. We have a long way to go before we're done here."

"You're right." Jean mumbled.

"It's just plain hard not to have your mom and dad. I happen to know that for a fact." She slugged back the Jameson's, and Jean sipped the rum. Blanche went back for refills.

"All the more reason I'm sorry, Blanche. You've had it worse than me. Except you had your Gran. And Cap and all."

"Yeah, we sorta lucked out in our own way. I had Gran, you had Dad. And now we're looking for mom." Blanche raised the bottle.

"Do you think we should be doing this?" Jean giggled as she drained the rum.

"What? Having a drink? I'd say it's the best idea I've had in the last fifteen minutes."

"Do you remember your mother?"

"I do. And I feel she's with me. In fact, last year, I was dumped in a Florida desert and left for dead, and my mother came to me and saved me." Blanche tossed an empty Jameson's into the wastebasket.

"What?"

"Yeah, it's true. I don't think I would have made it if she hadn't. She talked me back. I wanted to go with her, to heaven, or wherever she is, but she told me to stay. A mother's influence and love and presence are pretty strong, whether she's standing next to you or not. Whether she's alive or dead." Blanche leaned on the side table, both arms taut. "Don't forget it. Your mom did well, caring for your future. She loves you, wherever she is."

"Oh, God, Blanche. You and Sister Joseph are right."

"Well, yes, I guess." She stood up and raked her curls. "Wash your face, and let's get it together. We're going out. And we are not going looking for a convent."

———

Blanche caught her reflection in the hotel lobby mirror. *Not too bad.* She adjusted the errant black curls under the red headband. She and Jean wore simple sheaths—Jean's blue, Blanche's red. "We look awfully … American. All we need is some stars and stripes, and we'll look like flags," said Blanche.

"Camouflage wouldn't help. We kind of stick out," said Jean, who seemed a good three inches taller than everyone in the country. Blanche's pale Irish face and green eyes drew stares.

They spun through the revolving door of the hotel and into the path of three motorbikes coming at them on the sidewalk. Blanche grabbed Jean's arm. "Remember what Thuy said. Blend, like fish in the water."

"They *will* go around us?"

"I hope."

It was close to nine o'clock. Their hotel was in a "lively" district in the center of Saigon with restaurants, lounges, and clubs—Blanche was wondering where it wasn't lively. She wasn't hungry after that breakfast, then lunch, and several bottles from the mini bar, but a bar and some music weren't out of the question. She'd talked Jean around. They walked along the river—a black mirror reflecting the lights of skyscrapers. A few longboats lazily plied the ripples.

Blanche breathed in the humidity, the late February air weighing like an invisible blanket. "The heat and dampness," said Blanche, "even heavier than Florida."

"This river country isn't quite the same heat, is it."

"Uh-uh. Just think of being out in it every day, carrying stuff? Working? Our dads..." She imagined her father wading through the lowland, humping fifty pounds of Army gear, the sweat, and fatigue. The Vietnamese seemed undaunted, no matter the task or the load.

Jean scuffed along, her eye fixed on the silent river. "I like being here. Sharing it. You know what I mean?"

"I do," said Blanche.

Jean had rallied considerably. Blanche was glad they were out in the night though she felt aimless. *Where are we going with this whole thing?* The street smelled faintly of onions and fish sauce, the streetlamps shining an eerie golden light on the faces and chrome and storefronts.

They turned away from the river down a narrow street of restaurants and shops. The music of Three Dog Night blasted from an open door: "Mama Told Me Not To Come…." They looked at each other and laughed. "Let's see about that," Blanche said. The sign overhead said, "The Follies."

The bar was dark and smelled of whiskey and beer … and lemons? Four women sat on bar stools. Red, yellow, blue, and white satin lined up along the long, polished counter. Their *ao dais* shimmered. The women turned to Blanche and Jean and then back to the mirror behind the shelves packed with glassware. Their eyes shone like black jewels. Blanche and Jean had stepped into another world, and now Blanche's feet wouldn't move.

A booming laugh came from the back of the bar. A character straight out of an adventure movie? A Marvel comic book? The man was tall, as wide as the doorway he stood framed in. Shoulder-length white-blond hair, a flimsy tank-top, and silver bracelets. Blanche's eyes traveled down the length of him. "What's this?"

"Really," said Jean. "Should we leave?"

"Hell no."

Seven

Ride 'Em Cao Boi

THEY STOOD JUST INSIDE THE BAR. Jean had one index finger on her lip, deciding, but Blanche had already made up her mind. They could bolt, should the need be. She stared at this vision. The tall blond man came forward. "Lovely ladies," he said, holding out his hand. The four beauties lined up at the bar turned as one and chittered like birds.

"Hi," said Blanche. She was a terrible poker face, unable to hide it. It was odd finding a friendly version of The Hulk right in the middle of Saigon. He was clearly not Vietnamese; he looked more like a cowboy related to a surfboard. "So nice to meet you," she said. "Where you from? Texas?"

He laughed. "Nah, I'm here, always been here, it seems like. But o-rig-i-nally, from Florida. A long way from my surfing and rodeo ridin.'"

Florida. His jaw was square as the Rockies, his hair like Alaska snow. Blanche squinted at his chest. A tattoo of a palm tree—*a marijuana leaf?*—stuck out of his shirt, and on each bicep, a green shamrock came to life as he flexed. The rest of the outfit was black Vietnamese pants for a giant.

"We're from Florida, too," Blanche said. She shook his hand, which was like a huge, rough paw. "Blanche Murninghan. My friend, Jean McMahon."

"I'll be," he said. "Welcome to The Follies! 'Stick' Dahlkamp, your host. Please. Have a seat." One long arm took in the bar area. "We have all the beers in the world and booze. If you don't see it and you want it, we'll get it. Our Eagles tribute band starts in an hour."

The bartender yelled, "Mr. Stick!"

He made the peace sign. "I'll be there."

He ushered Blanche and Jean to a red vinyl booth, a cozy half-circle with a view of the bar, the stage, and the door. "Joy to the World" blared in the background. This was more like the south Tampa hood than an Asian hideaway.

"Stick from Florida? You don't look like a stick. You look more like a tree." Blanche clapped a hand on her mouth. Too late. *There I go again.* Jean stifled a laugh.

He seemed game with that hundred-watt smile. "Walter Winchell Dahlkamp the Third. But I prefer 'Stick.'"

Blanche said, "Walter Winchell? Named for the iconic newsman? With the hat?"

"The same. I was born late in life to my dear father. Rest in peace. He wrote for the old *Tampa Bay Gazette.* Inspired by the famous Walter—favoring his temperament, like a bulldog, rather than his politics. Dad had always wanted to be at The Five O'Clock Follies when the military lied to the press during daily briefings. I named the bar after the follies. Figure Dad is floating around here somewhere. Maybe Walter, too."

Blanche and Jean slid into the booth. Their host crossed his arms and grinned. "I digress. You must be thirsty. What can I get you? A pop? Dinner?"

"We're good on the dinner, for now. But whiskey? Jameson's?" Blanche suggested it, and Jean nodded. The bar rocked with international variety, and specks of light flashed under a disorienting but not unpleasant disco ball. Stick sauntered away and returned with a nicked tray, sloshing three shots of Irish whiskey and three Saigon Special beers. Blanche noticed that the backs of his hands were scarred, like crinkled tissue paper. He wore a ring with a green stone near the size of a ping-pong ball.

He put the drinks down. "Would you mind if I set a spell with y'all? I'd welcome a bit of news from home."

For an answer, Blanche scooted over in the booth, but Stick pulled a chair off the back wall, turned it around, and straddled it. He glanced over at the door, then back to his guests. Lifted his beer. "*Slainte!*"

He drank off half the beer and grinned, revealing large teeth and one dimple. His eyes settled on Blanche. "Where ya from in the land of margaritas and alligators?"

"West coast. Tampa area," said Blanche. "Both of us."

A huge hand slapped his chest, and his face got so red Blanche was sure he'd burst something. "Ya don't say! Old home week. Some of my best surfin' days out West, but I been mostly off the Melbourne coast."

"Cocoa Beach?" Jean asked. Blanche caught the scrutiny of a gaggle of men who came in. They quickly turned away, the bar girls fluttering around them. Blanche drank off half the shot and clicked the glass onto the slick tabletop.

"Sure, but kinda all over," he said. "Grew up east. Miami. West, school, Tampa. North, job Panama City, another job, back out east in Jax. Then I was outta there, more than thirty years ago. Haven't looked back since."

"Wow! How old are you?" Bang, at it again. "Sorry. Shouldn't ask a gentleman his age."

"Why, I'm old as heck," he said. "Made older by those years with the Ninth."

"Vietnam? That's why we're here."

"To start another war?"

"To end one," said Blanche. "My dad died here. Jean's mother is here. Somewhere. We want to find her."

"You don't say." He suddenly sobered. "We should talk." The music picked up and drowned out the conversation. Stick was summoned to the bar again.

Blanche and Jean exchanged looks. "Can't hurt, I guess," said Blanche. "Let's see what ol' Stick has to say."

As he lumbered away, Blanche noticed the un-Florida-like decor. An enormous Vietnamese flag covered one section of paneling behind the bar—the solid red banner with a single yellow star. On another wall, the front pages of curling newspapers, decades-old, from all over the world and shouting messages of war, escalating, de-escalating, deflating. A valiant tree in the front window somehow flourished in the dense air, its leaves clawing for whatever light it could get.

Stick resumed his seat. A little boy appeared at his side. He wore a new striped T-shirt, blue shorts, and brown sandals. His gleaming black hair nearly covered his eyes. He seemed content, but Blanche felt a stab of pain for his withered legs and his overall stunted growth. It was hard to tell his age. She smiled at him, and he smiled back, shy but open.

Stick put a hand on the boy's back and patted him gently. "Not now, Deebs. We'll talk later."

The boy hugged Stick's arm and scuttled off to the back of the bar.

"Deebs?"

"Long story." Stick craned his neck to see that the boy was settled. Satisfied, he turned to Blanche and Jean. "As aforementioned, Stick Dahlkamp, owner of The Follies. Not every night I get some beautiful American banditas in here."

"As aforementioned, Murninghan and McMahon."

"Up the Irish!" He called over his shoulder. "Please, Kim! Bring that bottle of Jameson's over here!" He swiveled around. "Before we drink the whole thing, tell me more. The war, your dad? Your mom?"

Jean leaned forward. "We're here to find her."

"She lost?" But he knew. Blanche could see it in his eyes now, softened and inquisitive. Stick was not a surfer boy on a toot; he was hardly a boy. He'd probably seen the worst if he'd spent any time here. A bit jaded? Blanche decided not. He was open, even naïve, yet he had the look of someone who had been around the world and back.

"Probably not," said Jean. "I haven't seen her in more than twenty-five years. My dad was an American soldier here. He met her in Hoi An, and here I am."

"You followed her trail to Saigon?"

"Sort of. I was born here. We think she may have traveled south to get farther away from the conflict up North."

"Any luck so far?"

"Nope."

He scratched his enormous chin. "Where'd your dad serve?" Laughter aside, Stick was all business now.

"Americal. He was a scout."

Stick frowned, the shadow of a wizened look crossing his face. "One of those righteous 'legs.'"

"Huh?" Blanche was perplexed.

"Scouts were crazy brave. They got on with it, long-range recon patrol. Light carry but heavy on the ammo. Most of them small, even went down in those tunnels after Charlie. Got their heads blowed off, too. Regular," said Stick. "I'm sorry, maybe too much info…."

"No, no. That's ok," said Blanche, her voice catching. "You were with the Ninth Infantry?"

Even in the dim bar, Blanche could see his eyes cloud over. "Ended up on the Mekong. I was pretty good at writing, believe it or not, mostly thanks to the dear old dad genes. I was support for a while; then they sent me out with a rifle almost as soon as I got here." He stopped like he'd run into a wall, and his gaze bounced between them. "It's good to see you both."

"Good to see you, too." She took a sip of the whiskey. It struck her that he might be around her dad's age and Hank McMahon's. Maybe closer to fifty-five. The hair, the outfit, the jaunty manner had put her off. He was a Vietnam survivor. "How was it? Tell me."

"It's not stuff for polite talk. For anyone." He jiggled the shot glass back and forth, but Blanche noticed he hadn't finished the whiskey. "Excuse me for going on about it."

"We both lost our dads to the war. My dad was a scout. Jean's father just passed," Blanche said. "I'd like to hear what you have to say." Her tone was insistent, almost tinny, and her throat dry. She doused it with whiskey. "Full disclosure, I'm a journalist." She had no idea why she added that. She wasn't about to write another *Fire in the Lake*.

Stick leaned back, hands on his hips. "You don't say. Following a long line of scribes, are ya? Sean Flynn, Peter Arnett…"

"More like Catherine Leroy and Kate Webb. But that's not it. We could use some background."

"It's a big place. Complicated," he said.

Blanche took another sip of the whiskey, the warmth of it flooding her with anticipation. She couldn't leave it at that. She leaned close to Stick. "What was it like for *you*?"

Jean tugged at Blanche and whispered. "Maybe it's personal, Blanche."

He heard it. "Oh, it's personal, all right. Everything about that war is personal—at least, to me. I lost people. I lost time. I almost lost my life."

Blanche and Jean sipped, waiting for him to fill in the spaces.

His brows knit together. "It's hard to describe what it was like. You see it in the movies, you hear it second hand, but it's different for everybody." He brought his hands together in one large fist on his chest.

"I want to understand," said Blanche.

"Of course, you do. So do I." He shook his head, drummed his fingers on the tabletop. "Don't think you'd like what you hear. But maybe you *should* hear it."

"Try me," Blanche said. Jean gave a thumb's up. "Me, too."

"Your daddies were scouts?" He hesitated. "Don't need to overthink it. You'd 'preciate knowing somethin' about my friend Phips...."

Eight
Pieces of Heaven

"MY BEST FRIEND WAS JACKSON GADY PHIPS, so dark you couldn't see him at night 'cept if the moon was out, and then you'd only see them remarkable teeth and eyes. We was buddies, went through boot together at Fort Polk, Louisiana—or Camp Swampy, as we called it. Marksmanship, survival, sergeant spittin' in our faces. Phips took it all better than me. He was good. He was great.

"As luck would have it, or un-luck like we used to say, we ended up together. Ninth Infantry Division, in the Delta. And then Phips went about making himself kinda famous as a 'forward observer.' A scout. The army is famous for calling stuff what it ain't: rations for food, P-38 for a can opener, Charlie Foxtrot for an f-upped maneuver, fatigues for the uniform, Lima Charlie for 'loud and clear.' On and on and on." Stick enumerated each on his fingers and clapped his hand on the table.

"Whatever. It was a whole separate world we lived in, but Phips had it down. Like I said, down tight. He'd find the enemy out there, every tunnel in the village, every suspect hole in the ground, and then he'd call it in. He could shoot the eyelash off a gnat if he had to. Had his stuff packed real tight, like I say. And he was always lookin' real strack. At least when we was stateside.

Time we got over here, we'd kinda lost it. We just hung on to each other in our team and hoped we'd make it out while we watched one after 'nother of our buddies get blowed away.

"Between patrols, we'd sit for hours, playing cards, drinking warm beer, jawin'. Then, 'cause we was bored, and 'cause Phips had a mind like a steel trap, over time—felt like years—he made up a code, and he taught it to me. We'd tap out that code with our fingers, or a pen, or whatever, for all kinds of stuff, make up stories about the lieutenant who was a West Pointer and didn't know shee-shee from shinola. A real 'cadidiot.' First sergeant had to pull him through. It was bad, half the things he wanted us to do that he wouldn't think to do hisself, like going down in the tunnels. We knowed Charlie was in there. We lost men who went down in those tunnels. Why go down there? We shoulda just popped him one good, blowed him away, and be done with it.

"We was always kinda on edge. It was impossible to sleep, relax, to forget about the war for even a minute. So, Phips and me, we'd go off in another world. We'd code if we felt something bad was about to happen, or even something good, like so-and-so pulled some good R & R in Hawaii, and he was going to see his old lady. We'd make a game of coding; I was nearly always wrong, and Phips was right. He had uncanny radar, that guy. We hardly ever used the code for serious stuff, except to practice for someday when we might need it. Sometimes, he'd code me I was about to get the clap or dysentery or extra guard duty, and I'd code him his girlfriend run off with Jody. It was an intricate code, one with an alphabet and numbers, and half the time we had to fill in with real words 'cause we was so messed up, tired or drunk, we didn't know what we was saying.

"Anyway, one night, I heard those knuckles beatin' on the side of a footlocker next to my bunk. I was dead asleep, and at first, I didn't get it. I was annoyed and groggy. But Phips kept on. He was a smart guy. I shoulda remembered that, but I was asleep. It was too bad I didn't wake up and listen better. He'd been a lucky guy, and I stood by that. I slept by it. He'd been in the war about nine months, survived a tripwire on a hump, more than once, lived through patrols into the jungle, so thick you'd cut for an hour and only go a hundred meters, slump down exhausted, smoke some, get up and do it again.

"Phips was rappin' steady that night on the footlocker. Thought I was dreaming about rain, 'cause, you know, it rain here all the time, never seem to stop. But this wasn't rain. It was knuckles; Phips's knuckles.

"I wake up and say, 'What, Phips. It's zero-dark three in the mornin'. We gotta hump comin' up, and I'm in no mood....' Anyway, if I'd been fully awake, I woulda know'd he meant business.

"He meant business all right.

"The code say: Don't freakin' move.

"So, I finally was awake enough to realize I shouldn't move a nose hair. I just lay there, like a stone or a boulder, I guess.

"Phips had these eyes, ya know, something clear out of the ordinary. Some kind of black stars. They shined like they was about to explode. And behind them eyes was a lot of intelligence. A lot of caring. He put on like he was some hard guy, 'cause I guess he had to, being the only Black guy in the squad. But I knew him good. He was the best soldier I ever knew."

Stick paused the story and took a hefty slug of the whiskey. His eyes were old then, vacant and flat, like he'd gone back a hundred years, but he'd only retreated to the battleground thirty-plus years before—a lifetime—Blanche's and Jean's.

"If you knew Phips, you'd know what I mean. That night was the first night his eyes lit up like they was real scared. We stared at each other. I think it was seconds, but who's to say? I'll never know.

"He pointed to my weapon. Then he moved off real stealthy—no time to talk about it. Phips was short and wiry. A swimmer, of all things. Passed with high marks in survival. Could carry a man twice his size, at least in the Mekong...

"He crawled across the ground. We was in garrison, temporary quarters, guarding a firebase near My Tho, and it weren't like this was some fancy barracks.

"I lay still watching him. I had no idea where he was going or what he was up to. But then I heard it. The rustling, so slight you'd think it was a tree branch or animal out there. But it weren't.

"I saw the profile of dark figures. It was like they melted through the walls or under the door. Not a sound among them. It weren't someone visiting for a cup of joe or a game of cards. This was Charlie, and somehow these mf-ers, pardon the language, had gotten past the guards and were making the rounds.

"Phips jumped the first of 'em. Me, finally I come around, and I got my weapon, but it was so dark I couldn't figure what was going on, and besides, it all happened in seconds. Phips knifed the first, then the second one, right off. It was the third one that was a real problem. Three was not a charm, not for my friend Phips.

"My eyes was adjusting but not good enough. I don't know how he managed to take care of them two so quick. But, like I say, Phips had it all together. It was the third one haunts me. I think I screamed, but I don't remember. I didn't hear the sound of my own voice. Besides, we was supposed to be quiet. If there'd been other VC nearby, it would have alerted them. Come on by, boys. Help your buddies out here...

"They roll around on the area inside the hootch. I'm clutching my rifle, and it's not doing one dang bit of good. Last thing I remember, the two of 'em are out in the dark, fighting out there hand to hand, and then I sees this white flash. I thought for a split second, this was it. Heaven, or hell, here I come. Phips must have seen it with them black stars of his 'cause he was on top of it. Threw himself on it."

Stick shuddered, reliving the whole thing. He poured a whiskey and cast his eyes away. Far away.

"End of story. Next, I knew I was on a chopper, medevaced out of there. Took me six months to recover, but if it weren't for Phips…."

"What happened to your friend?"

His mouth tightened. He drew a breath. "My friend's in heaven, and I know he's savin' some poor fool from up there." He drank off the shot.

Blanche and Jean hadn't moved—riveted on every word. Jean said, "That night. How did that happen?"

"I tell you, they came up from underground. They had whole cities down there under the country. Came up and cut through the wire, half a dozen of 'em. Spread out, killed off some of the guys. Phips got the last of 'em."

"I am sorry," Jean whispered. Blanche finally let out a breath.

"You say your dads were scouts. Phips was a scout. Thought you'd like to hear the story of Phips," Stick said, raising his glass. "Here's to Phips. Here's to your dads."

Blanche took note that Phips, and the scouts, were properly remembered. The bottle of Jameson's was drained.

———

The "Glenn Frey" guitarist and the "Don Henley" vocalist rocked. Blanche guessed that "The Eagles" and the beer were popular draws at The Follies, but it was probably Stick who sold the place and packed them in, talking and laughing. He made people feel—at home? If home could be neon beer signs, vinyl bar stools and booths, and that smoky combo of barroom cigs and whiskey.

Stick was called away again. He stood at the door, shaking hands with several tall, light-haired patrons who towered over the

Vietnamese. He seemed to know everyone as he moved around the bar. Stick made his way back to Blanche and Jean's booth with a beer in one hand and a whiskey bottle in the other.

Blanche said, "That's some story, Stick."

"The pits and the heights. My friend was all of it, wrapped up in that war." He lifted the bottle. "How 'bout it? To Phips."

They had one more to Phips. Blanche was past the warm cozy feeling and onto worrying about a hangover tomorrow, but it seemed worth it. "To Phips, and tomorrow morning. My grandmother always said to keep my wits about me."

"Well, you got us." Jean hiccupped. Blanche laughed. Stick scratched his head.

"Did you lose a lot of friends, Stick?" Blanche still held half a shot.

"About 55,000."

Blanche slumped in the booth. "Think of all those families."

"I'd rather not. Phips was s'posed to get married. His mama never recovered neither."

They sat with their thoughts while the bar jangled around them. It sunk in. The explosions and the people and the war.

Finally, Stick stood up. "Just a few blocks, then?"

"Yeah, but it might as well be a few blocks on the moon. Not anything like my little Florida island."

He nodded. "Will you give me a minute? Don't go yet."

"Sure."

Jean turned her shot glass upside down, her eyelids beginning to droop. "I'm ready when you are. Hope I can walk. Wonder what he wants?"

"Maybe he knows something or someone. Come on. *Cam un.* Perk up."

"Oh, Blanche, your Vietnamese is getting better!"

"Witchy Woman" was winding down, and the band was taking a break when Stick reappeared, the back of a chair in his grip. He sat down next to the booth. "I'd like to help. In the search for your Mom. I might have a contact or two." The young boy was stuck to his side, like Velcro. Stick pulled him up and sat him on his knee. It was a bizarre picture of friendship or paternal affection, the hulking blond and the black-haired boy. Stick bounced him once, and the boy laughed.

"Who is this little guy, Stick?" Blanche grabbed some coasters and started building him a tiny house, to his obvious delight.

"The Deebs?" The boy put down the coasters and took a bun out of his pocket. He held it up shyly. Stick ruffled his hair that lay flat and shining over his eyes.

"Hi, Deebs," Blanche said.

The boy extended sugary fingers and Blanche took them. He was still smiling, but the corners of his mouth drew down.

"Deebs doesn't talk," said Stick. "Maybe someday."

Blanche tilted her head, waiting for details.

Stick said, "He's my right-hand man. Right, guy?" Deebs burrowed under Stick's left arm. "Just shy, is all."

"Adopted?" Jean smiled at the boy draped over Stick's arm. He went back to nibbling on the bun.

"No, not exactly," said Stick. "Should we tell the ladies all about you?" Deebs chewed thoughtfully, glancing at Stick in adoration. Stick hugged him. "Yeah, he has a story. We'll get to it. One of these days."

Stick stood up and sent Deebs scurrying toward a room in the back. "Anyway, I want to help."

He didn't wait for an answer. He didn't seem the type. He was a presence. Rather like a bulldozer, thought Blanche. The boys in the band were banging out, "Already Gone."

"Will you meet me back here tomorrow?"

"Well, sure, Stick, but what for?" Blanche asked.

"You'll see. Want you to meet some friends of mine. Promise you'll come back?"

"Promise," said Blanche.

Jean wore a slightly startled look. "Sure, I guess."

"Okay, then we're on, ladies. Back here at ten in the morning. Think this'll be a help to ya, I hope." He saluted, fingers like a pistol. Winked. The bartender called him over.

"What did we just promise?" Blanche was puzzled and a bit drunk.

"We'll find out, won't we? You're game?"

"Game definitely on."

Blanche didn't realize until much later that they hadn't asked for the tab.

Nine

Snake Juice and Coconuts

"SHOULD WE GO BACK THERE TOMORROW? Really?" Jean's voice drifted from somewhere deep in her queen-sized bed across the room.

Blanche was sunk in a cocoon, about to wend her way to dreamland. "Uh-huh. Sure."

"Do you think he can help? Or do you think he's just full of it?"

Blanche could hear the rustling of sheets and pillows. It was dark in the suite, but not so much that she couldn't make out shapes. Jean's head bobbed in the ambient light from the windows. She was sitting up, wanting answers from Blanche, who couldn't say what day it was.

"Uh-huh."

"What?"

"Uh-huh."

"Oh, Blanche."

Jean's head hit the pillow with a *thunk,* and, for Blanche, the world of Vietnam blinked out.

———

The sounds of fierce sloshing and brushing came from the bathroom. Jean called out to Blanche. "Well, I slept on it. I'm going to get hold of Thuy through the agency and let her know we've got some business to attend to. We'll see her tomorrow. We can go to the consulate then," she said.

Blanche yelled back through a foam cloud of toothpaste: "Roger, that."

"In the meantime, let's go see Stick. You haven't had second thoughts, have you?"

"No," Blanche called back.

All Blanche could do was stare at herself in the mirror and wonder how it had come to this. She considered this scenario: halfway across the world with a person she barely knew. They were about to revisit an ex-surfer soldier—and do what? It was all sort of odd, but she had to admit, she liked the idea. In fact, she was anxious to see where this was going.

But first, coffee. Her head was pretty clear, considering the amount of whiskey she'd guzzled. Her brain was on overload, but it didn't ruin her mood. She appeared in the bedroom, wrapped in a terry robe, and sat down at the table set with white linen and a carafe, cups, crescents, and fresh fruit. The aroma of coffee was a pleasant wake-up. "No coffee egg pudding today?"

Jean sat on the bed cross-legged. "I figured you'd want a dose of regular old joe. Especially after last night. It was fun, but my head is full of cobwebs."

"Is that what you call it? Sorry, blame me."

"I partook willingly." Jean grinned. "You know, I'm still trying to figure that guy out."

"He's a character. He doesn't seem like the shy type."

"Hardly. He comes on kind of strong."

"Well, he may just have some strong connections."

"We'll find out. I left a message for Thuy while you were finishing your ablutions."

"I'm abluted. I'll be ready to go when you are."

"Back to the bar by ten." Jean was already dressed. She hopped off the bed and began packing a bag with a water bottle and a notebook. "Morning shot and a beer?"

Blanche groaned and took another jolt of coffee. "No thanks. Can't stand the thought of whiskey."

Jean stuffed the rest of the papers in her bag. "Oh, I've heard that before."

"When?"

Jean laughed. "Come to think of it, never."

"It's the drink of the devil," said Blanche. "But I love it." She shredded a crescent and sipped. "Wow, this is so good."

"A specialty here."

Blanche held the white china cup and savored the strong, rich taste. The pleasure of caffeine at the start of the day. *How did my dad start each morning? Not with a china cup…*

Jean stood there, clutching her bag.

"Girl, have a seat. Relax. We've got time," said Blanche, giving up on the dragon fruit for a good old Florida-style orange.

"All the time in the world," Jean murmured. She sat and poured herself a glass of reddish juice. "I don't know, Blanche. Sometimes I feel like this is all kind of crazy."

"Crazy can be good," said Blanche, neatly separating sections of the orange.

They made their way, carefully, out of the hotel and down the street, with every assortment of wheeled vehicle swarming about them. It was almost ten. The scent of noodles and broth from the pot of a vendor wafted toward them. A woman sat on a low stool, her back to the street, ladling the soup into bowls—a rich, hearty breakfast for working off the morning.

Outside The Follies, Stick was lounging against a shiny, black-and-silver Honda Dream motorcycle parked on the sidewalk. The rims flashed in the sunlight, the black leather seats were high gloss. He extended his arms wide. "Ladies of the night! Glad you could make it!"

Blanche had to laugh. Stick's white-bleached hair, the holey jeans, and scuffed boots stood out next to the bustling Vietnamese dressed in subdued, sensible clothing. Heads down, intent on getting to wherever it was they were going. His spanking new tank top said, "I *heart* Vietnam." He patted his chest.

Regular billboard for tourism. Blanche couldn't help smiling. He seemed so welcoming.

"Firstly, good morning to you," said Blanche. "We owe you for last night."

"Don't owe me a thing. Your daddies paid all the dues."

Stick handed them helmets and strapped one on his head. He patted the bike. "Hop on."

Blanche and Jean stood there, staring at him. Several motorbikes whizzed past them within inches. "What?" Blanche was the first to break the silence, except for the cacophony of traffic and hawking wares and the musical chant of a male singer pouring out of an overhead flat.

Stick held the bike's grab bars. "Yeah, we'll head out toward the Delta near Ben Tre. Contact there is sure to have a lead on just about anything you want to know. At least, she always claims so." Stick affixed the strap under his chin.

Blanche turned the helmet every which way and mumbled to herself. She sized up the motorcycle.

"We're going on that?" Her voice rose to a screech. "All three of us?" It was hard enough to negotiate the streets and sidewalks, but now he wanted all of them to *ride*? On *one* bike? Blanche stopped to think. She and Jean together were less than one Stick.

"You have a better idea?" Stick was all grins.

Blanche finally shrugged, clapped on the helmet, and slid onto the cycle behind Jean, who looked surprisingly placid—or resigned? A U-shaped silver bar on the back of the bike was all that separated Blanche from the crazy driver behind her. She held onto Jean. Blanche sent a prayer to Gran. *Get me back to Santa Maria Island in one piece. Please.*

Stick revved the thing and blended into traffic smoothly, surfing among the vehicles and people as they became part of the flow. At first, Blanche closed her eyes; then, she opened them. The breeze was a relief from standing still in the humid air on the street. The other motorcycles and bikes were less luxurious than Stick's, and they carried the usual variety of cargo—some of them jammed up with four people. One rider balanced a kumquat tree, another a bushel of leafy vegetables, and a table. Stick swerved around the old man waving a white handkerchief and walking across six lanes of traffic, steady as he went, not looking left or right. Blanche closed her eyes again. She leaned towards Jean's left ear. "Wake me up when it's over."

Jean turned sideways. "I'm kinda liking it. I hope it's not over any time soon."

"I hope it's not over-over any time soon." Blanche shifted and held onto Jean for dear life.

"How we doin' back there? About an hour or so more. Ya good?" Stick turned slightly, but this was no time for chit-chat. "Hold on," he said and sped off past rice paddies and bamboo, buffalo, and workers hefting bundles. Traffic was light, the cars small, the carts giving way to fast vehicles.

He veered off the well-paved highway and onto a road that turned to dried channels of red mud. A sign up ahead in Vietnamese lettering showed pictures of coconuts and snakes, and in English, "Coconut Factory."

Stick ground to a halt in front of an elevated wooden building. A long porch stood across the front, its roof a mass of palm thatch. Stick hopped off and reached for Jean, who wobbled to her feet. Blanche rolled off the back flank of the bike. "First stop," he said. "You ladies are some good riders."

"Well, that's some horse," Blanche said. Her legs felt like rubber after hours of tense grip on the bike.

"We aim to please," said Stick. He tucked his hair behind his ears and yanked at his jeans. He waved for them to follow as he walked ahead, Blanche noticed, with a limp.

Bales of palm fronds and heaps of coconut husks were neatly piled about. Workers threaded their way through the assortment. They didn't seem to sit and relax in Vietnam, and if they did, they were weaving, stirring, or selling something.

"A factory? For coconuts?" Blanche squinted in the hard sunlight. Dust rose up from the wheels.

Jean shrugged. "This should be good. Not sure what this has to do with finding Mom, but, hey."

Blanche brushed off her thighs and bottom and wondered what her hair looked like now. She'd think about it later. She was curious as all get out. Stick stood up on the porch, holding the door. They entered the "factory."

A tiny woman, thin as a new tree branch and old as the hills, stacked small boxes behind the counter. When she saw Stick, her eyes lit up, her arms crossed over her chest. "What you do here, GI? I sell you snake juice?" She came around, and Stick lifted her off the ground. Blanche guessed the woman was a hundred years old and weighed eighty pounds. "You put me down. I break."

"Oh, heck, Granny, you'll never break."

The two laughed, and Stick lowered her gently. "This here is one of my best friends, Phuong Di Ling," Stick said, introducing the little woman, who wore a simple, faded, perfectly ironed red *ao dai*, her hair pulled back severely. She was fit and healthy, it seemed, but in a fleeting moment, Blanche wondered at the years of terrible things she'd seen.

"We want to say hello, and I want some of that great soap and lip balm for my visitors. Don't think we can carry much more today."

"No snake wine? No cobra?" Phuong laughed, gazing up at Stick. It was a picture Blanche would never forget—the huge, gruff ex-soldier and the lovely, ancient Vietnamese friend.

"Next time. You know I got plenty of venom in me already."

"No, you sweet boy. You good boy," Phuong said. She held Stick's arm and nodded from Blanche to Jean. "You know, he save me. And my family. He no talk about it, but, yes. Mr. Stick. Good."

"Phuong. You makin' stuff up again."

She stood straight as a poker. "No, I do not. I no lie." She folded her hands serenely. "I never forget. Some things I forget, but not you."

"Better not forget me." Stick grinned at her. "You know, I'm always turning up to remind you. I'm here, checking up."

She laughed then, and Blanche wondered about her story. Everyone seemed to have one.

"I get things for you, then we talk." She scooted off to the back of the showroom. Samples of products made from coconut trees lined the shelves: candied ginger and coconut ribbons, oils, salad tongs, soaps, ointments, lotions, mats, and fabrics. It seemed endless, the things that a coconut tree could yield. Stick handed Blanche a pack of fruit candy. "Her own family recipe, made with durian, I think—and peanuts." Blanche tasted a piece. It wasn't too sweet, with a pleasant, almost oily nutty flavor.

On top of a glass case, a large cloudy jar of liquid featured a dead cobra. Blanche said, "Look at this guy. Yuck."

"Don't be harsh," said Stick. "That's snake wine. A local favorite."

"Yum." Blanche winced.

His hand smoothed over the glass-topped case packed with coconut cosmetics. "She has the best here. You'll come back to Vietnam for the soap and coconut oil. Maybe not the snake wine."

Blanche stepped away from the snake and nudged Stick. "What does she mean? You saved her family? You sort of slid right over that."

"She exaggerates," he said, pointing to Phuong, who walked toward them with a bag of products.

"Hmmm."

"I'll tell you later," he said, stepping toward Phuong.

"All your favorites," she said.

Stick pulled out his wallet and grabbed a wad of bills. He hardly counted it. He put it in Phuong's hand as he took the bag.

"Mr. Stick, you want more than product. I don't think you come only for coconut, but I know you love it." Her eyes rested on Jean. "What is going on with you and friends?"

"You are never wrong, Phuong. What is it? That seventh sense of yours? We *are* here for more than coconut."

"And?" Phuong had an expression of practiced patience.

"Jean here is looking for her mother."

With that, Phuong took Jean's hand. "*Con cua toi.*" The corners of her mouth turned down with concern and sadness. "My child."

Jean seemed to relax in Phuong's grasp. She poured it out. "My family is originally from Hoi An. They came to the Saigon area during the war—maybe to the Delta southeast of the city, not far from Ben Tre. I want to find her. That's why I'm here. With my friends." She gestured toward Stick and Blanche.

"Ah," said Phuong. "And does this mother want to be found?" It was not said unkindly. "What family is your mother?"

Her expression pinched, Jean looked to Blanche for support. "Dang. My mother is Dang Tam Li. Her father owned a hotel in Hoi An, but I think they fled in the early 70s. My father was an American soldier here. I was born in Saigon."

"Ah, *bui doi,*" Phuong whispered. She clutched Jean's hands and gently pumped them up and down.

"Yes," said Jean. "And now my father is dead, and I need to find my mother."

Stick planted his boots wide apart. "I figure, Phuong, with all your commercial interests and connections, you may know someone who knows someone who owned a hotel in Hoi An and later settled down here."

"And I say, with your *commerce* you know same same," Phuong snapped back, but she chuckled. "Mr. Stick, you know much, and you know many people here now."

"True, that. Hooray for commerce. I'm thinking of leads down this way but thought it'd be good to run it by you," he said. He rubbed his chin. "This is far different territory. My bar in Saigon isn't much of a connection, and you've got a whole network around here. You might know a name or a place that might help out. Just askin.'"

"It is good to ask," she said. "I think about it."

"That's great." Blanche squeezed Jean's hand.

"You want that I make calls now?" asked Phuong. "You have time?"

"Sure. But don't want to tie you up, Phuong," said Stick. "How much time you got?"

"Time. I have it. We will take it," she said. "In truth, it does not belong to us. It is here, and then it goes. No matter, we like or not." She half muttered to herself and shook her head. She waved them toward the back of the showroom. They followed her.

Blanche turned to Jean. "Why do I feel there is more going on here?"

Ten

A Peace Sign

PHUONG LED THEM TO A SEATING AREA behind the factory showroom. Tables and chairs were set up in the middle of a tangle of palms, ferns, and bamboo. Blanche had never seen such thick walls of green growth, even in Florida. The patio was like a small flat stone set down in a jungle.

"Khah, bring you sweets and something to drink. *Bia*? Or tea?" Their hostess offered the choice to them.

Stick laughed. "Phuong. Tea?"

She shook her head. "For you? You, snake juice." She laughed, showing small, even teeth. "Or you drink coconut wine? Cool and sweet with coconut flavor? Won't make you drunk, but just a little groggy, maybe something special in the throat."

"Hmmm. Maybe I'll just stick to tea," said Blanche.

"Nah. Bring us the snake juice, Phuong."

"Oh, go on. Khah will bring many drinks. How 'bout that? I make calls now." She turned, the delicate ends of her *ao dai* swishing with her quick steps. Khah appeared minutes later bearing a tray with baskets and fruit, a teapot, *333 bia*, and a glass jug of suspect milky liquid. They all stuck to tea, except Blanche, who could never turn down a beer.

"So, tell, Stick." Blanche sipped and then leaned forward on the table. "What did you mean? Commerce?"

"Well, there's Jean's mom, who may be in business."

"There's that," said Jean. "But it seems that you and Phuong have a special connection. Commercial?"

Stick shifted on the chair, a look of discomfort crossing on his face. "Let's just say there was some commerce during the war—some rations and basics that needed a wider distribution." He leaned forward, too, his tone casual. "The people here were starving; we'd lost the f-ing war, and, yet, we were still bombing the life out of them." He sat back, and his eyes drifted away. "She says I saved her, but she, and her family, saved me."

"Come on, Stick. Tell us." Blanche coaxed, her green eyes like go lights.

He looked at her sideways and then poured it out. "We was in the Delta. Me and some of the squad got cut off from the platoon. Patrolling, looking for an NVA ammo dump. Instead, we walked up on this village. You gotta understand about the village in Vietnam. It's everything; it's the world. At least it was. Enclosed in a hedge of thick bamboo and elephant grass, for centuries.

"The families, tight, handing down the field of rice and paying respects only to the local chiefs.

"And then we come along, following the French. And, I gotta say, the Chinese, the Japanese, the Portuguese got in there, too. Seems like the Vietnamese never got a break.

"I don't even know how we happened upon Phuong's village. The grass was so thick, like razor blades, and the bamboo surrounded the place. That's the design of the village. A protective measure, but not always."

He stopped there. The lush setting, the colorful tablecloth, tea things, the beer, fruit, and breads all belied devastation. He stuck a chunk of mango in his mouth and seemed reluctant to relive the old Delta.

"I mean, we screwed it up enough, destroying all their lands and jungle with Agent Orange and bombs, and our hacking and killing. At least the French left architecture and education. We spent millions and millions and left nothing but devastation."

"You walked up on their village?" All Blanche could picture was her father in the midst of the burning and the misery. What Stick described must have happened thousands of times during the war.

Stick's eyes went blank. "Yeah, we walked up, all right. And there was nothing there. Except funnels of smoke lifting into the air after the burning—charred remains of houses, I guess, you'd say, huts. The trees, skeletons. Like the people. The bodies." He shook his head. "There was nothin' left. A B-52 zapped the area; the Air Force left them the gift of Agent Orange. You could say it was toast. Literally." He lowered his head and clenched his fists.

"All I saw was Phuong. At first, I didn't think she was human—a mound of burned cloth next to the frame of a bamboo hut. I came up on her slowly 'cause there's VC all around. Ya just don't know. But there she was, cradling a bundle. The body of a dead child. She was rocking and singing, and the sound of it still drives me crazy."

Stick's voice hitched. Blanche and Jean didn't move, sitting in this green cocoon in the middle of nowhere. A loan cricket, or bird, peeped in the bushes.

"That day, there was not a soul left in the village. That I could see. We'd been humpin' through the jungle. Me and Freddie and The Neck. The three of us. Covered in mud, like a trio from hell walkin' out of the brush and into Phuong's village. At that point, I didn't care who was around. I was numb. All I remember is kneelin' next to her. I took the body of the child, and she followed me to a patch of mud off the path, and we buried it. It was a little girl. In a tattered red dress. Phuong's granddaughter. All the rest of the villagers were gone, burned to charred bones, or run off.

"I didn't know what to do then. Freddie and The Neck went to sleep in a kind of a shell of a temple down the way. I had some peaches, I took 'em out, and opened the can. Spoon fed Phuong, her eyes the color of the dead field all around us. I can still remember the look on her face when she tasted the syrup. Believe me; it was the only sun I'd seen for days.

"Then, out of nowhere, I heard the sound of AK-47s, the unmistakable poppin' sound. NVA. Very unfriendly fire. The bad stuff and they were out there, and they was close. I stashed Phuong behind some jars of grain and ran with Freddie and The Neck, but it was too late. My M-16 jammed, the boys went down and out, nearly vaporized by the rounds. And I just lay there, hit in the leg. Waitin' for the end of it…

"Phuong grabbed my leg, dragged me, pointin' like a wild woman. The shootin' had stopped, and there was blood everywhere. We low-crawled to a small depression about twenty feet from the hut, and Phuong said, 'Go in.' A hole opened up under some branches, so narrow, I didn't think I'd fit, but I did, and down I went into a tunnel that widened into a small cave and then larger—a whole world down there under the ground. Phuong was right behind me. She shushed me, wrapped my leg. A cold something on my head. That's all I remember.

"She saved me, an American soldier, responsible for the death of her grandchild and the end of her family and the devastation of her village. I'd given her a can of peaches.

"I woke up down there on a pile of palm branches, and she says, 'I know you no bad man. Vietcong, they come and burn us out if we do not cooperate. They want us to join NVA, give them all our rice, hide them from the ARVN and Americans. It is all bad business. All war, bad business. But some people, good.'"

"How'd you ever make it out of there?" Jean croaked, her eyes dark.

"I did. I made it out, back to my platoon. My leg looked like it was just about rotted off, but Phuong took good care of me. She and her people carried me, helped me find my way, and then they crept back to their village. I found Phuong years later when I returned to Saigon. Felt I had unfinished business here."

"Unfinished business?" asked Blanche. "More commerce?"

"Yeah, I guess you can say that. But more than that. Makin' some kind of amends? Seekin' peace? It can't hurt. Like the Buddha say, on the road to 'mindfulness,' one must extinguish the fires of hate, greed, and delusion. It's a tough order, but it helps make it right."

"Mindfulness?" Bang went at it. Jean raised her eyebrows.

"Gets rid of egotism. Limits our potential."

"Are you Buddhist, Stick?"

"I wish. My road to enlightenment has many stumbling blocks."

"Why?"

"You want to be enlightened, Blanche?" Stick relaxed. His shoulders drew down. "There's a parable about the Buddha, that he was born from the side of the mother near her heart. Come to mean, only when we live from the heart and truly feel pain of others do we become human."

"Sometimes it's hard to be human," said Blanche.

"In the ex-treme," he said.

Phuong shuffled toward them over the patio stones. "You go see Uncle Five. He know people in Hoi An." She squared her shoulders and folded her hands.

Stick stood up, his arms wide in gratitude. "Ah, I know Uncle Five. Good one, Phuong. We'll follow up."

She pulled him over, an attempt at privacy, but Phuong's raspy whisper carried. "The new computer and printer come. You, very good, Mr. Stick. Khah can fix, put all together." She took his hands and squeezed them, beaming up at him. "Business is good."

Stick clearly was embarrassed. He hugged Phuong and turned to Blanche and Jean. "I should call her Peaches, not Phuong. That sunny smile and all."

Eleven

The Buddha Talks

UNCLE FIVE HAD TO BE PUSHING SEVENTY, and he was halfway up a palm tree when Stick, Jean, and Blanche pulled up on the Honda. They'd traveled over a rutty road through a tunnel of overhanging palms, past bamboo huts, rice paddies, and a grunting buffalo or two in the field. At last, the bike veered onto a narrow, hidden path with a clearing and a house at the end of the world.

"He's called Uncle Five after his birth order. He's actually number four, but in Vietnam, they number the first child 'two,' and the remaining sibs are numbered from there on. I don't know why. Uncle's real name is Huc Vin Tong." Stick threw one leg off the bike seat and helped his traveling companions climb down.

Uncle Five's house was a long, low yellow building with a red tile roof. Under an overhang on the walkway, dozens of buddhas posed in welcome: gold ones and ceramic, male and female, smiling and serious. One seated on a stepped altar of glistening tiles. A variety of blue and white vases—some taller than Blanche—overflowed with lilies, roses, and orchids. At one end of the house, a spray of hot pink bougainvillea spread up a trellis and onto the roof.

Uncle Five shimmied down the trunk of the palm. "Welcome to my home!"

"Some home," Blanche said under her breath.

"Look at this place." Jean was gaping.

Stick attempted introductions. Uncle Five bowed. "Ah, Mr. Stick, and esteemed ladies. So nice. One moment, please." He bowed again to his guests and hurried into the house.

He reappeared minutes later, rolling up the sleeves of an impeccable white shirt. He wore loose black trousers and rubber sandals typically made of recycled tires.

Just then, half a dozen frisky puppies scampered down the walkway. Blanche picked one up. It licked her face and climbed up her arm. Jean bent down and tickled the rest.

"I hope the little devils do not bother you," Uncle Five said.

"Oh, no, I may have to take this one back with me to Florida," said Blanche. The puppy was making a valiant effort to burrow into Blanche's bag.

"Then you will have to take my son, Huong, with you, too, because he will not part with doggies." He chuckled. "Please, come. We need to have discussion and tea." Inside the dark entry, statues of Joan of Arc, Moses, and Jesus stared benignly from their pedestals.

Uncle Five paused, noting Blanche's surprise. "The practice of Cao Dai. We express reverence for the great leaders—Buddha, Muhammad, Victor Hugo, Sun Yay-sen, and the Pope. It does not hurt to listen to many, to invite the ideas of wise leaders." Blanche remembered reading about the popular sect of the 1920s that had spread and gathered followers in the Delta.

He gestured toward a large Buddha surrounded by candles and flowers, its hand pointing to the earth. "One with nature, sitting under the Bodhi tree. Nature is our friend, helping to achieve enlightenment." Uncle Five folded his hands and narrowed his eyes. "The world religions are not contradictory. Buddha does not reject help of other gods. But, mostly, we Vietnamese revere the Buddha. May his greatness guide you."

He bowed slightly, and Blanche hoped she would remember his words. They made some sense of the world.

"Thank you. Hope so," Jean murmured.

Blanche's eyes adjusted to the dim interior. The furniture was heavy and ornate—chests with intricate brass trim, large carved sofas with an abundance of silk pillows. They walked through the narrow house to an area in the back where a certain amount of industry was in progress. A shed spilled over with equipment, and a boy sat on the ground whacking away at bamboo with a machete. He stood up and bowed when his father introduced his guests.

"Huong, please, tea and cake, *s'il vous plait?*" The boy ran off into the house. Their host gestured for them to sit on the padded wrought iron chairs arranged around a table.

Blanche said, "French? You speak French and English? I wish I knew some Vietnamese…."

Jean laughed. "Blanche, please don't try."

"I know, right? I get things mixed up with cod and eggplant."

Uncle Five's eyebrows shot up. "Yes. Well. It is an interesting language. Tonal with Latin influence," he said. "I attended the French School in Saigon as a boy. Huong continues with the studies." Now that he was out of the tree, seated in an armchair with legs crossed, Uncle Five was poised and soft-spoken, like a professor or an executive.

Huong returned with a silver tray loaded down with a teapot, cups, and a basket of cakes and biscuits. The boy went back to his chore, this time sorting the bamboo he'd trimmed into bundles while the pups and their mother huddled next to him, yipping and whimpering. Stick crouched on the ground next to the dogs, tickling and rolling them around, much to the delight of Huong.

Uncle Five relaxed. His hair was slick and black, his vulpine features pleasant. "So, you enjoy Vietnam?" He looked intently from Blanche to Jean, and his eyes rested on her.

"Oh, yes, the energy on the streets, the food, the people…" Jean's enthusiasm made Uncle Five smile.

"But, I hear, you are not in Vietnam for the food and energy. You want to find mother?"

"Yes, that's it," said Jean. "And Blanche…"

"My father died here," said Blanche. The words spilled out, hard and uncomfortable, but she couldn't hold back. Her father was all around her in this country, and she wanted him to be part of the journey.

Uncle Five's expression didn't change. "I am sorry, Miss Blanche." His level gaze made Blanche look away. "It is difficult." He rested one hand on the table as he leaned toward her. "I share your sadness…."

All of a sudden, it was too much, but not enough for her to turn away. She had that choking feeling again. *Where does that come from?* She swallowed hard.

Stick looked at Blanche and loudly scraped a chair up to the table. He picked up his teacup, like a thimble in his large hand. "Uncle lost them all in the war. His family. They were among the three million Vietnamese soldiers and civilians. Gone," he said. "And, no, that does not make it easier or any better. For anybody."

"We are recovering," said Uncle Five, sitting back. He sipped the tea. His son dropped the machete with a clatter and began playing with the pups. No one had taken anything sweet from the tray.

A cloud of shared experience and understanding hovered. They had all lost someone and many things.

Blanche's thoughts found her way back to the mission: *Find Jean's mom. Maybe find out more about my dad.*

"I want to help," said Uncle Five. "Miss Jean, Miss Blanche, what can you tell me? Phuong said little on the phone."

"My mother's parents owned a hotel in Hoi An, and my mother kept the books. Her name is Tam Li. The family of Dang."

"I know of a prominent family in Hanoi of that name. Their daughter was a doctor during the war, and she was killed in Quang Tri province. Her diaries became quite the sensation. I doubt if there is a connection, but I will look. The name is fairly common, I'm afraid." He tapped his lips set in a thin line. "They were charitable people, and they had brothers in the South. Sometimes charity casts a wide net. That avenue may be a place to examine." His thinking echoed Sister Joseph.

"That is what we've heard. I hope that net is wide," said Jean.

"It is not so unusual here, but there are many outlets, agencies—religious and secular. It may be just as well to follow the business contacts."

"Maybe," said Jean. "I don't recognize that family of the North you mention, but I haven't had contact with my mother for many years now. I haven't felt her hands, hugged her in ... twenty-eight years."

His expression softened. "It was a bad time. After the Americans left in 1975, the North Vietnamese sent many to the re-education camps. Your mother may have been sent away or, my dear, worse."

"I know. I have thought of that, but I have to believe she is still alive. Her family would have sent my father a notice or something. They weren't very communicative, but I hope they would have tried to tell us such news."

Uncle Five sat up straight, animated, and eager. "Now I am thinking. Again, the business. You know, for all their cumbersome bureaucracy, the Communists do make use of talent. They may have employed your grandparents, and your mother, in one of their bureaus. I will check for you. I know some people."

"More doors to open," said Jean with a forlorn look. "Hope they're not dead ends."

"You must keep looking. Your family is of the educated class, so it is likely your mother continued in business," he said.

"And you, Uncle Five? What is your experience?" Blanche asked.

"I met my countrymen to the North the hard way," he said. "The world was blasted out from under me."

Uncle Five had been a prominent landowner and later a driver for the South Vietnamese army. But being industrious worked against him. In those years, mistrust among the Vietnamese was rampant. The North Vietnamese Army infiltrated the villages, worked to turn one against the other, further complicating civil unrest. No one's beliefs or privacy were safe.

Uncle Five was turned in to the Communists by a cousin who was afraid of being arrested. "I spent three years in a re-education camp reading Lenin and Marx and building roads from five o'clock in the morning until I dropped. It was boring, and we were not re-educated. I returned here to my village and began again. That is all I could do. That is all anyone can do. Begin again and make the past the past."

"I'm sorry," said Jean. "Here I am, asking you to dig up the past."

"Oh, no, no." He raised his teacup to Stick. "We are friends. I will ask about the Dangs, their charity work, and the doctor's and see if there is connection. And the business dealings. This is the past we want to recover. I hope you find your mother."

Twelve

Moon Gazing

BLANCHE, JEAN, AND STICK walked down the gravel path away from Uncle Five's house. They left with nothing solid to go on. Nothing but a couple more slim leads—possible connections to charity, and to the Dangs of the North, and the same encouragement to look for Tam Li as an entrepreneur in a new town with a new life.

"I don't think my mother is part of that family." Jean shook her head. "I would have heard something."

"He's going to check," said Blanche. "What do you think, Stick?"

"Like we were talkin', gotta throw out that net," he said. "Phuong and Five know a lot of people down here. They'll ask around. It can't hurt."

"It could work," said Blanche as she climbed on the bike. "I feel we're getting closer."

"Or further," said Jean.

"Don't say that. We're here, we're searching, and we won't quit."

Blanche and Jean held on tight as Stick sped down Highway 1 back into Saigon. A conical hat moved through the tall grass amid bomb craters that had been turned into lakes and stocked with fish. The humid countryside filled Blanche's head. The scenery was spectacular, the air golden above the patches of green neatly laid out in the different phases of farming. It lifted Blanche's spirits, and she hoped it did the same for Jean.

Blanche leaned into Jean's ear: "Beautiful, isn't it?"

Jean gave a thumb's up.

It was refreshing, but all the while, Blanche thought of soldiers wading through the waist-deep water with M-16s over their heads. Scared out of their wits. Her father among them. Everywhere she looked, she wondered about him—whether he had stood on that hill or the other, rumbled over this road in a Jeep, or flown over it in a chopper.

The bike heaved around another pothole, her stomach going with it—and oddly enough, she was hungry after a day of mostly fruit and cake. They swerved. A knot of fear coiled in her chest. Stick seemed to be a competent rider, but she worried they'd be tossed into a rice paddy. She tried to relax as the motorcycle flew toward town, hitting bumps and cruising past the occasional cart or small vehicle.

Stick turned his head. "Y'all hungry?"

"Did you hear my stomach?" Blanche's words were lost in the wind.

"Gonna take you to one of my favorite places. Be *real* hungry."

Jean yelled, "No problem!" And Blanche held on tight.

———

Stick pulled up to a bistro near a park in Saigon. A banner sign in red and yellow over the door to the restaurant read, *Politburo.* Stick wedged the bike into a snug space next to the brick building and locked it.

They sat against the wall at a table with a padded bench and chair under a mural with workers raising their fists, farmers in conical hats, patchworked fields, tall buildings, parks, and bridges. A collage of Vietnam, old and new, in every color.

Blanche ordered crunchy red rice with vegetables, Jean chose the sea bass with lemongrass and chili, and Stick selected most of page one on the menu: shrimp spring rolls, dumpling soup, pho, beef and broken rice, and two baguettes. Cuban rum, Swedish vodka, Irish whiskey, and tsipouro Greek grappa were listed on the back page. They all ordered the featured *333 bia*.

"Did you have trouble opening your bar, Stick?" Blanche was considering a shot of the Irish.

"Some. Dealing with the bureaucracy here is like turning the Titanic on a dime. But you can do it."

"Are you glad you did? Seems like you went through a lot during the war. Why would you stay?"

"The short answer is, I guess the mud got to me." Outside the window in the park, a tree waved droopy branches over the brown river.

"The mud?" Blanche put the menu down and followed his gaze.

"The fields, the earth, the good and the bad. Vietnam gets to you."

"I can see that," she said. *It's sure got to me.*

"I'm an old dog. Can't change now," he said. The spring rolls arrived. He slid the platter towards them. They all dipped into the chili-garlic sauce and fell in silently.

"Everybody's been so hospitable. That's mostly 'cause of Stick," said Jean, as she finished a dumpling.

"Nah, I can't take no credit. It's just I been here so long. Longer than I lived in the U.S."

"You miss it?" asked Blanche.

"The big C's? Competition, Congress, and Confusion?"

He was so large and blond that Blanche had a hard time imagining him fitting in. Yet, he seemed to manage just fine. She guessed it was his attitude. She hadn't heard him raise his voice except to laugh. He hadn't said a negative thing. The big C's he spoke of were fact.

Of course, Blanche was *curious* with a capital C. "But, Stick, you fought for it. And then you left it all?"

"I did and would again. I went back for a while but didn't fit in. They got plenty of the C's here, but it's a simpler life. And I ain't judged, believe it or not. The Vietnamese don't believe in regret and lookin' back. Waste of time and energy, they say." He dug into a mountain of shrimp fried rice.

"Buddhist philosophy? Seems you've picked up some of those beliefs." Blanche watched the mountain disappear.

He set down his fork. "It's their belief that suffering leads to enlightenment. Can't avoid it. Buddhism's been around for 2,500 years. They must be doin' somethin' right."

"Yes, determined." Blanche thought for a moment, her beer poised in midair. "Focused."

"You could say that. There is somethin' to being focused. You can win wars like that." A wry smile appeared. He seemed to forget the platter of marinated prawns he'd ordered, but then he dug in. Looking down into the last of the rice, Stick shook his head. "Whatcha all think about our outing today? Want to follow up with Uncle Five?"

"Absolutely. Even if he can't find us a solid lead, I loved meeting him. He got my hopes up," said Jean. "Tomorrow, it's the consulate. Right, B?"

"Right." Blanche sat back, stuffed with shredded bok choy and carrots. "I can't help thinking that Uncle Five said the 'charity' connection might be a lead. I want to talk to Thuy about that."

"Charity? Thuy? I don't follow," said Jean.

"Your mom went to the sisters when she was about to give birth to you. She might have paid them back in some way. And Thuy knows her way around. She might be able to dig up some clues. Follow the trail."

"Seems like Sister Joseph, or Thuy, would have said something."

"Maybe, unless they just don't know. Or don't want to say for some reason." Blanche unraveled her thoughts out loud. "So, the business, the charity, the family name. Nothing real solid, but I still have a good feeling."

Stick grinned. Jean's recurrent doubt and anxiety simmered down a bit. Blanche drank the last of her *bia*.

She made a grab for the check, but she was no match for Stick. "It's thousands and thousands," he laughed. "Of dong."

"What?" Blanche leaned over the table.

"Two hundred thousand *dong*," he said. "You just had a five-star experience for a few bucks a plate. Besides, I ate everything on the table."

"Not quite," said Blanche. The crunchy red rice alone was worth the trip. She'd never tasted anything quite like it. "Thanks, we'll get you back."

"Your charming company is payment enough."

"Right," said Blanche. "Bet you say that to all the ladies."

"Nope, just you two."

Jean rolled her eyes and grinned. "Thanks, Stick."

"Right now, I want to show you something," he said. They walked out of the restaurant toward the Honda. The humidity lay like a wet cloud. The moon and the red and silver lights of the buildings reflected off the river, and the gnarled banyan trees stood in a ghostly line along the bank. Blanche had read in Vietnamese mythology: The dark spots on the moon are the banyan tree, next to the man who flew away from his wife on earth to be with the Moon Lady and the Jade Rabbit. The culture seemed to find never-ending ways to explain nature and all the world—a trait that served up one puzzle after another. Blanche stopped at the edge of the park and looked across the sky.

Jean tugged at Blanche, who lingered over the moon. "Earth calling!"

Blanche snapped back. "Sorry, got carried away."

Stick waved them over to the bike. "Well, let me carry you a bit farther. Just a short ride, and then I got to get you ladies home."

Thirteen

The Landing

STICK DROVE THE MOTORCYCLE out of the fashionable section where the French colonial buildings and wide boulevards were reminiscent of Paris. The classical white buildings gave way to ramshackle plywood fronts as he headed into narrow, congested streets. The conical hats bobbed, one cyclo next to the other. People scurried with large vessels and branches and rolls of fabric. It was getting close to night, and everyone seemed to be hurrying to get the rest of the day wrapped up.

Stick zigzagged, slowed, and revved up, clearing motorbikes and pedestrians. The beeping was incessant. The smell of diesel from cars and grilled meat at the street vendors' carts clogged Blanche's senses as she held onto Jean. One-hundred-year-old pagodas leaned up against aluminum-front stores with neon signs advertising everything from cookers to noodles.

Stick's maneuvering was just as gutsy as that of the Vietnamese. He seemed competent, even as the motorcycle wobbled, stopped, and came to grips with the traffic. Stick planted his feet on the pavement when congestion was too thick to move, and then he kicked it into gear. There didn't seem to be any lanes, and no one stopped for lights or signs. Blanche had to remind herself that Stick had decades of experience on the streets of Saigon. The ambiance was hypnotizing; she was becoming numb to fear, and the beers at dinner helped.

Up ahead of them, a motorbike balanced a cage full of ducks. More ducks hung off the middle of the chassis, each bird nestled in its own little cocoon, but the sound was not warm and fuzzy. The quacking from those yellow beaks sticking out of the pockets and between the bars was enough to drown out the beeping bikes. The cage was tall, the driver sitting ramrod straight and driving on, compensating for the weight of his wieldy cargo. When the ducks went right, he corrected left.

"Oh, my God," said Blanche into Jean's ear.

She turned. "I know. Duck soup?"

"I hope not."

Stick tried to pass the driver with the ducks. He pulled alongside, but the man did not give an inch. Stick sped up and swerved around to the left. The ducks went left, too. The driver's hands worked the grab bars to steady the three-story bamboo tower of ducks, but it was not to be. Blanche saw it coming. She shut her eyes, then opened them in disbelief and clamped herself to Jean's back.

The motorcycle skidded sideways over a slick spot on the road. Blanche was about to lose the red rice, *bia*, and everything else she'd eaten that day. Several wheeled vehicles came at them in the opposite direction like a shiver of sharks. One tried to stop. Last thing she saw were Stick's white knuckles gripping the bars for dear life.

It was metal on metal, bamboo on pavement—the explosive quacking of furious ducks—a cacophony from hell.

In the middle of it all, Jean's arms shot up. She and Blanche went flying into a group of horrified Vietnamese who had been drinking their *bia* and *ca phe,* seated at a low table outside a restaurant. In an instant, Blanche was draped over a young man and a girl seated tightly together. The alcohol and caffeine splashed everywhere, the shrieks nearly deafening her. She struggled to her feet and got her bearings.

"Oh, I'm so sorry. *Very sorry*," she said. She patted herself all over; nothing felt broken. *I'm still alive, and so are they!*

She looked frantically for Jean. She was standing in the wreckage, yanking at her shirt. Blanche exhaled with relief that they were intact, except that they'd managed to destroy a table, several bottles of beer, a few cups, and the peace and quiet of those relaxing on the sidewalk. And the ducks! A great deal of chattering in Vietnamese added to the confusion.

"I am *really* sorry." Blanche straightened herself out. She kept nodding at the young man and woman, who smiled back with concern. He held out a wad of napkins. Blanche swiped at the stains on her front and at Jean, and then she dabbed at the young man. He laughed at her jerky attempt to clean up the mess.

"The Americans have landed." He grinned. "Again."

Blanche was glad he seemed amused and that they hadn't killed anyone this time.

A waiter emerged from the restaurant with a broom and began to sweep up the detritus. Blanche made a move to help, but the girl held Blanche's arm. "You sit. You had major air travel tonight. You need rest." She was grinning, too. They all did, with relief.

"Stick!" Blanche suddenly walked off. The crowd had congealed, and she couldn't see past the heads. *Where's Stick? And his motorcycle?* The driver of the ducks and his cargo were pulling themselves together amid a great deal of quacking. She dodged the pedestrians.

An officer came toward Blanche, one outstretched palm held up. He wore a tan uniform, and his features were hard to read. He didn't seem like the welcoming committee. Now he had both hands up, threateningly close to her face. "You!" he said. "Much problem, much trouble."

"My friend, I have to get to my friend," yelled Blanche. "And I'm so sorry about the ducks." She peered around the officer, but he did a side-step. Blanche did the same little dance and then stopped in her tracks.

"The friend, he lives. The ducks, not so sure," the officer said. "You stop now."

Blanche could see an emergency wagon of some sort. The back door was open. Stick was bundled on a stretcher, sitting up. He waved. *A thumbs up?*

"Thank God," she breathed. "May I see him, please?"

"No, he go to clinic. You see him other time. Tomorrow. Maybe," said the officer.

Blanche smoothed her damp shirt that reeked of beer and coffee. And fish sauce? She was in a daze. The officer sniffed disapprovingly, and the stolid expression cracked into one of disgust. Then, for an instant, he softened. "You all right, lady?"

Now the hospitality. "I think so." But she couldn't think. She craned her neck. Stick chugged off down the road in the van, his bike under the care of officials in tan uniforms. The ducks were gone.

"What you do here?" the officer asked.

"I don't know." Blanche was suddenly confused. She kept her hand on her fanny pack.

"Passport, please?"

Blanche unzipped and reached in. Reflex. The moment she handed it over, she regretted it. An American in Vietnam? Relinquishing a passport? Not a good look.

The officer flipped the passport open. Blanche waited a beat, then thrust her hand out to retrieve it. He backed away, his mouth in a tight line. Blanche was intrepid, if nothing else; she peeked at the precious little booklet that he held upside down. He snatched it from view. "I keep. Tomorrow you come to Bureau of Security Police. Maybe get passport back."

She was stunned. "No. I need it back now...."

He walked away, the boots clomping down the sidewalk, an arm swinging.

"Hello! Hey!" She pleaded, but he was gone.

The young couple who had been Blanche's landing pad stood at her elbow. "Miss?" The girl tugged at Blanche's arm. "My name is Nhung. This is Bac," she said, seemingly oblivious to the passport drama. The front of Bac's shirt was soaked. His glasses were slightly askew, and yet he was *still* smiling.

Nhung held on to Blanche's sleeve, her cheery face framed in a fringe of shiny black bangs. "Come over and sit. Your friend, Jean, is waiting. We will talk."

Blanche gestured at the retreating officer. She was inclined to chase him down. "He has my passport."

"Tsk," said Nhung. "It is protocol. You will get passport back. Perhaps."

"*Perhaps?* There is no perhaps about it."

Nhung said, "Do not worry. They—the traffic police—are posturing. You give ten dollars. Maybe more. You get passport back. It is the way."

"What? A fee?" Blanche asked.

"More like bribe. Too bad you no give now."

"That wasn't in the guidebook."

Nhung laughed. "Many things not in guidebook. The traffic police, they do nothing when they should do something. It best to have little to do with them. You foreigner, you in the wrong, no matter what you do. Too bad. Look!"

Across the street, two motorbikes had collided: one carrying four people, the other balancing a large bundle of vegetation. Leaves and branches were scattered on the pavement, and the riders picked up their bikes and cargo with a lot of chattering. No one seemed to be in charge of the chaos. Blanche's eyes watered in the gray metallic haze of the traffic fumes, and she knuckled away the irritation with her fists. The traffic policeman lounged against a small grocer's display, ignoring the mishap entirely.

"Give them 'tax' and get passport." Nhung waved dismissively. She picked up a fresh beer off the table and handed one to Blanche. "*Hakuna matata.* No worries, for rest of life."

"You know *The Lion King*?"

"Who does not know Lion King? From the Great Mouse at Disney."

Jean seemed to be quizzing Bac on the intricacies of the police state. He didn't have another idea outside of what Nhung told Blanche. She was anxious, but there was nothing to do about the passport predicament now. She'd have to get Thuy on the case. They all sat down at the low plastic table, now righted, and once again covered with bottles of water, beer, and coffee.

Nhung turned to Jean. "Sister, you *Viet kieu?*" She addressed her respectfully as a peer. Jean knew what *Viet kieu* meant: a Vietnamese returning home from another country.

"Yes, I guess I am. Half Vietnamese returning here. My father was an American soldier. Some call me 'child of dust.'"

"Oh, you no dust, friend." Nhung slapped the air. "*Viet kieu* of endless interest. Many say, you rich, you lucky, you live in land of opportunity and wealth and freedom. We are curious, sometimes jealous." But Nhung's smile was welcoming, clearly not showing signs of jealousy.

"I'm not wealthy, and I am glad to be here," said Jean. "I'm looking for my mother, and my friend Blanche is helping."

"Ah," said Nhung. "Where you look?"

"I feel like we're looking all over. We have appointments and some contacts. Stick, our friend who was on the motorcycle, is helping us."

"That is good. You will need much help. Many people. Vietnam is a big place," said Nhung.

"Much bigger than I thought."

"Sometimes unraveling strings is easy when you look for simple way out of tangle."

"We'll try," said Blanche. She filed that piece away. Sometimes she did make things more complicated than they needed to be.

The group had recovered. They were all sipping beer and coffee together like long-lost family, communicating in a mix of English, Vietnamese, and a little French. Blanche perched on the frightfully small seat. Her shirt had dried, but it was a mess. "Better to drink it than wear it," she muttered.

"I'll say," said Jean. "You okay?"

"I'll live. Didn't look good for some of those ducks."

"I saw the driver get up. The ducks, not so much, but I wonder about Stick. I'll ask Thuy to call over there."

"Stick waved at me. That's a good sign. The officer said he's all right, but I got the feeling he was placating me."

"Ya think? We need to get that passport back."

Nhung chimed in. "You will do this tomorrow. It seem bad, it not so bad. You will see."

"I hope you're right," said Blanche. "I like it here, but I do want to go home. Eventually."

"You take me with you?" Nhung asked, but her tone was playful. Bac was leaning forward, nodding.

Blanche cradled the beer bottle in her hands, her shoulders hunched. "I wish I could do whatever you want. You have all been so hospitable and warm to us. Despite our busting up the party."

"You *make* party. We like flying American girls," said Bac with a hint of mischief behind those crooked glasses.

A wave of exhaustion swept over Blanche. It was not only the accident. She and Jean seemed to be veering further afield. Now they needed to visit the police—and connect with all those leads on new contacts. It seemed like something was always getting in the way or taking them in a new direction. *We're here to find Jean's mother? Where the heck is she?*

It was piling up, but she *would* get that passport back. And Stick would be *fine*. He'd waved, and that was a good sign. Right now, Blanche needed sleep … and maybe one more beer.

Have to think positively. What would Uncle Five say? The words of Buddha—and Gran: Do not dwell in the past; do not dream of the future; concentrate the mind on the present moment. Oh, Buddha!

Fourteen

There'd Be Days Like This

THUY MET THEM IN THE HOTEL LOBBY the next morning. She had changed hats, this one a cloche with a large red bow on the side. She'd applied lipstick to match, and her outfit was a sensible white blouse and mid-length black skirt. Happy and smiling, and always helpful, Thuy was a lifeline.

"You ladies. Very busy in Saigon," she said. "Now. We have much business today."

"Thanks for adjusting our schedule, Thuy. I'm sorry about all the confusion," said Jean. "Our friend Stick is in the hospital, and the police still have Blanche's passport, and we need to get to the consulate…."

Thuy bowed her head slightly and clasped her hands. "We do all. One thing after other. First, we look at Mr. Stick, and then we get passport back." She gestured toward the waiting car.

"What would we do without Thuy?" Blanche murmured.

"We'd be quacking with the ducks. Poor ducks."

It was a short ride to the clinic where they had taken Stick. The entryway was a dour greeting with bile-yellow stucco walls, bars on the windows, a single, sagging vinyl settee against the wall. A poster with an obvious list of rules featuring bullet points hung on the wall behind the desk. Blanche couldn't understand any of it, but the rules appeared to be stark and ominous with warning signs and bold letters. An intimidating statement. *Do or die.* Thuy chattered away with the attendant, a miserable-looking older man with a down-turned mouth who kept shaking his head.

The trip turned out to be useless. They would not allow visitors. That was clear from the animated, somewhat infuriating discussion between Thuy and the attendant at the information desk. Unrelated parties were not allowed to see the injured. His final report: Stick was recovering. Check back later. Or never.

Blanche shuddered. She felt partially responsible for Stick's accident. If he hadn't been so kind and accommodating, he'd be intact. Adding to it was the frustration that she couldn't do a thing about it. "We'll go over to The Follies later," she said. "Maybe the staff will know something. And maybe we can help somehow."

"Glory, Blanche. We've done enough damage."

"I know. I hear you."

"Do not worry," said Thuy, bustling ahead of them toward the door. "I'm sorry we cannot see Mr. Stick, but we know he is resting."

"I have a feeling he won't be dancing under that disco ball any time soon," said Jean, a frown etching her forehead. "I bet the condition of his bike worries him more than his arms and legs."

"Oh, no. He *loves* that bike," said Blanche.

"No love bike. Bike is two wheels, no heart," said Thuy. "Mr. Stick, he will be fine."

Thuy drove them the short distance to the Office of Security Police. The same sad, rundown façade and barred windows of a once-grand building. There was not a sign of Vietnamese hospitality here. It looked more like a prison.

Thuy held the door open. "Now we get passport."

—✺—

The decorator for the Security Police was the same one for the hospital. Although the outside of the building promised a nostalgic glimpse of old French colonial architecture, the inside was the same depressing yellow stucco and a waiting room that held the smell of stale smoke in the gray air. Two young kids with backpacks were sitting on metal chairs. The hole in the wall framed a gruff officer who took their names and said, without looking up, "You wait."

"Ugh. Communism," said Jean, under her breath. "Sometimes I feel like I'm in two countries here."

"Well, this better be the land of reasonable, or I'll be spending a lot of time in Vietnam without that passport," said Blanche. Thuy didn't seem inclined to chat or sit. She stood stiffly at the window of the dour officer, making her presence known while he shuffled papers. "We need to finish this business. *Tout suite.*"

Blanche and Jean exchanged glances. "She means business," said Blanche. "Doesn't that mean quickly?"

"Right now," said Thuy, firmly.

On cue, the official retreated, and the door next to the hole in the wall sprang open. The traffic officer from the duck incident stood there with a look of disdain, taking them all in.

"Officer, sir," said Thuy. "I wish to present Misses Blanche and Jean. The passport of Miss Blanche, *s'il vous plait*?" The throwback to French seemed to deepen his frown.

"Yes, I meet Miss Blanche. In street," he said. His little arched brows shot up.

In street? What? She didn't like the sound of that. She ground her teeth and determined to cool it, which was a stretch. They hadn't even started the business at hand.

He turned. "*Pffffft,*" he said as he ushered them into an office and gestured for them to sit. The accommodations were like the lobby but with the addition of a long table that doubled as a desk, four more metal chairs, and a high dirty window with bars. The same stale air nearly made them gag.

The patch on his uniform said "Bung." Blanche had not noticed his name the night before in her state of confusion, nor the stamp of meanness of his downturned, tight little mouth. He lost no time getting to the point as he pulled up a chair and sat. "You cause destruction of many ducks." He folded his hands on top of the table.

The ire crept up Blanche's back, and with it, heat to the top of her head. She clamped her teeth on her tongue to avoid causing more trouble, but it did no good. "Well, doesn't this duck delivery person have any responsibility? He was weaving and bobbing all over the street." Blanche stood up and put both hands on the table. "And what do the ducks have to do with my passport?"

Jean coughed discreetly and croaked, "Bang!" She tugged at her friend's sleeve. Thuy made an effort to step forward, but the officer stared back at Blanche. Implacable. The eyebrows arched once again.

"Ducks and passport," she said. "They are not related." The spurious connection was obvious.

Jean and Thuy stood on either side of Blanche, who answered his stare. "Sir, Officer Bung," said Jean. "We are sorry for the fate of the ducks. We did not cause their destruction. But we are sorry. Definitely."

"Sir…" Thuy began.

He ignored her. "You, Miss Blanche, you riding with American bandit when this occurs. You involve. You…" He seemed to be searching for a word. "Cul-pa-ble."

At this point, Thuy straightened her cloche and leaned forward. A hardening of her features: *enough is enough.* She burst into a flaming rant in Vietnamese while Blanche and Jean sat down, wide-eyed. At first Officer Bung did nothing. His hands remained folded, his mouth clamped. His gaze flicked over Thuy and landed on Blanche, where it stayed.

"Someone must pay for ducks," he said, obviously not willing to budge.

Thuy's thin shoulders lifted. She turned to Blanche. "It is a … penalty fee, he say. But if you pay for the ducks, you get passport."

They were on a double highway to nowhere, see-sawing between Vietnamese and English. The officer chose to argue with Thuy in Vietnamese. He could understand Blanche perfectly yesterday though his reading in English may have been lacking. He now threw out the occasional demand when it suited him. She was exasperated. She looked at Bung. "How do we know the duck farmer will get payment?" She could barely speak through her teeth.

"He get pay."

"How much?" Jean was already digging in her bag, seemingly ready to give him the money and get out of there.

"Two hundred dolla." His hands clenched in a knot on his desk. "You American, you create chaos. You pay." He looked straight at Blanche. She wanted to jump over the table and stomp the crooked smile off his face. Jean put her hand on Blanche's arm. In an aside, she said, "Believe it or not, my dad warned me there'd be days like this. Don't worry. I can take care of it. Let's get out of here. The sooner, the better."

"This is a rip-off, Jean." Blanche was losing control, and it was making her furious.

Jean shrugged, her lips barely moving, "Just wait."

Thuy resumed arguing with the officer, but he didn't back off. "Pay, or no passport," he repeated, in English, looking straight at Blanche, who was as unmoved as Bung.

"Two hundred dollars! How many dong is that?"

Jean was adamant. She pulled Blanche into a huddle. "Don't worry. We have a fund."

"He's taking advantage, Jean, and you know it! It's not fair."

"Life's not fair, Blanche. This is the cost of doing business, and you are my friend, and I don't care. Let's do this and go." Through gritted teeth, she said, "I got this."

Blanche backed down into her seat, her fingers squeezed into a ball in her lap.

Jean plopped the dollars on the edge of the desk and said, evenly, "I'd like a receipt, please, and the passport."

Officer Bung's eyes lit up; then the light went out. Jean kept her fingers on the bills as he reached for the money. "Not until I see the receipt and the passport," she said. Then softly, straightening up, she said, "And we drop *all* charges against Mr. Dahlkamp and recover his bike for him."

Jean still eyed the officer. She slowly withdrew the stack of bills from the desktop and squared them off neatly in her lap. She took her time about it. She fished a one-hundred-dollar bill from her bag, put it on top of the stack, and placed all the money back on the desk. Bung watched every move; the last bill was a fine dollop of "screw you." Jean's index finger rested on the money. Blanche tried to keep a straight face. "Please draw up the papers in regards to the release of the passport and Mr. Dahlkamp and his property," Jean said. "It would behoove you to do it now."

The officer hesitated, but not for long. He needed to fill the air. "You are visitor to Vietnam. You must obey rule."

"Yes, we obey the rule. We pay, and then we go. On these terms," said Jean. She still held down the money. Thuy didn't make a peep, her eyes blank and cold as she sized up the officer. Blanche got a whiff of victory.

Jean's hold on the situation ticked on. Blanche watched the long hand on the wall clock and didn't breathe. She bit her tongue. Officer Bung's features softened, his willingness to concede in the face of a stack of American dollars wavered. The push and pull played out between them, and the time called for a summoning of dignity on the part of the official.

"One moment, please." He stood up abruptly and left them there. No one moved. Blanche stared at the door, waiting for some fresh hell to return.

Officer Bung came back. He thrust a sheaf of papers at Thuy. She sat and reviewed them. "It is good." She folded the pieces and gave them to Jean. The officer quickly grabbed the money then handed Blanche her passport.

"I hope you have safe journey," he said with a slight bow, his officialdom restored for three hundred dollars.

Thuy answered his farewell in kind, her own considerable dignity intact. Savvy and firm. Blanche exhaled with relief. *What a lesson ... in Communist bureaucracy?* She hoped she'd never need a refresher.

They headed out of the dull office building and into the sunshine. Blanche tugged at Jean's sleeve. "You're the bomb."

"I'm glad I didn't blow up," she said. "Ya know, Blanche...."

"I know. I'm sorry. I get so frustrated," she said contritely. "You saved us."

Jean laughed. "Had no idea what I was doing, but it worked. You got your passport, and Stick gets his bike back. I hope."

They trailed out behind Thuy, who was marching quickly toward the car. She fumbled with the keys. "He one big dope," she said. "But do not say I say so."

Fifteen

In the Fold

"I COULD USE A *BIA*, and it's barely eleven in the morning," said Blanche. They were back in the car and headed to the consulate. *Finally, and it's what? Day four?*

Jean clutched her notebook with a list of questions for the US government. She and Blanche had gone round and round about their approach. Would they help find her mother? In a sea of millions? *How?*

"I don't know how you do it, Thuy," said Blanche, wincing at the traffic.

"Must have good horn to drive here," said Thuy. She checked out her passengers in the rearview mirror. "*Bia*, now? You thirsty, Miss Blanche? You hungry, ladies?"

"Guess we could stop," said Jean, "after dealing with the institutions of Vietnam."

Blanche slumped in her seat. "Yeah. Enough with the ducks and the Bungs. A beer or maybe one of those egg-cellent coffees."

Thuy drove the car up on a sidewalk next to a café. She parked amid a tangle of motorbikes while a uniformed attendant waved at her furiously. She blasted him with a few choice words, and he sauntered off. Blanche was now leery of a confrontation with anyone in a uniform.

"Are we all right? The parking here is interesting, Thuy," Blanche mused as she threaded her way through a jungle of wheels and handlebars.

"Parking? What parking? More like dropping and leaving. Wherever. It is the way of many strange ways here."

They sat inside the café, though it seemed most people were outside crowding at low tables. The wall facing the street was open, so they were part of the general hubbub. Blanche watched the chaos with a mix of amusement and trepidation, reminded once more of the challenge they faced in finding Tam Li. She could be *anywhere*. Blanche's attention diverted to the whirl of humanity as she waited for her egg coffee. "Have you had run-ins with the traffic police, Thuy?"

"What? No, they all dopes." Thuy perched on the stool opposite, flicking through an open binder on the table. She eyed Blanche through funny-looking half-spectacles. "What? No *bia*?"

"Later," Blanche said. "I like that strange confection of egg and coffee. Don't know how I'm going to go back to a regular diet of plain old joe."

"And I don't know how I'm going to go back to plain old noodles. I love the *pho*," said Jean.

"First things first," said Thuy. She straightened up. "Miss Jean, your questions for consulate? We have appointment now. Today, soon."

"I think we've got it together. My dad gave me as much information as he could, and Blanche and I have been working on it. You know, Uncle Five in Ben Tre suggested that maybe my family went to work for the Communists after the takeover. They had a background in accounting."

"Maybe," said Thuy. She did not look convinced. "I need say, the consulate is not good source for Communist, how to say, industry? The consulate better with local agency. They know contact." She nodded vigorously from Blanche to Jean and adjusted the cloche tightly over her ears. "Ah, *ca phe*, good here, no?

"Superb," said Blanche.

Despite what Thuy said about the Communists, Blanche hoped the consulate could help with leads. Not only for Jean but also for herself. She wasn't sure what direction she would take, but she was determined to find out more about her dad. The thought of it made her stomach flutter.

—∕ᴠᴠ∕—

The consulate was on the grounds of the former US Embassy in Saigon. The iconic picture of the Vietnamese trying to get on the last chopper out in April 1975 was imprinted on Blanche's brain. And so was the picture of the ambassador holding the American flag to his chest as he escaped at the last minute. The old embassy had been torn down and moved to Hanoi. The new consulate on the spot was a long building fortified with the ubiquitous mustard-yellow walls. Blanche was beginning to wonder about the use of yellow; it was a Vietnamese thing, that and the red tile roofs. The consulate was impressive and discreetly shaded behind a sidewalk forest of trees.

Kathy Martell sat at a desk in the middle of a warren of desks and cubbies. She stood up and shook hands with each of her visitors. She was a pleasant-looking woman with a round face and a bubble of a hairdo. "I hope I can help you. Please." She indicated for them to be seated, her movements unhurried and casual.

Jean held the notebook open and studied the pages in front of her. She seemed tense. Her pen tapped the paper nervously. Blanche put her hand on Jean's arm.

"I am trying to find my mother, once married to an American soldier. She was from Hoi An, but her family probably moved south to the Saigon area. The family is Dang." Jean looked up with a penetrating gaze. "Would you have any clues as to how I might find her?"

The lines on Kathy Martell's face softened—Blanche could tell she likely had a soft heart, too. "You have followed your leads?" Miss Martell asked.

"We've tried," said Jean. "And, I'm afraid, failed. So far. Do you have an agency that might help?"

"I'm sorry, we can offer you little. There was such chaos after the war. So many records were destroyed. You do understand?"

"Yes," said Jean. "But is there a bureau in the Communist government that might be willing to help me?"

Kathy smiled, rather like she was facing an idealistic student. "They are a very … closed society on the matter, I'm afraid. They talk of rebuilding, not looking back. They are not sympathetic in this regard." A diplomat to the last letter.

Jean pushed on. "What about private—especially religious—agencies? Here in Saigon?" Kathy was still smiling while she flipped through a Rolodex. "Let's have a look." She made some notes on a pad.

It did seem incongruous, this gray and white American setting in the middle of Saigon, but so did everything else. Blanche looked around at the hodgepodge of government workers going about their business. There didn't seem to be any formal arrangement to the space. *But someone in here knows something.* They moved slowly, even picking up the phone in slow motion. Shuffling from one gray metal desk to the next. A miasma of papers and folders and dust. The wheels of industry abroad. The US carried on in the wake of a lost cause. It had a dampening effect. Blanche shook it off and concentrated on Jean and Kathy Martell.

A man walked over to their tight little group. He was tall and rangy with gray hair. He had striking blue eyes and, Blanche noticed, a large coffee stain right above his belt. He nodded at each of them and then approached Kathy: "Sorry, Kath, to intrude, but couldn't help overhearing. You know that Quaker group? They've had some success in reuniting families."

"Hey, Rob," Kathy said. "I hadn't heard." She picked up the notepad. "Let me look up that number and add it to the others, Jean. You never know."

Rob smiled. "Who's looking for a parent?"

Blanche and Jean, at once, said, "I am."

It was quiet for a moment, except for the tentative clicking on a lone keyboard and the scraping of chairs and feet. The air smelled faintly of some awful fake air freshener. The high dirty windows let in some light, and potted palms mitigated the desolate look of the place.

Blanche fiddled with her bag. She felt her neck, her face, reddening. *This isn't about me. It's about Jean.* "My friend, Jean, is searching for her mother." She straightened up. "And I'd like to know more about my father."

Something was not right, and everything seemed wrong all at once. Blanche had lost her father, and Jean was trying to find her mother, and the world was tilting.

Rob pulled up a chair and inclined his head with interest. The tired office pallor vanished. "I heard you talk about your mother, Jean. But, Blanche, is your father lost, too?"

Blanche couldn't help it. The egg coffee roiled in her stomach, and the tears started up. "Yes," she said. "He is lost on some rice paddy. Blown up. Probably around May 10, 1970." It was a relief to get it out there. It would never be erased, and she was tired of carrying it around, wondering what exactly happened to him.

Rob sat back. "Miss Blanche. We are still looking for your father. We are still looking for all of them. More than 2,000 missing in action. They are out there. They may be MIA, but, to us, they aren't lost."

It was then that Blanche let loose. She bent forward. She couldn't bear for them to see it. Hidden away, protected by her grandmother and mother and Cap, she'd never faced it. Until now. All at once, it seemed unbearable. She bit her tongue and swiped at her eyes.

He leaned closer, empathetically, and his hands clenched together. "Let me see now," he said. "Do you have information about your dad?"

Blanche looked up then, her throat constricting. She opened her bag and pulled out the picture of Thomas Fox. "This is him." She would not say this *was* him.

"Ah." He looked from Thomas to Blanche. "The map of Ireland, I see. What else? Do you have papers? Any information?"

She gave it all to him—documents, letters, the photograph, her birth certificate, and her passport. He shuffled through the papers, then stood up. "May I make copies?"

"Yes."

He started away, then turned. "And may I ask? Murninghan? Your father's name is Fox?"

"My parents never married. My mother wasn't notified when he was killed. She happened to find out from his mother, and I just found her letter."

He didn't look at Blanche as he read through the small stack of papers. "I see. In any case, your family probably wouldn't have been notified—about anything. But there are records. We can cross-reference the information here."

His tone made Blanche hopeful, and she couldn't say why. It was an open-ended comment—a thread to the past, and she'd pull at it until she got the rest.

Blanche lowered her head, her fingers laced tightly. "I'm sorry, Jean. I know this is about your mom. But I've got this thing...."

"I know." Jean put her arm around Blanche and jostled her. The warmth of friendship grounded her. Thuy sat, immovable, primly.

Kathy was clearly sympathetic, but her tone was business-like. She looked up from her notepad and files. "It is not so uncommon, this sad searching. Unfortunately." She slid a page of notes toward Jean. "Here are the contacts for local agencies. I would try the Quaker group, and the Lutherans, maybe Catholic Charities. But I don't want to encourage you unnecessarily. These reunions often happen by accident or through a lot of shoe leather, calling, and asking locals. If you put it all together, something might come up."

Rob came back and handed Blanche the originals. In addition, he waved a brand-new folder.

"What's this?" Blanche reached for the folder as Rob opened it.

"See here? We put the information about your dad in the system—not that we don't have it already. But it doesn't hurt to shake up these channels. Much has been done with finding and identifying soldiers. As I said, the search is ongoing." Rob held up her passport, which he'd also copied. "And you're in the system. Right next to your father. We'll notify the Department of Defense and ask that your certificates, contact information, and passport be added to his records."

Blanche stared at the official notes Rob had made, her name next to Thomas Fox, "father." It was a big thing, after so many years. She was closer to him. His numbers and photo right along next to her numbers and birth certificate. All attached in the same folder. Yes, it was *something*.

"We'll have all of this formalized soon and notify you. And in the meantime, we keep at it," he said.

It was worth a trip to hear him say that.

Sixteen

Silk Dream

BLANCHE AND JEAN WERE just about to leave the consulate. Thuy had left them to run an errand, and she'd promised to bring the car around in thirty minutes. Kathy Martell did not rush her visitors away. "I know of one woman in London, the half-Vietnamese daughter of an American soldier, who found her father by posting his picture in newspapers. She spent a lot of money on advertising, but she finally found him. In Lexington, Kentucky." Kathy's friendly, dimpled smile was encouraging. "They were happy to find each other. I always loved that story, Jean. Don't give up. And you, too, Blanche. I have your phone numbers. If anything surfaces, I'll get in touch."

Rob stuck his head out of a nearby cubicle. "Just curious, Miss Blanche. It said in these records that your dad was in the 23rd Infantry Division. I was, too." He came around the desk. "The old Americal. They saw a lot of action, especially near Chu Lai. What was your dad's MOS? Sorry—military specialty."

"He was an infantryman, a rifle carrier. Did a lot of scout patrols, as I understand from some of the letters." Even as she said it, something froze inside. "Did you say Americal?"

"Yes, the 23rd. One and the same."

Blanche turned to Jean, who had her head in the notebook, her face averted. "Your dad, my dad. Were they in the same division during the war? At the same time?" Blanche gulped. "At the same place—and *job*. You called it the Americal, Jean. I didn't know it was the same…."

"It was a big war," said Rob.

"Not that big," said Blanche.

Still, Jean busied herself over her notes.

Kathy watched Rob avidly. "Now, that is some coincidence," she said.

"I don't know," said Blanche. "I don't think so." She stood up. "Jean, what do you know that you're not telling me?"

Now Jean was standing. Her face reddened, a look of surprise. She even looked terrified. "Blanche…"

"Don't Blanche me. What do you know that you're not telling me?" She had a hunch. There had been hints along the way, but suddenly she felt blindsided. The feeling was overwhelming, strangling her with confusion.

Jean flopped back into the chair, the notebook sliding to the floor. She put both hands over her face. "I don't know what to say."

The words tore at Blanche. "Try," she said. Her voice was icy and sharp. *How could she do this? How could she hold this in, this truth? All across the ocean. All this time.*

Blanche clutched the papers, jammed them into her bag, and headed for the door. She didn't look back. She didn't know where she was going, but she was getting out of there, away from the lies and reminders of the thing that took her dad. She was going to walk back to Santa Maria Island if she could.

———

Blanche hurried down the sidewalk wildly, dodging motorbikes, vendors, and cyclos. *On the sidewalk, for God's sakes. They're always trying to kill you over here.*

The heat and humidity were intrepid, but at least she was short like the rest of them, dressed in neutral beige and white. She blended in. She was glad of that; she wanted to be invisible, to think, and walk off the confusion that boiled over inside her. She needed to sort herself out. She must be wrong, but her feelings rarely failed her. Something was up with this whole trip, and something was up with Jean. Her deception. Blanche felt the lie like someone had wrapped her in it, cold and unyielding, insistent and oppressive. She wanted out of there, and at the same time, she needed to get to the bottom of it.

She walked fast. She wasn't far from the hotel in District One. She passed a bookstore, more noodles—noodles galore—and the broth they swam in: cafes and souvenir shops and antique dealers with blue-and-white plates and jugs overflowing onto the street. One woman approached her with threads drawn between her fingers. She held up the threads to Blanche's face. "I want to make brows beautiful, pull hairs on American lady," she said.

"God, no, thank you. *Cam un*. And *tam biet*."

Blanche pushed through the crowd, her anger dissipating some. She felt smaller and smaller, and for some reason, she felt better. She wanted to forget. She was not the center of the universe; it was a big place, and she was a pip at the bottom of it.

She stumbled into a tailor shop. Bolts and bolts of silk in every shade and pattern lined the walls. One woman in a yellow *ao dai* tossed a length of flaming red silk onto a long wooden table; another woman measured a customer from nape to waist. Blanche held back near the door and watched the deft hands and movements, the graceful features of the women working with the silk. They whispered and smiled while they smoothed and flipped the fabric. *Not exactly like the industry in a newsroom, but fascinating*. Blanche chuckled when she thought of her chosen profession, with old crusty Bill, her boss, and the smell of ink and old paper, compared to the women here. Worlds apart yet both compelling.

The scissors clicked. The shaft of silk settled in the sun beaming through the large front window. The room was cool with noisy fans high in the corners, rotating and whirring. Blanche let herself be lulled. She fell back onto a small metal stool near the door. She didn't want to move. She didn't want to think.

"May I help?" The woman in the yellow *ao dai* approached Blanche. She perked up as if coming out of a dream, but that was how it happened sometimes. She'd escape down that rabbit hole of imagination and emerged, reluctantly.

Blanche stood. "Oh, I'm sorry. I'm just looking." *Actually watching. I am so weird.*

The woman bowed slightly, her thin fingers clasped, held closely against her chest. Her eyes were like Jean's, dark and soft, almond-shaped. Blanche looked away, feeling a wash of regret that she'd come here.

"*Lam on,*" the woman said. Blanche was puzzled. "Please?" The woman tried again, tentatively. She took Blanche's hand and guided her to the wall with bolts of silk. "Choose pretty fabric. Green?" She pointed to Blanche's eyes. "Green go well with yellow in Vietnam, many shutters on buildings. Green. Eyes. Beautiful."

"*Cam on,* you are kind," said Blanche. "I'm wondering about yellow here. It's everywhere."

"Yes, yellow is royalty, success, and prosperity." She waited, tilted her head first one way and then the other. The woman didn't use a tape measure, but Blanche felt like she was being sized up.

Blanche studied the silks and chose a kelly green with a pattern of tiny gold fans. She had no idea why she was doing this. She just did it.

The woman yanked the bolt out of the wall and whipped it across the table. The shimmering beauty of the fabric stunned

Blanche. She had to have it. "This is so beautiful. I would like to wrap myself in it and take a nap."

The woman's delicate eyebrows shot up. Then she laughed. "No, no. Not for sleeping. I make lovely tunic for you for wearing. All day."

"Oh, I don't think that's possible. I'm only here a short time."

"Two ow-a. Done"

"Two hours? How is that possible?"

"We do it here. *Immediatement.*"

The woman held the tape measure across Blanche's shoulders, up and down and sideways. Blanche was amused at the efficiency and completely removed from herself and her depressing thoughts.

"May I ask, what is your name?"

"Mai Lin. You, lady?"

"I'm Blanche."

"You, Blanche, you look sad when you come in here. Now you look happy."

"Yes, I guess I am a lot happier than I was."

The measurements were noted, the order was in. Mai Lin took Blanche's hand and led her to the back of the store. Down a narrow hallway and out into a small courtyard, overhung with fruit trees and palms. Mai Lin pointed to a round table and chairs. "Here, sit, please. I bring tea."

"Will you please join me? You will have tea with me?"

Mai Lin bowed, her face soft and pleasant. Blanche sat down in the middle of this small cocoon in Vietnam. *How odd to be rescued in Vietnam.*

Mai Lin brought the tray, set it on the table, and poured the tea. A cup for each of them.

"Now, tell, why sad?" She held the teacup under her chin and waited for Blanche to respond. Blanche was taken aback, but then she spilled the story. Of her father and Jean's mother, of the deception she felt, and the loss.

"Now, she look for mother, you look for father. Ah," said Mai Lin.

"We might find Jean's mother. I'll never find my father."

"Yes. But mother, father always with you. No matter you see them, touch them. Believe that." Mai Lin nodded. "Vietnamese people study the past. Buddha say, much to learn in history— how to live in good invention of past. Improve history. Build on past! But with all that, concentration on present." Her small fist shot up in emphasis. "It is confusing?"

"No, encouraging. Thank you, Mai Lin."

How oddly comforting. She'd lost her way, sunk in the misery of imagining what her father went through and then having it hidden from her. That history was sad, but maybe she wasn't looking at her own past with open eyes. There was more to this trip, and this country than her and her father and all the American loss put together.

Mai Lin offered Blanche a small plate of biscuits. She nibbled at one. "Let me tell you story," she said. She put the biscuit down, and her face settled into placid lines. She smiled at Blanche.

Seventeen

Tam and Cam

THERE WERE ONCE TWO STEPSISTERS named Tam and Cam. Tam was the daughter of her father's first wife, who died when Tam was young. He took a second wife. A few years later, the father died, and Tam was left to live with her stepmother, Mong, and stepsister, Cam.

The stepmother was harsh and mean. She made Tam care for the buffalo and chickens, feed water fern to the pigs, fetch water, and husk rice. While Tam worked, Cam played games, ate sweets, and wore pretty clothes.

One morning, Stepmother Mong gave Tam and Cam baskets and told them to go to the paddy fields to catch tiny shrimp—tep.

"I will give a yêm—a lovely bodice of fine red silk—to the one who brings home a full basket of tep," the stepmother said.

Tam knew well the task of finding shrimp in the rice paddy, and soon she had filled her basket. Cam waded from field to field, but she could not find the shrimp. She saw Tam's full basket and said to her stepsister, "Oh, my dear Tam, your hair is covered in mud. Get into the pond to wash it, or you will be scolded by mother when we return."

Tam hurried away to the pond and began washing her hair. Cam quickly snatched Tam's basket and all of her shrimp. She ran off with the stolen tep to claim the silk yêm. Tam discovered her empty basket and burst into tears, knowing she'd be punished.

Nearby, a Buddha sitting on a lotus in the sky heard Tam's sobs and came down beside her. "Why are you crying?" asked the Buddha.

Tam told him what had happened. He said, "Child, do not cry. Look into your basket and see if anything is left."

Tam looked in the basket. "There is only one tiny bong fish."

"Take the fish and put it in a pond near your home," the Buddha said. "At every meal, save a bowl of rice for the fish. Call him: "Dear friend, Rise and eat the golden rice.""

The Buddha disappeared. Tam did as he instructed. Day by day, the bông fish grew, and Tam became great friends with it.

Seeing Tam take rice to the pond, the stepmother became suspicious and told Cam to spy on her stepsister. Cam heard Tam call the fish. She rushed to tell her mother the secret. The next day, the stepmother told Tam to take the buffalo to the far field. "It is now the season to harvest vegetables in the village. Buffalo cannot graze here."

Tam set off on the buffalo. When she was gone, Cam and her mother took rice to the pond and called the bông fish. When it rose to the surface, the women caught it. They then cooked and ate it. Tam returned and took rice to the pond to feed her friend. She called out but only saw a drop of blood in the water. Tam knew something terrible had happened, and she began to weep.

The Buddha appeared. "Your fish has been caught and eaten. Now, stop crying. You must find his bones and put them in four jars. Then you must bury the jars under each of the legs of your bed." Tam found the bones of her beloved friend in the rubbish pile and did as the Buddha instructed.

Some months later, the king proclaimed a great festival. All the people planned to attend, and the road was packed with well-wishers. Cam and her mother dressed in their fine clothes. They smirked at Tam, who wanted to go. Mong mixed a basket of unhusked rice with clean rice and said: "You may go to the festival after you separate this grain. If there isn't any rice to cook when we return home, you will be beaten." With that, the stepmother and her daughter set out for the festival and left Tam hopeless and in tears.

Once again, the Buddha appeared. "Why are you crying?"

Tam explained her task. "The festival will be over by the time I finish."

"Bring the baskets to the yard," said the Buddha. "The birds will help you." They pecked and fluttered, dividing the rice into two baskets. Not a single grain did they eat.

"Thank you, dear Buddha, but I cannot go dressed like this."

"Go and dig up the four jars," ordered the Buddha. "You will have all you need."

In the first jar, she found a beautiful silk dress. In the second, a pair of embroidered shoes that fit her perfectly. When she opened the third jar, a miniature horse appeared and shot up into a noble steed. In the fourth jar was a richly ornamented saddle and bridle. Tam dressed in the gown and rode off to the festival. On the way, she lost one of her shoes in a stream. She was in such a hurry, she didn't stop. She wrapped the other shoe in her scarf.

Later, the king and his entourage riding elephants arrived at the same spot. The elephants refused to enter the water, bellowing and trumpeting. When no amount of goading would force them on, the king ordered his followers to search the water. One of them found the shoe and brought it to the king.

He said, "The girl who wears such a beautiful shoe must indeed be beautiful. Let us go on to the festival and find her. Whomever it fits will be my wife."

When the women heard the king's announcement, they eagerly waited to try on the shoe. Cam struggled to make it fit but to no avail. When the stepmother discovered Tam waiting, she sneered. "How did you come here? Did you steal those fine clothes? I am going to punish you severely when we return home."

Tam said nothing. When she tried the shoe, it fit perfectly. Then she produced the other from the folds of her scarf. The king was delighted. Everyone cheered the future queen as the king ordered his servants to take Tam to the palace in a palanquin. She rode off happily under the furious and jealous gazes of her stepsister and stepmother...

Mai Lin stopped there. "The story goes on. And on. We Vietnamese love our stories and poetic justice."

Blanche sat with her hands tucked under her chin, her eyes laser-beamed on Mai Lin. "*What happened?*"

Mai Lin sighed. "You must know... The evil stepmother later killed Tam, but she came back as a *vang anh*—a bird—and the king fell in love with its singing. The stepmother and daughter killed the bird. The king planted the feathers. They grew into a beautiful tree, which the evil pair cut down and burned. The ashes grew into another tree that bore one piece of fragrant fruit—from which Tam emerged and later reunited with the king. Cam was jealous and plotted further to do away with her stepsister. But this time, Tam was ahead of her and saved herself. She warned Cam not to pick the peaches on a forbidden tree. Cam ignored the warning, and reaching for the fruit, she fell into a pot of boiling water. Tam made a sauce of the water, and the mother ate it and fell dead when she saw the skull of her daughter in the bottom of the jar."

Eighteen

The Double Good

"WOW," SAID BLANCHE. "Not exactly Disney."

"It is an old Vietnamese story told many times, in many ways, but you see the similarity? To Cinderella?"

"Yes, but what does it mean?"

"The cycle of life, from the people to the bird and the fruit. You cannot stop it. At last, goodness and salvation emerge. And the evil shows face. You understand?"

Blanche sat back, the last of the tea drained. "I think so. The good is lasting, and the petty not so much."

"Petty. What is this?"

"Unimportant things," said Blanche.

Mai Lin studied Blanche's serious expression. "Your friend, she want to know truth? You also, Miss Blanche. You are both here for reasons. Go find answers. The Buddha say delusion and ignorance stand in way of enlightenment."

There's Buddha again.

Blanche didn't want to distrust Jean, but she was holding something back. Blanche was sure of it, and it nagged her. Her curiosity was the itch that never went away, and somehow, she was paying for it. She could make this venture work out or not.

They had come this far, together. She stood up. "Will you come back into the shop, Mai?"

Mai rose, and they went back into the workroom with its walls of silk. "What color would go well with very dark eyes, light skin, and black hair?" Blanche studied the rich colors of the bolts of fabric and turned to Mai Lin. "I'd say she's about your size, except taller."

The shopkeeper went to a yellow-gold silk with green birds and drew out a length of silk. "Very nice one. You two, twin beauty. No Cam and Tam. Blanche and Jean. Double good." She laughed.

"Yes, double good."

Blanche watched the deft craftsmanship of the tailors, their fingers cutting the fabric and running the seams up on the machine. In a couple of hours, they finished tops for Blanche and Jean. Blanche even picked up a pointer or two on sewing, although she knew she'd never have the patience for such art. She hugged Mai and left the shop with two silk tunics wrapped in brown paper and string.

She was not far from the hotel. She walked past the low tables and vendors on the sidewalks, dodging motorbikes, catching the scent of grilled meat and vegetables. She began to get hungry. It was around six, and she hadn't eaten much all day. Her brain and emotions had taken over and left an empty stomach. She hurried back to the Caravelle, hoping to find Jean and go off to eat and drink. And talk. They had a lot to settle.

And Stick! What was happening with their new best friend? She was not eager to set off to The Follies at night, alone, in Saigon to find out. But if she had to, she would.

Jean was not in the room, and there was no sign she'd been there. Blanche wasn't surprised. What did she expect? Jean would be sitting there, waiting to greet her? *So sorry you ran out of there like you were on fire. We need to talk.* It would have been nice.

It would have been a start. But this one was on Blanche. She'd closed herself off without a word and blasted out of the consulate. In retrospect, with a cool head, it didn't seem quite fair.

Blanche unwrapped the two tunics, put them on hangers, and hung them on the drapery hardware. She stood back. Jean would see them when she walked into the room.

Blanche looked around for clues that Jean had been there that afternoon. No note, no mussed towels, no open suitcase. The beds were made up so neatly that she could bounce a penny off the duvet. The bath salts and dragon fruit were replenished. Blanche threw herself on the bed and closed her eyes. She was just going to rest for a minute, investigate a possible place for dinner, and figure out how to get hold of Stick. She wanted to be ready and have something to offer up for discussion with Jean. For a truce. *What am I going to say?* All of these thoughts tumbled around in her brain, and she couldn't shut her mind off—until she did. Soon she was off in dreamland, with Cinderella and Cam and Tam.

—⁓—

Blanche's eyes shot open. Jean was leaning over her, shaking her gently. And she was wearing a kelly green tunic with tiny fans on it. It was stunning, dressed up with the beige, nubby-silk cigarette pants.

"You shouldn't have," said Jean.

"Yeah, I shoulda. And by the way, that's mine." She reached up and grabbed her friend in a hug. "I guess the green does look pretty good on you."

"Where did you go?"

"To a tailor shop. I drank tea and heard a story about a Vietnamese Cinderella."

Jean flopped onto the bed. She put several small bottles of vodka from the mini-bar in her lap and uncapped one. "I gotta hear this." She handed Blanche a bottle. "Wake up time."

"What time is it?"

"Around seven. Who cares?"

"The tailor told me a story based on Cinderella. It kinda made me think—about sisters and relationships and how good will win out. Finally."

"Well, that's a relief. You had a kind of epiphany? About our little journey together?"

"I guess. I just want to be fair, and I want the *truth*, Jean."

"Don't we all."

She and Jean clinked bottles. "Down the hatch." Blanche winced and sat back on the pillows. *When did I ever wake up and start drinking vodka? First thing?*

Jean crossed her legs in pretzel fashion. All sincerity and innocence. "You have to tell me, exactly, Blanche. Why did you leave? You were upset."

"You tell me. Too much coincidence if you ask me. Our dads."

Jean sighed, looked down at her hands, and smoothed the front of her new tunic. "I really like it. So sweet of you to do this. I heard they make them on the spot, but this...."

"Don't deflect. I'm not buying you off with a silk tunic. But I do want the truth. I want to know what you know."

"Oh, Blanche. I didn't want to throw all of it at you at once," said Jean. Then her face changed, a realization striking her. "I was selling you short, and you have to know. Now."

"Know what?"

"Our dads were together, that final day, and for days going up to it." Her voice was soft and wavering. She took another slug of vodka.

Blanche could feel her insides freeze, like a cold vice had taken hold of her. "What are you talking about? And what do you think you're protecting me from? *What happened?*"

"It's complicated, but I'll try to sort it all out for you. I need to start talking. I'm going to tell you everything I know." She stood up—firm and uncharacteristically in control. "Come on, Blanche, get dressed. We need food and more to drink. Fuel."

Feeling like she was sleepwalking, Blanche went into the bathroom and looked in the mirror. The same familiar face stared back at her, a bit paler, but there it was. Maybe she was closer to the truth. Her eyes were dark, deep green pools. In a mild state of shock? The vodka had taken the edge off, but she still felt raw.

She splashed cold water over her face, neck, and arms. It felt good. She threw a handful at the mirror and watched the stream of droplets run over her image. No tears. Relief. It swept over her, knowing that soon she might hear more about her father. Maybe not *everything*, but *something*. It was better than what she had now.

Nineteen

A Terrible Time

BLANCHE AND JEAN LEFT the Caravelle Hotel and headed down Le Loi Street toward the Hoi An Restaurant. It was a starred Fodor choice and Jean's pick. She insisted on splurging.

"It's a treat," she said, walking at a fast clip along the river in District One. "We need this."

Blanche was drained after a day of drama. She skipped to catch up. "We don't have to get all fancy, you know. I just want to talk."

"I dragged you all the way over here, across many ponds. We need something special—for our talk," said Jean. They dodged a couple of cyclos that revved down the sidewalk and a vendor who slowly repositioned his dumpling cart. It was a regular obstacle course to walk a block.

"Before we get to our dads…" Jean took Blanche's arm. "I asked Thuy to check on Stick. She says he's doing well. Guess they won't let us into the clinic to see him, but the good news is he's getting out in one piece."

"That's progress," said Blanche.

"Another thing. Thuy is looking up some of those contacts who came up during our recent excursions," said Jean. "Mom didn't stay put. We may have to do a bit more traveling if the leads pan out. We'll know more tomorrow."

"Our agenda is filling up." Blanche was good with that if it helped clear things up. Plus, she longed to cover some of the ground her father had seen. "Travel? Where to?"

"I don't know, Blanche." The words trailed off.

Blanche quickly changed the subject, eager to stay with a positive vibe. "Don't go there. Tonight? It's all about our dads, right?"

"You got it." Jean grinned, but there was a sadness in her eyes. "They were a team, Blanche. You'll see. Like us."

"Yup," said Blanche. "We're dressed up enough for this fancy place, right?"

"We're dressed." They wore skinny sheaths, Blanche in cranberry and Jean in black. Their sandals clicked over the pavement. They stopped in front of an elegant brick building under a sign with black cursive on a white background, *The Hoi An Restaurante.*

"Let's go to Hoi An," said Jean.

"Let's," said Blanche. "This place is gonna cost some dong. I'd be satisfied with a dumpling off the cart that almost ran us over."

"Nonsense. We need a nice place to talk. Maybe then you won't yell and get up and do a dance out the door."

They were both in a fairly frisky mood after finishing the vodka in the minibar. It had drowned some of the anger and tension of the day, but now the booze was wearing off. Blanche burned to hear what Jean had to say.

The host was dressed in crisp black and white, which seemed to be the color scheme inside, except for the yellow glow of candles. "Ahem." He smiled and bowed. "Mesdames? You have reservation?"

"No, I don't think so," said Blanche. Something smelled divine. A lavish bouquet of fresh herbs, garlic, and grilled meat?

"Yes," said Jean. "Two under Jean McMahon."

"Ah." He held enormous, leather-bound menus and led them to a table in a room full of dark wood walls and furniture. Pear-shaped lanterns hung from a sky-blue ceiling with an overlay of white lattice. The tables gleamed with linen, flatware, and a candle set in the middle. They sat down, and the host deftly opened their menus.

"Prepare to feast," said Jean. "I'm famished. What a day."

Blanche flapped through the pages of the menu, her eyes lighting up. She leaned over to face Jean. "This is lovely." She put aside, for a second, the anticipation of a cruel, hard story. It seemed a long way from this Paris-inspired table.

"Yes, it is." Jean smiled but then looked around distractedly. "Ya know, I got a kind of a hate-love thing going on with Vietnam." She bent over the menu. "But I guess it's mostly love."

They ordered—Jean the roast lamb with curry, bok choy, and pickled ramps, and Blanche, grilled sturgeon marinated in turmeric. The first course arrived. Blanche's white endive, like dove's wings, held three large prawns on a lotus leaf. Jean tasted the lobster soup, a creamy concoction of heaven on a spoon, and nodded. They chose a cabernet sauvignon from Mendoza to accompany the dinner.

Blanche lifted her glass. "To our dads," she said. "And to your mom, I hope, soon. And my mom, wherever she is."

"Wouldn't they be happy to see us here? Dressed up and enjoying the best food in Saigon?"

Blanche sipped. "They would. It's a kind of celebration, I guess. Maybe a little premature, but we do have a lot to be thankful for." She put the wine glass down and folded her hands on the tabletop. "Now. Shoot. And don't spare the details."

Jean seemed startled. "Where to begin." She signaled for a refill of the cab.

"How about at the beginning? And don't leave anything out. Remember—we are in this together." Blanche held the ruby wine to the lantern light. "And you're right. This is helping it go down a bit more smoothly."

"Our dads were in the same division in Vietnam. The Americal, or the 23rd Infantry Division. In fact, they were in the same battalion—company—even, the same platoon." The words shot from Jean as if she'd been holding it in.

"The same platoon?"

"Yes, Blanche, about a dozen soldiers. But let me back up here. The whole division was more than ten thousand of them. Somehow, our dads ended up in one of the smallest units."

"That came out today, that they were together. You said your dad didn't even get to Vietnam until the fall before May 1970 when my dad was killed...." It was still foreign to hear it, to say it. Blanche had never said it to anyone. Gran never talked about it, and here she was in the land where he was buried. Part of this beautiful, sad place.

"That's right," Jean said. "They met during training and ended up together in the same unit in Vietnam. What are the odds?" She leaned toward Blanche, hovering over the salad. She'd barely touched her dinner. "Blanche, it was a terrible time. The My Lai massacre happened on the American's watch in 1968. It didn't blow up in the news until late 1969, just about the time our dads went in. Vietnam was in mourning for Uncle Ho, who had just died. They revered him...they still do. Then the Kent State massacre happened on May 4, right before your dad was killed."

It flooded back, what little reading she'd done about the social context of the time. The events—including assassinations and political unrest at home--all added to the misery of low morale, drug use, and racial tension in Vietnam.

"Blanche, my dad said soldiers were killing the officers. 'Fragging,' he called it. Some refused to go out on patrol. It made it hard for the rest." Jean sat back and frowned. "And, as if it wasn't bad enough with all the killing, they were covered in jungle rot and sores and leeches...."

Blanche gulped. Her fish stuck somewhere in her middle. She chased it with wine.

"...starved and thirsty, wet, filthy, suffocating in the heat—and scared shitless." Jean shook her head. "Even the M-16s they were issued jammed. It was terrible."

"How do you know all this?"

"Dad told me. Over the years. He wouldn't say anything at first, but I got it out of him. Especially at the end."

Blanche had read about the war, but now it seemed too real and chilling. It was all coming home to her. She imagined her father with his skin peeling from the rot, covered in mud. Exhausted and wanting to be back with Rose. To get married and wait for the new baby. *Me.* She thanked her father silently for the sacrifice, but it made Blanche heartsick, once again.

"Jean, did it give your dad some relief? To talk about it?"

"I don't know. Maybe. He'd say, the war played in his head, round and round. In the early days, he wouldn't tell me anything, but I knew it got to him. I had to hear. He seemed to be holding back. And he was. Finally, he couldn't help but talk about it. That's what I have to tell you."

Blanche sat very still. The clink of silverware and the low buzz of patrons were normal, but nothing seemed normal.

"About my dad. And your dad. And the awful day that Thomas Fox died." Jean's eyes locked on Blanche. "Oh, Blanche, please listen and understand."

Blanche put her hand over Jean's. She was about to burst, but she fought to reassure herself, and Jean. "Look, none of this is our doing. It was our dads' time. It's just the way it was and is."

"You're right. But when he talked about that day and your father, I lived it with him. It seemed to happen all over again."

Blanche sat back. "Honestly, Jean, nothing ever gets better when bottled up. You need to talk."

"Yeah. I've been carrying it around. Now I won't have to do that alone."

"No, you won't."

Jean smiled. "Try to imagine it. When my dad remembered bits of that day, he wrote it down. Even what they said to each other. He said it helped him. And now, some nights when I can't sleep, I go over it. What he told me is like a film going through my head."

"Tell me. All of it."

Jean set her shoulders. Her voice was firm. "This is how it went...."

Twenty

May 1970: What He Said

THEY CALLED THEM "MAC AND MAC"—son of the Fox and McMahon. The two Irish guys hardly ever separated. Specialist Thomas Fox and Private Hank McMahon finished off a week of downtime together, training at Chu Lai. The beach had been good, the movies hot, and the beer cold. They'd even attended a mess hall performance with a stripper who teased the men and, at the end, whipped off her black wrap, threw it over their heads, and then disappeared behind a curtain to the hoots and taunts of the GIs, most of them barely twenty.

It was time for the platoon to head out and join B Company in the field. Thomas and Hank climbed in the chopper with sixty pounds of gear each, their packs loaded with ammo, ponchos, tools, socks, foot powder, pens, a book or two, C-rations, and some grape jelly. They sat in the door, their boots hanging over the opening, as the helicopter dipped forward and wop-wopped out of Chu Lai, leaving the beach and beer and girls behind. The sand and rice paddies and trees sped along under the skids. Thomas shouted, "We gonna get it there, or over there? On that hill of sand or in those trees?"

Hank held his helmet down tight and elbowed Thomas. "Shut up, guy. Be cool. We're not gonna get anything, except Charlie."

His words did not match the way he felt. He was scared. He tried to convince himself. He was more than halfway through the tour and lucky so far. But, deep down, he didn't think luck had anything to do with it. If he'd been lucky, he wouldn't be here. He was glad for the shot that zinged past him—the shot he could hear was the one that didn't kill him. He had to make it past the next search and destroy mission and the next. One at a time.

—⁓—

Firebase Sally was a sorry flat hill and a half where B Company waited for Tom and Hank and the rest of them. A valley sloped down to a canopy of trees on one side, and a green patchwork of rice paddies stretched far and wide on the other side. The Huey skimmed the treetops and hovered over the dirt, blowing up a dust cloud that choked the load of soldiers as they jumped onto the landing zone. The helicopter swung around in a half-circle and dipped beyond the trees. Hank watched it go, wistfully, as he grabbed his gear. "Bye, bye, flying friend."

"Okay, Mister Rogers," said Thomas. He hefted a crate of C-rations. "Grab that one. Hope there's a nice double cheeseburger and hot fries in there."

"Yeah, hot and fried," said Hank. "That's us." They lugged the crates off to a supply tent and then went to the perimeter to set up. They made tents with makeshift uprights and commo wire, their ponchos for cover. They dug foxholes and filled sandbags and hunkered down for what sleep they could get on the hard ground.

It was six the following morning, and Hank and Thomas were warming up canned ham and eggs over heat tabs. Thomas had fashioned a coffee cup out of an empty C-rations can of pears, the top artfully folded into a handle. The thing always hung off his pack, ready for the next blast of caffeine.

They were quiet. Each had killed a man. Hank had killed an attacker. Thomas had shot a young VC through the eye. One of the guys had wanted to take the soldier's ear off for a souvenir, but Thomas had raised his arm, blocking his friend as he came down close to the dead soldier's head with a blade.

"Hey," Thomas said, with authority. The dead soldier wore a clean uniform, had combed his hair and shaved that morning. A suitable preliminary to sacrificing himself to the god of war. Hank saw Thomas turn pale. Like he was sleepwalking, he'd picked the soldier up and laid him on the pile of dead. Closed the other eye.

Breakfast was sustenance, but it was also a diversion from what they did. Hank put hot sauce and grape jelly on his eggs and ate them with hard crackers. "Eat up," he said, glumly. "We're gonna need our strength. We're moving out. Intel says there're night invaders out in the tunnels farther south. Toward Saigon."

"*Word coming down.* You ever wonder about that? Some colonel on a gilt throne in a plywood shed near Chu Lai? Holding an M-16? Shit." Thomas finished the last of his eggs and chased them with the tepid instant coffee. They had cigarettes and candy for dessert.

"Colonel Dandry's usually holding a bottle of Wild Turkey."

"When we leaving?"

"Zero eight hundred hours."

"Hurry up and wait. Colonel gonna brief us."

———

Jean sat back with a faraway expression and took a sip of wine.

Blanche was equally dazed. "Why do they name these firebases after women?" she murmured, imagining Hank and Thomas dropping out of helicopters and into position for war. It didn't make sense. Any of it.

"Must have been some kind of comfort to them. I know my dad would have liked to name one Tam Li, and your dad, Rose."

Twenty-One

May 1970: Firebase Sally

THE COLONEL CHOPPERED IN for a briefing. He ordered a search and destroy mission to begin ASAP. He wanted body counts. If he didn't get it, it was well known that he had ways to make it happen. On record, one dead VC and four wounded would add up to five dead. "Just stands to reason," he'd argue. "Those who get whacked ain't gonna make it, given the expert capability of the United States Army." He had a barrel chest and a stiff-legged strut. The colonel needed an "effective kill ratio." Successful VC sapper attacks at several other firebases had been demoralizing, and he had ground to make up. The men were getting "lax" on pot, depression, and war fatigue; he meant to change that with "victory over the VC."

Thomas and Hank were soon wading in mud and thigh-deep water through the rice paddy, their rifles over their heads. Six on patrol. On the lookout for caches of weapons and tunnels where the Viet Cong persisted. According to intel, the VC were hiding away tons of rice and ammo, even managing to set up quarters and hospital rooms underground.

It had been dry on the hill top, and now wet in the rice paddy. The mud sucked at their boots, making progress slow. "Keep your powder dry. Haha."

"How 'bout them feet?"

"F that. I'll never be dry again. If I can help it."

Their patrol was near a village and had little reason to keep quiet with humans around. Yet, the lieutenant continued to admonish them. "Listen for orders." He sent the message down the single file. The farmers bent to their task, ignoring the intruders, their conical hats pulled down over sullen expressions. On the path between the rice paddies, an occasional buffalo lumbered past pulling a wheeled cart.

They came into the village. Old women and children quietly crouched on the ground, some eating noodles out of bowls made of coconut shells. The kids stared, wide-eyed, and then they attacked. "GI, GI, candy, you give candy!" And they did. They tossed M&M's and cans of peaches at them, but it was never enough. The lieutenant coaxed an old woman to give him information about the area. *Where are the men? Where is papasan?* But the women didn't respond except to shake their heads. The children were like small dogs, yapping and hungry and just being kids.

Thomas and Hank looked about and turned over palm fronds, high and low, and cut through brush. They searched for openings in the ground. Then they all trudged on.

So far, the day was a bust, and they were happy about that. They didn't want to meet Charlie. They set up for chow at the edge of a long string of rice paddies. The slog had been exhausting. Now they could take off their boots and dry themselves off, but it was a losing battle with the heat and humidity. At least they were sitting still, even if they were nearly comatose from the morning's march and hacking at the bamboo.

Thomas and Hank sat on empty ammo crates. Thomas heated a can of ham and limas over a heat tab.

"How can you eat that crap, T? I got some beef and noodles—you want it?"

"Thanks, limas aren't so bad with pear juice and coffee creamer." Thomas stirred the beans with a plastic spoon.

"Jeez, our taste buds is what's dying over here."

Thomas finished the can of beans and busied himself making coffee over a heat tab. Hank drank a Coke and smoked a cig.

They ended the meal with peaches and pound cake, and then they did what they most often did: talk about Rose on Santa Maria Island, walking on the white sand, near the Gulf, her lovely belly getting bigger with the baby coming in July. And Hank talked about Tam Li, missing her with a terrible ache. They consoled each other that the women were safe, waiting, and it wouldn't be long now. *What? A few months?*

Thomas idly shoved the cans and wrappers together with his foot. Hank lit matches and threw them on the pile. They ignored the sounds of guffaws and yelling. Someone popped a flare—for fun. They fixed their attention on the small fire, watching the paper and brown cardboard catch, the cans blacken.

Then they repeated their ritual. Hank took out a picture of Tam Li, one taken in Hoi An at the river, her long black hair shining, her white *ao dai* snug on her tiny frame. Thomas held a photo of Rose, a head shot of a young woman with black curly hair, a wide smile, and those eyes. He looked about to fall into that picture. He set it down on his bag and stared at her. The black-and-white photo was sheathed in plastic. Except for a bent corner, Rose was in pretty good shape, having been carried through the mud of Vietnam for months.

Hank said, "You're gonna stare a hole right through that picture, T."

"Yeah, I know, but she keeps me going."

Hank had seen the picture before, but he gamely looked it over. "She's beautiful." He'd said it before, and Thomas knew he'd say it again.

"Yeah, isn't she? Seven months pregnant, and here I am. Useless," said Thomas. He threw his head back and grimaced, like something struck him in the middle.

"Nah, not useless," said Hank. "What's the matter? Them lima beans got you?"

"It's just that I miss her."

Hank sat with his elbows on his knees, holding a can of Coke. "Whatdaya gonna do when you see her again?"

Thomas grinned. "Whatdaya think? There'll be more than just the two of us by then. I'll be going home to a reg-lar fam-i-ly. Gonna get married, right off." The heat tab made his eyes water.

"I'd cry, too," said Hank. "Daddy."

"How's Tam Li? When you getting together?"

"R & R next month. Fourteen days, six hours, and…" Hank checked his watch, closed his eyes, doing the math. "Twelve minutes." He dropped his head forward, a sheepish, faraway look on his face.

"What?" Thomas glugged the coffee, leaned forward. "Anything wrong?"

"Nothing's wrong, but when I see you all happy about Rose having a baby, kinda rubs off. Know what I mean?"

Thomas stood up. "Don't tell me. You gonna be a daddy, too?"

Hank threw back the last of the Coke and stood up. "Shake hands, Daddy? Tam Li's a couple of months along."

"Oh, man, that's great!" said Thomas. He ignored the hand and grabbed Hank in a hug. "Brothers?"

"Forever." Hank smiled ear to ear.

Joy and fear bonded them, but they knew committing to friendship was dangerous. In an instant, it could all be wiped away, leaving a hole of regret and loss and pain. It happened all the time.

—◦◦◦—

Thomas and Hank headed back out on patrol. The colonel had been relentless; they were to "get 'er done." Six of them, the lieutenant, and the radio operator. They wore bush hats and painted their faces green and black.

The trail out of the paddy ended at a sharp-edged wall of elephant grass as tall as a man. It cut the skin as they hacked their way through it. In half an hour, they'd only gone a few yards.

The day sizzled away, hot and tangled and confusing. The fetid jungle gave off a dank, sometimes rotten, smell. It was quiet, except for buzzing mosquitoes. Not a bird or animal. Not a peep out of the troops. They'd taped down their dog tags and secured other dangling, possibly noisy apparatuses, including Thomas's coffee can. The radio antenna was a beacon to the enemy, but they needed it. The operator kept it low.

It would be a long afternoon before they set up camp, but orders were to stay out until they made contact with VC. Find a trace of them, draw fire, mark the territory. The idea was to call in artillery, blow smoke, and blast Charlie to kingdom come. In the thick canopy it was likely they'd "Agent Orange" the place.

But with every step, they knew: Their efforts would never work. They were losing the war. The VC had a way of melting in and out of the jungle, burrowing down into their holes. Out of sight but not out of mind.

The line of troops pushed through the trail, stop and go. At times, a Vietnamese scout led the platoon—usually a captured VC paid to inform on his brothers. The Americans had come to rely on the scouts. They were adept at finding booby traps, especially when they had their own arms and legs to worry about. But the scouts were erratic, and in short supply. In truth, they were only helpful about half the time. Today, there was no Vietnamese scout. Thomas was in the lead. Hank followed behind.

The platoon was on its own. Every step they took was a careful one, eyes on the ground and all around. They were afraid but determined. What did the major say? Every good soldier is afraid. It means he's alive and feeling. Ready to act. Willing to go to war. Thomas had attended Recondo School in Nha Trang. He was trained to look for the rigged grenades and mines—the concave-faced directional mine, the Bouncing Betty, the M-14 "toe popper." All the many ways the VC removed limbs and heads.

Sometimes the rains washed away Betty's prongs and wires, revealing the trap. Reliable and deadly, the firing device was a ticket out of this world. Thomas scoured the trail, his eyes peeling away every bush and blade of grass. But he couldn't depend on the rain to show him Betty.

Rain. It came suddenly, soft and comforting. Thomas looked up at the sky. He hesitated, peering through the towering green jungle at the blue, blue sky, and Hank slowed behind him.

It was a mistake to take that luxury, to take his eyes off the trail. A minute of repose and thought and relief, to look up and away from the misery.

He was always longing to be back in the world with Rose. It was probably Thomas's last thought.

—⁓—

The line of soldiers trudged on. They feared every tree and bush, the adrenaline lifted that left boot, and the sixty pounds on their backs propelled them forward to where they didn't want to go. But they went.

Hank saw it the instant that Thomas did. Thomas, in the lead, a couple meters ahead, looked up. Hank did, too. The booby-trapped grenade sat precariously on a branch in a tin can, the detonator concealed, ready for the toe of a soldier to trip the wire strung across the trail.

Didn't Thomas see it? What was he looking at?

He did see it. Too late. Thomas's arms shot back, waving Hank away, but in a split second, it was done. The concussion of the grenade blew debris into Hank's face and shrapnel into his arms and legs. A regular shit storm, a hole blown into the narrow trail, throwing up clods of dirt and dust.

Hank's face was on the ground. He froze, aware that if he rose up and Charlie were around, Hank would be dead for sure.

He raised his head. "T," he called hoarsely. He saw Thomas's legs protruding from the brush. Hank crawled forward, reached out. Then he stopped. His head was exploding with pain, his vision poor. The men would come, but now they had their faces pressed in the dirt, measuring out the seconds for when they should get up and move. Hank was alone.

He blinked away the dust of the blast. Tried to wipe his eyes clean. He swiped at them again. Surely, his brain was playing tricks. The big cat's face stuck out of the clump of leaves and fixed a stare at Hank. Stripes and whiskers, not body, just this orange and black face, a magnificent face. A knowing face, a conquering face. Hank recoiled, scooting backwards. He called Thomas again, but he didn't move, and then he did. Thomas's boots, the toes dragging over the humps of grass and not of his own accord. He disappeared into the brush. It was the last thing Hank remembered of his friend.

They came up the trail and went in to look for him. They fanned out as best they could, hacking their way through the thick brush. They never found him. Only, at first, a narrow, bloody trail and drag marks that quickly mixed with the jungle.

Twenty-Two

No Regret

ACTIVITY IN THE DINING AREA included discreet sweeping and chairs moving upside down atop tables. It was after eleven o'clock. Blanche and Jean had finished nearly two bottles of wine. Blanche stabbed idly at the remnants of caramelized bananas, not even looking at them. The waiters were cordial, but clearly the Hoi An Restaurant was past closing time. It was quiet while Blanche's brain went round and round in a riot of questions with no answers. She was horrified, having just trekked through the jungle with Hank and Thomas, hearing details of Thomas's death and disappearance that involved a booby trap and a tiger.

Jean wore a look of concern and regret for the whole episode, her lips set in a tight line. Her face was a silvery block of stone in the low light. She put her hand on Blanche's arm. "I wish I'd never had to tell you. But now you know."

"Not really. Who's to know? We weren't there." Blanche whispered. She was numb and, at once, felt a deep-down relief that knowledge brought, even the deeply sad kind. It was other worldly, sitting in this Vietnamese restaurant, listening to this … story.

Jean sat back. "You're right. My dad knew that, too. But somehow it helped him to reconstruct what he could tell of it. I'm

146

not sure why. I think he got some relief from going over it. He'd be spent, drained, but the pain seemed to lift off him."

"Wish it were that easy."

"He also said he was sure Thomas's last thought was of Rose. He'd often look up at the sky and say, I'm looking at the same blue sky as Rose is..."

"They never found him?" Blanche could hardly bring herself to ask the question. "He was carried off by a tiger, or a cat, you said?"

Jean wrung her fingers. "That's the thing. My dad never could remember exactly. But parts of that day kept coming back and he'd piece it together. He remembered being thrown clear of the trail when the grenade went off. His head wasn't right, and the dirt and dust were blinding. He imagined he saw a tiger through the brush, but he could never be sure. Even as he relived the moment time and time again. He does remember the boots. Being dragged off..."

"And they went to look for him?"

"Yes, of course, and my father said it was impossible, the jungle so thick with growth. There were no trails, no pathways to follow. No VC. No sign of any life at all. They tried—they really tried."

Jean shook her head, near tears. She reached for Blanche and held on.

"Later, my dad heard about the tricks the VC sometimes played. Like ghosts, melting into nowhere. They made strange sounds. Eerie guttural singing and chants. They even wore masks. The 'cat' my dad saw could have been a mask. We'll never know.

"But he searched. He was frantic. They all were. They tore through that jungle looking for Thomas," said Jean. She added in a low, even voice, "Your dad saved mine from that grenade. He waved him back. Hank put your father in for the Bronze Star, for saving him and the rest of the platoon. For warning them on the trail."

"And my mother and grandmother never knew any of this?"

"How would they, Blanche? You and your family are not listed, officially, as survivors. Margaret Fox died soon after hearing about her son's death."

"Your dad knew all this and didn't find me and tell me." She could not hold down the bitterness.

"Courage is something that sometimes comes in an instant, or never at all. He regretted not telling you, but I'm telling you now. He carried it around, and it ate at him," said Jean. "My dad didn't have it in him to tell you what happened. He felt like it would open up an old wound."

"And now?"

"He told me before he died. He'd been keeping an eye on you all these years. He knew you were well cared for and loved. That was all that mattered to him, I guess."

"Ignorance isn't bliss, Jean."

"Maybe not. I don't know. He did what he thought was right. For you."

The waiter coughed, softly. Jean stole a glance at him. "I think we better get out of here. We're overstaying our welcome."

Blanche finished off the last drop of wine and pushed the glass away. The waiter whisked the glasses and bottle off the table, then stood nearby, hands folded. "Mesdames? You had lovely dinner? Yes?"

"Yes, thank you," they said, at once.

"*Ngon*," said Blanche.

"Now what?" said Jean.

"Delicious, for my stomach. And for my soul." She forced a smile.

Jean's mood softened, visibly relieved this night of storytelling was coming to a close. "We need to go. And I wish I could make it all go away. But I can't. And I wish I could tell you more."

"More? How much more?"

"That last day? Over C-rations? My dad told me they became brothers that day," said Jean. "They made promises."

"Promises?"

"I hate upsetting you, Blanche. I already have, plenty. But you need to know the truth. All of it."

"All of it?"

"I've told you what I know. It's a lot."

"Our fathers were brothers, and now I feel we've become sisters."

———❦———

They walked arm and arm along the river, past the kapok trees, and Blanche vaguely recalled the stories about the ugly pods on the branches that were likened to ghosts in Vietnamese folklore. There seemed to be ghosts everywhere, in the dark shapes and white mist. It was a haunted place and compelling. It drove her to want to learn more.

The lights of Saigon and a near-full moon shined on them. Jean's revelations swept Blanche back into the jungle with her father. She tried not to dwell on the horror of his death, but it was hard to get it out of her mind. She told herself it was over so soon, that he never felt a thing. But she couldn't get away from it. *The truth? It's a kick in the head.*

"Come on." Jean tugged at Blanche. "You in another world?"

"I guess you could say that," said Blanche. She stopped then. "Is there more you need to tell me, Jean? Do I have it all?"

Jean shook Blanche's arm gently. "What more can I say now? We are sisters. That's all I want to think about now." She swiftly picked up the pace.

Blanche sighed and hurried along with her. "Think we ought to stop in at The Follies? See if they have news about Stick?"

"Definitely." Jean's spirit seemed to lift at the suggestion, brought back to the present and removed from Thomas's ugly demise. Blanche would leave it there, but she wanted more stories about what Hank knew. There was always more to the story. She tried to remember every word that Jean had told her, but she couldn't. She had to be grateful that Jean was a lifeline to the death of her father and all that went with it. What happened that day in the jungle bonded Jean and Blanche forever.

Blanche stared out at the moonbeams on the river. "What would they be doing? If they were alive today?"

"Hard to say. My dad had a difficult life, at times barely able to keep his sales job. But he did. Your dad? He would have had that little business he talked about."

"We wouldn't be here today. We'd be alive, but it would be all different. Did you ever think of that?"

"I think the only constant is that my mother would still be missing," said Jean. "And you're here, helping change that part of our history. For that I'm grateful."

The thought gave Blanche a boost. It was the one positive move they could make together. They couldn't change the past, but they could make the future better by bringing Tam Li back into Jean's life.

They kept walking, arms linked, both lost in thought. Jean filled the silence. "I haven't been able to find out anything more about Stick. I wanted to talk to you and tried to track you down. I was worried after you fled."

"No more fleeing. We're on a mission."

They strolled away from the river and down into the center of the district. They could hear Mick Jagger before they reached the door of the bar. They walked into the light of a swirling disco ball, the strobes catching the glitter and shine of jewelry, glasses, and long silky hair on the women, the satin sheen of jackets on the men. The air was eighty proof, the tobacco smoke clogged the senses. It was a shock coming from the soft night of beeping motorbikes and crackling palms along the river.

They weaved through the crowd and headed to the bar. "Whiskey?" Blanche leaned on the bar top.

"Oh, boy. Whiskey and wine. It's that kind of night, I guess. Sure." Jean looked around. "I don't see Stick."

"Hold on. The bartender looks familiar." They'd met him briefly the first night they visited. He swung back and forth over the polished mahogany surface, wiping small puddles as he went. "Ah, ladies of America! How are you tonight?"

"We are *fine*," said Blanche. "And you?" She extended her hand. "I'm Blanche, this is Jean."

"Fi, as in Hi Fi." Pronounced "hee-fee." He had a wide grin. His hair stuck straight up in a brush cut, and he wore a gleaming white shirt and black bow tie with polka dots. "Good to see you. What can I get you?" The towel went round and round, polishing the same spot.

"Whiskey? And an update? We'd love to know how Stick's doing."

"Mr. Stick, he doing well. Not here tonight. I tell him you call. He be glad to hear. Come back tomorrow night. Bet he be here, for sure." He'd already grabbed the Jameson's and was pouring two neats into old-fashioned glasses.

"That's a reason to celebrate," said Blanche. She lifted her drink and clinked Jean's.

"I tell him, for sure." The bartender winked, then looked over Blanche's shoulder. "I think you have company."

Blanche turned, and standing next to them, smiling, were Bac and Nhung, whom they had met unceremoniously at the outdoor café following Stick's accident.

"You are recovered from misguided trip into air," said Nhung. She tapped Blanche's arm lightly and smiled.

"Oh! Hi!" said Blanche. "Nhung and Bac? Right? How could you ever speak to us again after we ruined your night?"

"No, not ruined. Actually, quite interesting, and lively. Except for the ducks." The corners of her red lips turned down. She held a bottle of 333 beer. "You get back passport? Or you stay here in Vietnam forever?"

"Yes, got it. And you were right. About paying up, and all."

"Ah, you do it. Grease the palm?"

"A bummer."

"Yes, a bum."

Blanche wasn't sure about the translation, but she nodded vigorously. Nhung's hair shone under the strobe, she wore a tight glittery top and long, flowing pants. Bac was smiling and pounding the bar to "Jumpin' Jack Flash."

"And Mr. Stick? How is he?"

"No broken anything. But I am really sorry about those ducks. We took care of that with the bum, er, the Security Police," said Blanche.

Nhung laughed, then sobered quickly. "And curious…" She leaned toward Jean. "You find mother yet? How is search?"

"No, haven't found her yet. Search is slow," said Jean. They settled in the booth where they'd first chatted with Stick.

Blanche spoke loudly over the Rolling Stones. "Got any suggestions?"

"Ah," said Bac, sympathetically. "Vietnam is big country. Seem small, but millions here."

"I know. It is daunting. We're tracing her whereabouts through letters she wrote, memories my dad shared. I was born here, but I grew up in Tampa, Florida. My dad was in the U.S. Army…" Jean nodded toward Blanche. "Both our dads."

Their new friends drew patient expressions. Waiting. It occurred to Blanche that her dad, and Jean's, might have caused pain for their families. But there seemed to be no evidence of ill will on the faces of Nhung and Bac. Just interest.

Then Bac clapped both hands on the table. "You must go back to home of mother's family," he said, with finality. "The Vietnamese, they are tied to the land, even when there is nothing left there except their ancestors. Most important. That is best option."

"But they weren't people of the land," said Jean. "They worked in the city, at their hotel, as accountants. I don't have any record of ties to land, such as farmers would have."

"Bac is right. The land is the land. They had hotel, they had land. There is tie there, and it remains forever, even though the people only swim over land and then go away," said Nhung. "My grandfather died in his village. He not leave when soldiers come and tell him to go. When they return later, they find him, sitting in his home, on floor, legs crossed. Picture of his father in his hand. The fire from the sky burn everything around him."

"That is terrible," said Blanche, leaning forward, elbows on the table. "Did you … lose your families in the war?" The thought of all that destruction, death, and injury swept over her.

"Fortunately, no. But, yes, it was terrible. Many die or went to camps after the takeover. Now they work. We all work. Hard," said Bac.

"I am sorry," said Blanche. "I don't know what to say."

"It is enough," said Nhung. "And do not be sorry. Not your fault. Is fault of old government, not you."

"That's gracious, Nhung." Blanche raised her glass and clunked it against Nhung's can of beer. They sipped. Blanche had changed over to club soda and felt clear-headed, despite the hour and the booze.

"Oh, not gracious. Practical," Nhung said. "We are looking forward. It much better than looking back. Regret is waste. Revenge not good. We build, you see."

Twenty-Three

The Hold of Memory

BLANCHE AND JEAN MADE IT BACK to their hotel room well past one o'clock in the morning. Blanche curled up on the sofa and absently peeled an orange. Jean paced around, waving a bottle of Evian.

"Blanche, how about what Bac said? About going 'home,' to the land where my family lived. Back to Hoi An to look for my mom." Jean stopped pacing. "Should we go there tomorrow?"

"Definitely," said Blanche. She was in a fog after a day of wandering and revelation, eating and drinking all over Saigon.

"Blanche!" Jean smiled and dunked the bottle in the wastebasket. "If I said, let's go to the moon, would you go?"

"Oh, sure." Blanche snapped out of the daydream and grinned. "But your mom's not on the moon."

"We may get a good lead like Bac said. We'll have to fly to Hoi An. It's some distance north of us." Jean resumed pacing. "Tomorrow. I mean, today. When we get up. I'll get hold of Thuy first thing in the morning."

"Sure thing, but let's get some sleep before we run out the door to the airport."

"God, Blanche, you're such a trooper."

"A tired trooper." She yawned, popped the rest of the orange into her mouth, and came to. "The mission, Jean. The mission. We can check out that hotel in Hoi An, the one your grandparents owned."

"It's not open anymore, but *something*, or someone, has to be there. If what Bac says is true, we might be able to trace her from there. It's all my dad talked about at the end, how he met Tam Li in Hoi An, and the good times they had there."

"Do you have any names? Any contacts?"

"Not really. My grandparents are gone. My mother moved away quite a while ago. I think." Jean looked quizzically at Blanche. "But—what if we just up and find her there?"

"That's the dream." Blanche was skeptical, but she didn't want to discourage Jean. "We have to check out *all* the leads. Including what they gave us at the consulate. And Stick's contacts, too."

"I'm so wired." Jean flopped onto the bed and pulled the duvet up to her chin. She was shoeless, but still dressed for dinner. Her eyes were wide open, staring at the ceiling. "We've got to find her."

Blanche switched off the light next to the sofa and stretched. "We will, girl. We will."

———

The flight from Tan Son Nhat in Saigon to Danang took about ninety minutes on the new Vietnam Airlines. Thuy managed to get Blanche and Jean round-trip tickets for a hundred dollars apiece. The flight was a marvel of efficiency, although Blanche had the feeling the airline was run and staffed by automatons. They moved with unusual swiftness about their duties, lifting incredible loads, filling every need at each turn. They were delivered to a large and busy airport just a couple miles north of Hoi An. On time.

Thuy had arranged for a driver to meet them. Deng whisked them into his Kia and out of Danang. They drove along the China Sea to their hotel in the remarkably preserved ancient city, mostly untouched by the war and influenced heavily by the French,

Japanese, Chinese, and even the Portuguese. Blanche caught glimpses of white sand in front of resorts and homes on the sea, the opposite of the busy, bustling, industrious Saigon with its fits of toxic air. She'd heard the coast was a laid-back paradise where many Americans had trained for battle and relaxed between missions. Again, she thought: *Was my dad here? Did he see what I see?* It didn't matter—and it did. The surroundings were a comfort, and she felt an uncharacteristic calmness sink in. That he was with her, always, even if she would never know exactly where his bones were buried.

The driver pulled up to the white marble steps of a new hotel on the river. It had to be new, or capably refurbished. It sparkled as if a great geni had taken a magic brush to the whole front of it. The wide doors shone with brass trim, and each level of the building sported balconies with fancy black railings. Blanche's eye wandered over the magnificent detail all the way to the red-tile roof.

"Jean! Is this where your grandparents' hotel was? The one where your parents met?"

"Don't I wish." They climbed the steps together, each carrying a small bag. "This place is brand new. Thuy is a miracle worker. She got us a deal. And they have a pool."

Blanche turned and looked at the small arched bridge over the river. The sun sparkled on the water. The flags posted along the walkway flapped in the wind. The air was sweet and soft, and hot.

"Oooo. Let's go for a swim," said Blanche.

"In the river? Or the pool?"

Blanche hesitated, and Jean laughed. They crossed the lobby to the reception desk, past towering palms and red velvet sofas under a skylight of multi-colored glass.

"This is lovely, Jean. I'm getting a good feeling about Hoi An."

"I hope you're right."

—◦◦◦—

The next morning, after another staggering breakfast of herby omelets, odd fruits, honey and baguettes, Blanche and Jean checked their notes and map and walked out of the lobby. "My grandparents' hotel was only a few blocks from here." Jean looked down the street, wistfully. "Can't imagine what we'll find."

"At the very least, the building has to be there. Hoi An was virtually untouched during the war."

"True, but so much time, and so many things, have changed."

It didn't appear to have changed. Ancient Chinese and Japanese architecture lined the streets. Sanitation workers in blue tunics and conical hats pushed waste cans, and a few motor-powered vehicles crowded this part of town. It was still early. Lights on the bridge glowed, colorful flags flapped in the breeze, and the red tile roofs along the river pushed through the fog.

Blanche and Jean walked under hundreds and hundreds of multi-colored lanterns crisscrossing the street. Small, sturdy men on cyclos threaded their way through the thin crowd. The buildings were muted yellow, the food carts and vendors clustered here and there. The pungent aroma of dumplings and noodles and spice wafted out of a narrow restaurant.

A woman in a loose, flowered dress offered baguettes from her glass-enclosed cart, and Blanche couldn't resist. A thousand dong—about a dime—for a packet of bread? She shared with Jean.

"Yum, Paris on ... Nguyen Cho Street?" Blanche read the street sign.

Jean chewed distractedly. "This is the street. We should find it at 192A. That means there's more than one residence or business at that number." She folded the map and stared up and down at each storefront and doorway. The sidewalk was narrow, but one café owner had found a way to put a plastic table and stools outside. Several children ran in and out, picking up coffee cups and papers. One sold single cigarettes and ginger candy. Blanche checked around for signs of a hotel.

They stopped at an antiques shop numbered 192. The storefront's window, with a yellow ginger jar taller than Blanche, was crammed with stacks of dusty, blue-and-white porcelain dishware, ceramic ducks and cows, many Buddhas. A valiant bamboo tree hovered over the goods.

"This is the address, but I don't see any hotel. Do you?" Jean glanced down the street.

A dead end. The hotel was gone, and, so it seemed, the lead to finding Tam Li. Jean looked glum. Blanche had a sinking feeling, but she didn't let on. "Jean! The people in here may know something. They may even be relatives of yours!"

Jean anxiously peered through the glass into the dark shop. "You're right."

A bell on the door jingled. Blanche's eyes adjusted to the interior, crowded with crockery and shelves of books. No one was in sight. They waited. Nothing. Jean shrugged and wandered to a glass case full of old jewelry in need of polish. Blanche picked up a grimy but lovely blue-and-white plate with small figures standing under a willow tree. Gray barnacles clung to the backside of the plate. She turned it over curiously.

"From shipwreck. You like? You buy? Five American dolla." A small woman called out from the back of the shop. Her slippers whisked over the tile floor. She was smiling and rubbing her hands together, anticipating a sale, perhaps. Her hair was pulled tightly into a bun, and her cream silk *ao dai* with a pattern of flowers fit her snugly. An attractive, brisk, middle-aged woman.

"It's quite nice," said Blanche, replacing the plate in a bin of hundreds of old dishes. She did a quick calculation. Five dollars apiece would be a small fortune here... "I'm just browsing." She spied Jean on the other side of the shop. She looked up quickly from the row of jade jewelry.

"My name Marie Luong," the woman said. "Welcome to Flying Dove shop. I owner. I help you find something nice." She bowed.

Though the shop was bursting with dusty items, it gave off a warm welcome. Here was a careful collection of pieces of history, neatly arranged: bins of tiny porcelain animals and people, walls covered in intricate silk hangings, and a floor scattered with Oriental rugs.

Blanche plowed ahead. "Lovely to meet you. I'm Blanche. This is my friend, Jean."

The smile plastered on Marie's lips was an easy, automatic one, and it did not waver. But Blanche saw something in her eyes when she looked up at Jean. It was fixed and careful, but a look of recognition? Blanche filed it away.

"Please to help you," said Marie, all poise. "You look for Vietnamese goods?"

"Not really," said Blanche. "We thought there was a hotel here…"

"Actually, I'm looking for my mother." Jean left the jewelry case and came closer. "She once lived here with her parents, and grandparents. In the hotel…" She nodded at Blanche.

"Lotus Hotel?" Marie clapped a hand over her mouth and studied the floor tiles. "*Mon dieu!*" Her smile turned to shock.

"It was my parents' hotel. On this very spot." Jean looked around again, disappointment reflected in her eyes.

"What can you tell us about Jean's family, Marie? What happened here? Where did the people go?"

Marie bowed again. Blanche couldn't see her face, but her hesitation was apparent. Then, from the back of the store, came a voice, loud and strong. "*Viet kieu!*"

Blanche peered into a dim hallway. An old woman, no bigger than a fire hydrant, perched on a stool, her legs curled up under her. She was shrouded in black. She waved at them as if her life depended on it. "*Viet kieu!*" she shouted again.

"That expression. I've heard that before." Blanche turned to Marie.

"Yes, Vietnamese returning home from other country." Marie avoided Jean's laser focus. "You, *Viet kieu?* From America, England, Australia?" Marie seemed composed once again.

"America," said Jean. "We're both from Florida. In the United States."

The woman yelled again. She rocked back and forth and pointed. Blanche and Jean stepped closer to the pale figure, hunched on the stool. Marie blocked the way and hurried to the back of the store. "Ma!" Marie jabbered in Vietnamese—in what seemed to Blanche an urgent rant that did nothing to soothe the old woman. She leaned away from Marie and yelled, even louder, "Tam Li, Tam Li!" Now Blanche understood.

The color drained from Jean's face. Two red spots rose in her cheeks, and she didn't move. She stared back at the woman who teetered on her perch all the while Marie tried to steady and calm her.

"Oh, my God," said Blanche.

"Do not know what is happening?" said Marie, clutching the woman around the shoulders. "My mother, Hoa, suffers the dementia. She is in and out of the world. She say many crazy things, but this? I sorry old mother disturb you."

Blanche put her hand on Jean's arm and turned to Marie. "Tam Li! That is the name of Jean's mother. We are looking for her..." Blanche studied Hoa's face. She'd closed her eyes and quieted down and continued rocking and humming, seemingly alone with a memory. Then it came at Blanche in a flash: Hoa's urgent insistence, Marie's surprise and evasiveness. *Something funny is going on here, and I need to get to the bottom of it.*

Marie held her mother tightly, but she shrugged out of her grasp. The long, crooked fingers reached out. Now barely above a whisper, she said, "Tam Li."

"Aunt," said Jean, using the formal address of respect. "My mother is Tam Li. I am Jean."

Marie murmured at the old woman, but she paid no attention. She insisted, her voice rising. "No, no, Tam Li!"

"She is convinced you are Tam Li," said Marie quickly. "She says you come back. The war took you far away, and now you come back."

"But who is this old aunty? The war took Tam Li where?" Jean insisted as she held onto the woman.

"I will try to calm her, to get information, but she doesn't remember much," said Marie. "I do happen to know my mother was milk-mother to a young Tam Li. She nursed her for three years. When her parents worked with numbers at the hotel. That was many, many years ago…"

"Milk-mother? Like a nanny?"

"Yes, that is right. She say Tam Li's mother and father work hard and Hoa Sang care for baby Tam Li. She confused. She say you are Tam Li." Marie laughed softly. "You must look much like this person."

Jean did not let go of Hoa Sang. Jean was tall for a Vietnamese woman, and Hoa was small as a doll next to her. The old woman began crooning again, a one-note song. Haunting. Like a lullaby.

"Does Hoa know where they went? Tam Li, and her family? We have come a long way to look for Tam Li." Blanche spoke firmly this time. She would not be put off.

Marie translated. Hoa Sang seemed to have no recollection of the whereabouts of Tam Li or the family. But she would not release Jean's fingers as she fixed a vacant stare on her face. The three stood around the old woman, who finally stopped singing and closed into herself. Quiet and smiling, she muttered in Vietnamese.

"She holds on. She has many illusions," said Marie, dismissing her mother's outburst. "I do not know why she does that. Memory holds much pain."

Twenty-Four

Inspiration

"BUT WHERE IS THE HOTEL? What happened to the property?" Blanche had asked the question earlier and gotten no answer. Marie looked away. The old mother remained silent.

"Yes, what happened to it, Marie?" Jean appealed, insistently. "Can you tell us? It might help me find my mother."

Marie waved off the questions. She peeled the old woman's fingers off Jean and busily settled her mother on a cot. Blanche and Jean stood their ground, determined not to go away without answers. Marie dropped a light blanket over Hoa Sang. She stole a look at Blanche. "Please, come to tea. If you have time, that is. If you need to go, that is fine." The ubiquitous invitation, mandatory wherever they went and the summation of beverage consumption. The very definition of a tea-totaling society.

"Yes, we would love to have tea," said Blanche.

"We will sit on patio." Marie left her mother and hurried to the front of the store, where she flipped the sign to "closed" on the door. Blanche and Jean watched her quirky moves as she flit from the hallway to the cot to the front door and back to them.

She led Jean and Blanche to a small, square courtyard in the back. It sat among adjoining buildings with narrow alleys on either side. The surrounding walls were pockmarked, crumbling, and streaked, with the grime of millions of motorbikes, war, and time. All of it was reinforced with warped plywood and corrugated aluminum. The structures looked about to collapse but for the lattice of viney, hot-pink blossoms holding it in place, climbing to the darkened windows like eyes dead to the world. Not a movement came from behind those windows, nor a sound from the street except for the faint echo of motorbikes. A small rickety outdoor table—that didn't look, typically, like kindergarten furniture—was covered with a linen cloth and centered with a bowl of fruit.

Blanche tried to digest the whole scene. She set aside doubts, for now, and squeezed Jean's hand. "This looks promising. Hoa knew your mother!"

"What can she remember? Her mind's so feeble..."

Marie came back onto the patio minutes later, tray clinking with tea things, and set the cups and pot and biscuits down with a clatter. Jean and Blanche sat back. Marie poured the tea in a mechanical fashion. "I tell you now some things I know."

Jean's teacup hovered over the table. "Please, Marie." Her hand was shaking.

"One thing. I saw Tam Li. One time or two. That is all."

"Your mother as well, beyond being a milk mother," said Jean. *"She must have seen her."*

Marie smiled politely and ignored Jean's tone. "My mother is old. She not good. She give birth to me very late in life. She pass eighty now." Marie looked from Blanche to Jean who leaned in for the details. "I live in country. My mother come here to Hoi An to help with babies, many babies. Tam Li was one baby."

Blanche was figuring the timeline. Marie's story was possible. "Who took care of you while your mother was here?" Blanche asked.

"You do not understand. Vietnam is one big family—grandparents, aunts, uncles, they live together and care for each other. Share all, many people in one house. I have many great aunties."

"Was the hotel here?" Blanche looked around the courtyard, at the place that once was the back of the Lotus Hotel before the war, trying to imagine the lobby where Tam Li and Hank met. It was difficult to picture the time. The building was narrow and three stories tall. The other buildings abutted one another all around the courtyard, taking up every usable space. It was quiet and humid and only seemed home to that single bird darting in and out of the flowering vine.

"Yes, property was here but now divided, all gone," said Marie.

"Then how did you come to live here with your mother?" asked Blanche.

"My mother help family Dang, Tam Li family, long, long time. They give property to my mother Hoa Sang, and I come to help her, but Tam Li gone then." Marie twitched around in the plastic chair. She did not appear to be comfortable. "You take property now? You, daughter, granddaughter?"

"Oh, no, Marie. Never. I am looking for my mother," said Jean. "Do you have any idea where she is? Do you think my grandparents are still alive?"

"No, no. Grandparents pass on to ancestors. They good people. They die many years ago, but we lucky here in Hoi An. The bombs and fire from the sky fall all around. The war not come here. Yet, many suffer, many things change. The hotel close. One thing I know: Tam Li not here. She go with American soldier."

"Yes, the American soldier is my father, Hank McMahon."

"I think so now. Mother say you look like Tam Li," said Marie. "I wish I know where Tam Li go."

Blanche sized up the exchange. *Why is something wrong here? Why is this Marie rubbing her arm, moving her feet nervously?*

Blanche said, "So, let's be clear. You knew Tam Li?"

Marie cast her eyes down into her lap. "I see her. Briefly, long time ago, but then she go away."

"When?"

"Do not know. About 1970?"

Blanche and Jean nodded at each other. There were still blank spaces, years missing. The family mysteriously disappeared.

"This does not look like a hotel, Marie," said Blanche.

"The family sell off hotel property, little piece here, little there. This remains." She waved an arm to take in the courtyard and the small store. "There are rooms above store. That is all." She began to busy herself stacking teaspoons and cups, but Blanche concentrated on the odd nature of Marie's explanation. She held onto the teacup.

"Do you think we could talk with your mother, Hoa Sang?" Blanche stirred in a bit more sugar. "Just one more time. We don't want to disturb her, but she may have some idea of where Tam Li went. Maybe if we coax her a bit? Gently?"

Marie's eyebrows lifted in surprise. "Mother sleeping. She not well."

They looked up to see the old woman framed in the doorway. She seemed calmer, bent and walking toward them in halting steps, but clearly in a better frame of mind. She was smiling and pointing at Jean.

Marie's eyes darted from the old woman to Blanche. Hoa reached for Jean, and Jean obliged, twining her fingers in Hoa's soft hands. Marie spoke slowly to Hoa as she went through a musical one-side conversation while the old woman smiled.

"Mother need rest now," said Marie as she took her mother's arm and began to guide her back toward her quarters. Hoa resisted. She stood stock still.

"Can Tho," said Hoa, firmly. She repeated it. She raised one crooked finger and pointed it at Jean. "Can Tho, Tam Li."

"She suffers from bad memory," said Marie. "She say Tam Li go to Can Tho? But … I do not believe this."

"You don't believe this, Marie? *Why?*" Jean's face was red.

For answer, Marie hustled Hoa into the house. Blanche and Jean exchanged looks.

"Seems Marie is downplaying her mother's claims." Blanche leaned forward and spoke in a hoarse whisper.

"Hmmm. But Dad never mentioned Can Tho." Jean's tone was desperate, urgent.

"Think about it. Your dad left soon after you were born. Do you know any details of what happened to your mother—and you—after that?" Blanche's wheels were turning.

"Not really," said Jean. "The information in the letters is sketchy. No envelopes with postmarks or news about where she was staying, except Hoi An. My dad assumed she stayed here."

"Maybe not, if the property was divided and sold off and Hoa and Marie set up shop at one point. Seems to be a missing link *somewhere*."

"Yeah, and I don't know why my family would run off and leave the property."

"You know what I'm thinking? Follow the money, Jean. There must have been something in it for Marie and Hoa." Blanche's line of sight darted furtively toward the door to the shop.

"You don't think we're getting the whole truth?"

"No way."

"And speaking of following the money. If the grandparents did have any money, they may have helped Tam Li when they let the hotel go. *Don't you think?*"

Marie came shuffling back across the patio. She whisked away the tray with the teacups, avoiding eye contact with Blanche and Jean. "Grandparents very generous to give this space. I not know about Tam Li. Now, I am sorry. I must attend to business."

The insistence in her tone set something off in Blanche. *Again and again denying the whereabouts of Tam Li. Me thinks she doth protest too much.*

Blanche did not get up. "When did you come here, Marie?" she asked.

"I come from country before Communist takeover of the South in 1975. Hoa Sang here, and she begin to need help. We escape re-education camps because she is old and I caregiver."

"So, you have been here more than twenty-five years, and you've seen nothing, nor heard from, Tam Li?" Blanche hated to ask the question. It left in doubt that she was still alive, but Jean's father had heard from her over the years. *She must have escaped. But to where?*

Marie stood with her arms straight at her sides. She shook her head fiercely. "No. Hoa not mention Tam Li until you come. She suffer dementia many years."

Blanche and Jean rose, too. The discussion had turned awkward, and stiff. But Blanche felt there was little left to find out in the courtyard of the long-gone hotel with only the memory of a senile woman to guide them—and Marie's apparent stubbornness blocking the way. "Thank you, Marie," said Blanche. "If you think of anything, will you call us? We're at the Royal, and then at the Caravelle in Saigon for at least another week."

"At least until we find my mother," said Jean. Blanche nodded.

"I call you. But I tell you now, I not know more," said Marie. She stepped back from the table and swept one hand toward the exit. The women bowed to each other. A whispered, "Thank you" from Jean. Blanche and Jean headed through the shop and out to the street.

"Jeez, I could use a *bia*," said Blanche. "We need to talk."

"I'll say. She knows more than she's letting on."

"Yup."

"But we did find out something: Can Tho."

Blanche and Jean hurried down the street between Chinatown and Japan town with the homes of families descended from ancestors for hundreds of years. The Chinese had ruled Hoi An for a thousand years until the 10th Century, and the vestiges of that rule had left a permanent imprint. The French in the 18th Century touched Hoi An with colonial grandeur, the Dutch and Portuguese added their own, and the Japanese, briefly, made their mark. The result was a colorful confusion of lanterns, bright lacquered and tiled surfaces, and an endless delight at the table.

Blanche wasn't thinking about the wonders of Hoi An. "There're years and years missing, Jean. Maybe your mom went to Can Tho, maybe not. The old mother may be right. Her daughter certainly didn't think so."

"We should check it out. It came right from Hoa Sang's recall, such as it is." Jean walked in long strides, Blanche hurrying to catch up. "What's our next move?"

"I have to think."

They passed over the Japanese Bridge, an ancient, red-painted wooden structure, and headed toward the Chinese quarter. Blanche pointed to a stunning temple, a red and gold pagoda with a green barrel-tile roof decorated with a fantasy of animals. A young couple leaned over the carp pond in front.

Blanche tugged at Jean. "Let's go in here."

The air was hushed and redolent of burnt offering. Pungent incense made Blanche sneeze. Two young men were burning some paper—money, petitions, prayers?—over a large, shiny receptacle on a carved altar. Elaborate screens and silks, red lacquer and gold tassels adorned the altar and walls and sparse furniture. The sun shone on the fierce statue of Quan Cong, a revered general of the Chinese Han dynasty. A holy presence pervaded the 17th century temple. The great central space was packed, but people stood about reverentially in prayer.

"I like this." Blanche peered up at the general. "They say he was steadfast and righteous."

"And the horse he rode in on." Jean gazed wide-eyed at a life-size ceramic white horse near the general. "I like it, too. Got any inspiration? Brainstorms?"

"Brainstorm? How about a weird vibe instead," she whispered, hardly moving her lips. "Stay put, Jean. Just stare straight ahead like you're praying for all your might." Visitors milled about the edges of the main sanctuary, but Blanche held Jean's arm to her side.

"What is it?" Jean spoke through clenched teeth.

"You know how these people are moving about us, like fish, but one of them is not? He is watching us. I feel it."

"Where? We do kind of stand out. I've got to be three inches taller than most of the men in here."

"True, but it's not that."

Then, under her breath, Jean said, "I don't know where you get some of your ideas, Blanche." She looked down at her feet. They had removed their shoes out of reverence. "It's going to be hard to run out of here barefoot. I forgot where I left my shoes."

"Just give it a minute," said Blanche. She put some dong in a donation receptacle and casually looked up. The watcher was gone.

"Can I look? What now? Another brainstorm?"

"He's gone. Maybe it's nothing."

"Probably. People do stare."

"Let's get out of here," said Blanche. "And get a plan. Brainstorms mix well with noodles and beer."

Twenty-Five

Sprout

IT WAS THE MIDDLE OF THE MONTH and the time of the lunar celebration in Hoi An. All the electric signs and street lights were turned off. Overhead, the lanterns glowed in the moonlight, and the reflections danced on the river. It was the town's monthly toast to the full moon. Blanche forgot her wariness with the watcher in the temple.

"Wow, this is so beautiful," Blanche said. The motorized vehicles were parked, and the streets were transformed into pedestrian thoroughfares. People crowded the wide sidewalks and paths along the river, enjoying the warm night.

"Can't you see Tam Li and Hank sitting here?" Jean pointed toward the groupings of low tables near the river where young couples were drinking and eating.

"They're here. In spirit," said Blanche.

"We're here, in their spirit," said Jean, linking arms. "Let's find a seat."

They sat at an open-air café and ordered spring rolls and *bun cha,* grilled meat with vermicelli-style rice noodles—and several of those little packets of pork and rice Jean's dad had told her about. The waiter brought them a pitcher of *bia hoi,* a fresh, local draft beer. "I could get used to this place," said Blanche. "Twenty-five-hundred dong for a liter of beer. What is that, sixteen cents?"

"Your math skills are very good when it comes to beer." Jean took a sip of the *bia* and bit into the wrapping of rice. "We sure are a long way from the Peel 'n Eat."

Blanche smiled. "You're getting to do what you wanted to do, Jean: have that treat by the river in Hoi An."

"Oh, Blanche." She looked out at the river, dreamily, but then began moving her plate around in circles. "I'm worried. About what happened back there in the temple. You really think someone was watching us?"

"Pretty sure. Maybe. Or maybe it's just travel fatigue, and I'm seeing weird stuff." Blanche looked around the café, satisfied they were alone except for hundreds of people celebrating in the moonlight. The Vietnamese tended to stare at the two American women, but they seemed to do it briefly, almost courteously.

"You were uneasy, Blanche, even before we went to the temple."

"Marie was not telling the truth," said Blanche, leaning forward, her fingers drumming the table. She took a hefty sip of beer. "Your grandparents must have helped Tam Li when they sold off the hotel. I would think they'd take care of their daughter, and Marie would know *something* about that. Especially if she got part of the building. But she claims to know nothing. I think that's odd. Don't you?"

"It would depend on the timing. Maybe she hardly knew my mom. Only saw her a time or two, like she said. There is the age difference, and Marie was living out in the rice paddy."

"And now she's fully ensconced in what's left of your family's property."

"You're making sense, Blanche, but here we are. No closer to finding my mom. We're still without a solid clue, except for what that lovely little old woman told us." Jean frowned.

Blanche poked Jean's arm, gently. "Aside from that—and Can Tho is still a possibility. Think of this: Tam Li was educated. She worked at the hotel, with numbers. She was a professional. If she had money and backing, like I'm guessing, she probably went off to start a business. From what you've told me of your mother, she seemed quite capable. She did make some good decisions."

"And some hard ones. She didn't want to send me away, but she was right to do it. Famine, millions fleeing, people homeless and destitute…"

"The people here are certainly making up for it. This place is busy as a hive," said Blanche. While there were many idle strollers and sightseers, there were others working everywhere, selling food and sweeping the street, even cutting hair and tweezing eyebrows in a make-shift outdoor salon.

"Wanna get your hair cut?" Blanche added.

Jean laughed. "Nah, and I'll keep my eyebrows," she said, glancing at the woman with an intricately configured thread for pulling hair.

"Fine idea." Blanche mused. "Your dad raised you safe and healthy—and tall. Your mom must be strong, a survivor."

Blanche had a hunch about Can Tho, and she was giving into it slowly. She stared up at the silver moon and the gold lanterns above their heads. The festive lights and color of Hoi An were uplifting, even energizing. "We will find her. I feel it."

"Hope you're right." Jean sat back and gulped the beer. "If she did start a business, it was probably hard to do. You can't just waltz off in a Communist country and open your own hotel or boutique or whatever."

"True, but one thing is for sure—she was probably free to move about. Your dad never got word that she was sent to one of those re-education camps. And by the mid-80s, the government allowed limited investment and commerce. Say your mom was in that lucky group. We're just going to say she was. It fits, Jean."

Vietnam's semi-capitalist policy of *doi moi* was clunky with its permits, delays, restrictions, and paperwork, but the Communist machinery was geared up. Blanche didn't have to remind Jean of the difficulties; rather, she preferred to dwell on the probable hardworking resourcefulness of Jean's mother. *Purpose and positivity, Blanche.*

Jean sighed. "What should we do now?"

"We should get down to Can Tho. Even though Hoa's mind didn't seem right, she may have had a moment of lucidity. She seemed refreshed after that nap, and it could be the one bit of information we need. That one good lead."

"And Marie dissuaded us from taking Hoa seriously."

"Uh-huh."

"Can Tho is south of Saigon. There was a big Army base nearby." Jean's expression brightened. "Who would know about that?"

"Are you thinking what I'm thinking?"

"Mr. Stick?"

"Could be."

It was late. The moon traveled over the river, and the crowds began to melt away. On most nights, the streets thinned out by ten o'clock, but tonight the town glowed on. Even so, by five in the morning, the country would be up and at it again. Blanche and Jean headed back to the Royal with plans to pack up and fly to Saigon to get hold of Stick. They needed him on board with their plan to head to Can Tho.

"Plan A: we need Stick and a driver," said Jean, striding ahead.

"And Plan B: I need to figure out a way to get you to slow down," said Blanche, hurrying to catch up.

"Oh, I'm sorry. It's just that I'm so anxious."

"I hear you, and I am, too. But I've got short legs."

"Okay, Shorty." Jean grinned and linked arms with Blanche. Their sandals clapped down the sidewalk in tune.

"Plans A through Z and anything else we can think of," said Blanche. "We need to get down there, with or without Stick."

The lobby of the hotel was quiet. The clerk behind the reservation desk bowed slightly and smiled. He paused a second longer than necessary, and Blanche caught his eye following them toward the elevator, his watchfulness lingering. It was all Blanche needed to get that funny feeling in the pit of her stomach again. She swallowed, hard. Her step slowed, and she looked around as Jean hit the elevator button.

"Blanche! What's wrong?"

"I don't know," she said, casting a look toward the counter. He was still watching them. "Maybe I'm seeing things. Again."

"You and me both. I'm seeing my pillow and that yummy duvet." She yawned.

They walked down the hallway to their room. Jean put the key in the lock. Blanche fumbled in her bag, still distracted, searching. "Wait, I forgot to tell the desk we're gonna check out," she said. "And he's got some cash and papers in the safe."

Jean pushed the door open. "See ya in a sec."

The clerk looked up as Blanche approached the reservations desk—warily. He said, "Madame, good evening." There was that hesitancy again. "Did friend find you?"

"Friend? What friend? She's with me. Up in the room. You just saw us come in."

"No, no. A gentleman friend. He come to desk and tell me he look for you," said the clerk. "I no tell him anything." Which made Blanche think he'd told this "friend" everything, given the power of single dollar bills and dong. Her stomach seized in fear, a shiver went down her neck.

"What is there to tell?"

Blanche picked up the vibe. He was nervous.

"No, nothing," the clerk said, fiddling with a pen and ledger. "He look for you…"

Blanche turned and ran for the elevator. *No, the stairs. It's only three flights…*

She reached the door of her hotel room. No key! Blanche knocked, loudly. No answer. She pounded on the door, but nothing. *Maybe she's in the shower?* Blanche was frantic, the fear demons flitting through her head. Then the door opened a crack, and Jean's face appeared. She blinked furiously, left to right.

"What is it, Jean?"

"Bad…"

At that, the door burst open. A pair of arms yanked Blanche into the room, and the door slammed shut. The man threw Blanche into a corner. He growled. It had to be a man behind the mask and not a large animal, given the smell of nervous sweat and the bad haircut sticking out of the cap. Blanche blinked back her fury as he turned and shoved Jean across the room. Her hands were tied with a thin rope, her face the picture of terror.

Jean shrieked, "Leave her alone!"

"You no look for Tam Li," the man rasped, crouching ninja-like, dressed in black down to the gloves and boots. "Tam Li dead to you."

Jean sprang at him, her tied fists a mallet of destruction. "No, she isn't!" She swung at his head. He lost his balance for a second, but then regained his footing. Blanche was on her feet. She jumped on his back. He threw her off against the wall. From his waist he drew a short wooden club and went after Jean. Blanche yelled a warning, the adrenaline and anger driving her mad. She lunged at him again. Too late. The club glanced off Jean's head as Blanche charged him.

The man's arm came around and cuffed Blanche. She landed in the corner, jarred loose, maybe something broken. She sank into a limp heap.

The man tossed a wad of paper on the floor. "You look for Tam Li, you die."

He swung a heavy boot at Jean. She dodged but not before it landed on her leg.

He dashed out of the room.

Jean was moaning as Blanche shook herself and crawled across the carpet, her hand scraping the shards of a broken lamp. The guy had done a thorough job. The room was a wreck. The bedding, the suitcases, the desk, nightstand, and table accessories were scattered to all corners. He wasn't just looking to score a bit of dubious communication. He'd bent on indiscriminate destruction. Whoever *he* was. Blanche cast aside the pillows and reached for Jean. They had both survived, and Jean was coming to.

"Are you all right?" Blanche's head was spinning.

"Who was that masked man?" Jean managed a smile, one hand on her forehead.

"How bad did he get you?"

"I'm all right, thanks to you. Wow, you're a regular ninja-ette, Blanche. The look in your eye was killer."

"You're not so bad yourself. Nice move with the clenched fists. If you'd landed one, that turtle would have been toast," said Blanche.

Jean reached for Blanche. "You're cut!"

"I'm fine," she said. The superficial scrape was ugly, but it had stopped bleeding. She grabbed a wad of tissues and helped Jean up and onto the bed. "I'm going downstairs to have a word with that clerk." Blanche rubbed her neck, checked the mirror. She had a welt on her forehead where he'd smacked her. She straightened her dress and looked around for one of her sandals. She was furious.

—⁓—

The clerk stepped back as Blanche stormed toward the desk. "Where's security?"

"Madame? Security?"

"Yes, we were just mugged. In our hotel room." Blanche slammed both hands on the desktop and winced. The clerk backed against the wall. He saw blood on the counter, and blood in her eye.

"*Mon dieu!*" His hands went to his cheeks. "I call guard now."

"It's a little late for that. Who was this 'friend' you referred to when we came in? Did you let him into our room?"

The clerk shook his head fiercely. He reached for the phone and spoke rapidly in Vietnamese. A guard appeared, dressed in black. Bad haircut. The similarity made her freeze, but it wasn't the same man. It couldn't be. But suddenly the venom that ran like crazy from her brain to her toes changed course. *Now is not the time to blather on. Now is the time to be calm, to think…*

The guard smiled wickedly with bad teeth, his hands folded in front of him, the knuckles white. "Madame?"

"We were attacked in our room," said Blanche. She tried to make herself tall and failed miserably.

"This very bad. You good now? You look good, madame," he said, a leer curling one side of his mouth. "What happened?" He couldn't look innocent if he tried. A whiff of bad breath made her step back.

Blanche was dying to say, *you know what happened.* She said, "We need to call the police."

Both the guard and the clerk advanced. In unison. "No, no!"

"Why not?"

The clerk said, "Perhaps we compensate room for all visit. That good? That make better?"

Blanche was exasperated, but she covered it. "That would be fine. But I still think we should call the police."

The guard shot a glance at the clerk. "Madame, here in Vietnam. We avoid police."

"What?" She came to her senses. This was not Santa Maria Island. She was dealing in a Communist country, and obviously the rules were unique. "Well, all right. But I want to make something perfectly clear. Do not give a key to anyone or tell people off the street who is staying where in this hotel. It is a bad idea to do so." She measured out each word with force, trying to keep a lid on her anger—while an idea sprouted and grew.

The clerk seemed to shrink with each word she hurled at him. The guard barely concealed a smirk.

She lowered her voice, even softened it. "I appreciate your help with the room charges. We accept." Then she turned to the guard. "And, sir, are you on duty all night? I hope so."

"Yes," he said.

"Until?"

"Eight o'clock, madame."

"Good." Blanche retrieved their documents and cash. She turned and stomped off to the elevator. The idea was growing, and bursting, almost to full bloom.

Twenty-Six

Alley Cats

WHEN BLANCHE GOT BACK to the hotel room, Jean was sitting at the desk, smoothing out a crumpled wad of paper. She looked up at Blanche. "Our visitor threw this down. Remember?"

"What is it?"

"Beats me."

"Literally." Blanche peered over Jean's shoulder. "What does it say?"

"It's some kind of scribbling, half English, some French," said Jean. "Says something about 'go away, kill you.' My mother's name."

Blanche studied the paper, but couldn't make sense of it. "Great. They want us to go away and to kill us. Don't think both are possible."

"What are we going to do, Blanche?" Jean whined, crossing her arms and pacing the room.

"Exactly what we are doing. If they were going to kill us, they would have done it by now. And we are not going away."

Jean's eyes opened wide. "We ought to get out of here, right now."

Blanche ignored the suggestion. She folded the paper and put it in her bag. "We'll take this along. I don't want to talk to that bozo on the desk. Shady stuff going on around here, if you ask me." Blanche flopped onto the bed, but then sat up. She was far from tired. She was wired. "That clerk and the guard knew what was going on up here. I'm just sure of it."

She sprang to her feet. *What would Dad do? WWDD?* Sometimes, out of nowhere, he popped into her head since she'd arrived in Vietnam. He sent her strength, unexpectedly. *He died here. His spirit is here.*

Blanche grabbed a chair near the desk and wedged it under the door knob. "We're all right for now, Jean. Do *not* worry. I have an idea—and don't think I'm crazy. Let's try to get some sleep and talk more in the morning. I'm setting the clock for seven."

—⁓—

"Blanche, this *is* crazy."

"Maybe. But this is what we signed on for. This kind of crazy. A fearless crusade. Right?" Blanche's nerves were on edge, but she wouldn't give in to it. She needed all the temerity and spirit she could call on.

"But in broad daylight?"

"That's when it's easiest. No one suspects." Blanche's voice had taken on a strange guttural quality that was odd for someone barely five feet tall. She sounded like a small fierce animal, maybe one that would shoot quills or suddenly lunge with large canine teeth.

Jean studied her, briefly. "I guess so. I just wanted a nice little trip to Vietnam to find Mom."

"It's *lovely*, except for these side trips."

Jean coughed. "We are diverging. But I guess your plan can't hurt. Much. Unless they do try to kill us, and torture us first."

"Don't be silly. You got your mace?" Blanche planted her feet as if she was about to spring.

"Yeah, but it's not exactly a Glock."

"It'll get us out of trouble. Thank you, Stick."

They stood concealed in the recess of an abandoned building about half a block from the old Lotus Hotel, now home to the Flying Dove Antiques Shop. They watched the entrance to the shop. If Blanche's prediction was correct, the guard from the Royal would be making his way back to report to Marie. Blanche hoped he didn't phone it in. It was a long shot, but she and Jean had the whole morning to kill before their flight, and Blanche wanted to check this hunch off her list. She didn't trust the shenanigans of the staff at the Royal. And she had strong doubts about Marie, to boot.

"We talked about this," said Blanche, now hunched into a sort of ninja pose. "If he shows, I'm going to slip down the alley and spy on them."

"They may stay in the shop. And they'll probably be speaking Vietnamese. Unless you've become fluent in the last week or so, what good is it going to do to spy on them?"

"Maybe nothing, maybe a big fat something. It will confirm that Marie is in cahoots with that low life, for starters. And maybe they'll throw in a little French. What's Blanche, or Jean, in Vietnamese?"

"Blanche? Jean?"

"There you go. We know two words."

They kept their eyes peeled. They were dressed in dark clothing, their heads covered, sunglasses in place, and mace at the ready. Their getaway—and stake out—were planned. They'd snuck past the reservation desk at the hotel. Their things were stuffed into one bag for light carry, and now Blanche crammed it into a crack in the building next to their hiding place. Pedestrian traffic and business were picking up in the area, but mostly toward the café down the street. No one came near them while they watched.

"He said his shift ends at eight o'clock."

"Well, he's been off for half an hour already. No sign of him. Let's go."

Jean started to turn, and Blanche grabbed her arm. "Look!"

They hugged the wall, a piece of warped plywood over an old storefront. The guard from the Royal sauntered up and stood at the door to the antiques shop, looked around, and then slipped into the alley next to the building.

Blanche took some deep breaths. "I'm going. You watch. If I don't come out in twenty minutes or so, creep down there, and get ready to spray the suckers if you have to."

"Good Lord."

"Yes. Get Him for backup."

Blanche sidled out of their hiding place toward the alley way and stood at the entrance. She listened, hard. Not a sound came from the store, or from the courtyard in back. The closed sign was in place on the door of the shop. She entered the crack between the buildings and crept along the old brick wall. It was dark and smelled of rancid oil and mold. She hoped she didn't step on a rat. Blanche didn't like rats, except for the ones that lived in her palm trees. She was a long way from her palm trees.

Clumps of mortar and detritus littered the narrow passage, no more than a couple of feet across. She stepped carefully and she was glad she was small. It was one advantage. That and stealth, and speed trumped strength. At least, it had worked so far.

The building was deep, with the antiques store in front, then the living quarters, and the courtyard out back. Blanche stood at the end of the alleyway. Dim light from the courtyard slanted toward her, and she stepped into a patch of sun near the opening. She leaned flat against the sweaty brick wall, waiting.

Nothing. Just the peep of a scrawny bird dipping into the flowering vine.

Then a door banged open. Rapid Vietnamese echoed throughout the courtyard. It was Marie. Blanche didn't need to know the language to understand she was angry. The guard was sitting at the table. Blanche could hear the chair scrape over the stones. He jumped up, the chair went over. He yelled back. She heard, "Blonche, Jeanne … femmes … hotel…" Some of it in French, most of it in Vietnamese, but Blanche picked up some of the words. They were definitely talking about her and Jean.

But why?

Now they were mumbling. Blanche stepped closer to the opening, her ears straining to hear more. But it was useless. She began to retreat down the alley, out of the patch of light and into the darkness. She didn't see the shards of metal and broken brick. She couldn't see anything. She'd cleared it before, but now she stumbled. The metal clunked against the brick. She tried to right herself. To get out of there. Fast.

Too late. Startled, she looked up to see the goon silhouetted in the crack between the buildings.

"You! What you do there?"

He took a step in and grabbed her before she could run.

"Not this again," she said. "Let me go, you oaf."

"What is this? Oaf?"

Blanche gave him a withering look. "*You.*" She tried to shake his paws off her. He plopped her at the table in front of Marie, who frowned venomously, her arms folded over her chest. "Miss Blanche. You, here again. You come back to buy antique?" Her smile was cold.

"Very funny." Blanche sat up straight. "What was he doing in our hotel room? Or whoever it was you sent to mug us?"

Marie's fingers splayed over the front of her *ao dai* in surprise. "*Moi?*"

The goon-slash-guard stepped toward Blanche. "You want I kill her?"

A splatter of Vietnamese and French spewed from Marie, and Blanche picked up one word: *stupide.*

"It won't do any good to kill me. Jean knows where I am, she will alert authorities…"

Blanche realized instantly how weak her threat was. Her captors laughed.

She had to think. She took a deep breath and turned to Marie. "What exactly do you want? Why did you have us mugged? *What is your problem?*" Her hand inched toward her pocket where she'd stashed her mace. She was afraid to risk it. Yet.

Marie feigned innocence, but the goon spoke. "We tell you, Tam Li dead to you."

The twenty minutes were up. Blanche listened hard for Jean's step. She hoped Jean didn't stumble on that debris in the alley. She hoped she had her mace ready.

"Where is Jean?" Marie asked.

The answer was a blast of pepper spray from behind Blanche. She was ready. Blanche crouched low and clapped a hand over her mouth and nose, and Jean sprang forward and hit them again with another cloud of the blinding chemical. *The element of surprise.* Jean's aim had been perfect. Marie and the goon were bent over, coughing, and swearing—a string of Vietnamese words that burned the air.

Blanche didn't linger a second to see more. She had hold of Jean's shirt. They bounded toward the alleyway and dashed along the narrow passage between the buildings toward their hiding place. Blanche yanked the bag out of the crevice behind the plywood. So far so good. They were on their way. They sprinted down the street.

"Airport, here we come," said Blanche, her teeth chattering with fear, and also relief. She looked back, but they'd turned the corner. The bustling traffic of pedestrians, cyclos, motorbikes, and cars swallowed them up.

"What a plan." Jean held on to Blanche's arm as her legs took them far and fast away from the antiques store.

"We're not there yet." The words stuttered out between breaths. Their enemies were still out there, and they were onto them. It seemed there was no safe place to run to, but they ran.

They had staked out a taxi stand beforehand and now they jumped into the old Hyundai. Blanche slammed the door a good one.

—⁓—

Blanche and Jean strapped into their seats on the Vietnam Airlines flight to Saigon, barely making it on time. They'd planned it well, their whole morning route and early departure from the hotel—which had been gratis, thanks to getting jumped in their hotel room. Blanche did not feel this was a good way to save money, but she would file it away for future reference. It was the secrecy, the off-the-grid approach that appealed to her. *Gotta think on my feet, especially when I get knocked in the head.*

Blanche had not notified the front desk they were checking out. She hadn't wanted them to know, at least in the early hours. It gave them extra time. She'd had the presence of mind to pick up their documents and cash the night before, after that dust-up with the clerk. Around seven o'clock in the morning, they'd crept out to the street undetected, as far as Blanche could tell.

"Now we've really stirred it up," said Jean.

"Maybe so, but I guess we know one thing for sure. Some people, whoever *they* are, don't want you to find your mom." Then it hit her. Blanche slapped her forehead. Hard. She twisted around toward Jean, straining the seat belt.

"What's the matter, Blanche? You look like you stuck your finger in a light socket!"

"Don't you see? This is good. Your Mom is alive! If she weren't, they wouldn't be chasing us."

Jean's mouth was set in a tight line. She nodded. "I hope you're right. You were right about Marie."

"Yep, she knew where we were staying. And I told her. Thanks, Blanche. Bigmouth." *She's not the only one. Thuy knows, too.*

Jean pounded her head back against the seat. "Well, how the heck would you know? Marie seemed so *nice*."

"Yeah, nice like a snake. She set that guard up to try to scare us off."

"Was he the one who attacked us?"

"I'm not sure. All that black, the hat, the mask. The clerk said a 'friend' was looking for me. I think Marie got to that guard, and he went in or hired some thug to go in there. I don't know. The whole place is shady. They just want us off the trail. That's all I'm sure of."

Jean looked plenty concerned. "Are you afraid, Blanche?"

"No, we don't have time for that," she whispered hoarsely. "But we should check in with the consulate, and we need to find Stick. Get down to Can Tho." She gulped the rest of her *bia*, and choked on a handful of peanuts.

"Something's not right," said Jean.

"We're gonna make it right."

Twenty-Seven
Dive In

"WOW, AM I GLAD TO SEE YOU!" Stick was leaning on the bar when Jean and Blanche walked in the door of The Follies. He grabbed them in a hug. He was thinner, his hair slicked back in a ponytail, and he smelled like limes. His T-shirt read: *Surf's Up. Are U?* "Where have you been?"

"On an adventure?" Jean looked skeptical.

"We can say that again," said Blanche. "How are *you*?"

"I'm good, on the mend." He tapped vaguely at his head and his collarbone. "Glad you ladies didn't get hurt in our little, er, mishap. Thuy says you landed special delivery on a bunch of kids at an outdoor café."

"Yes, once more the Vietnamese prove how gracious they are. They brushed themselves off and ordered us beers and snacks," said Blanche.

"You went to Hoi An?"

"Sure did," said Blanche. "To Hoi An and back, and it was *not* purely enjoyable, thanks to some creepy peeps we met."

Stick's eyebrows shot up. "Gotta hear this one." They filled him in on their meeting with Marie and friends, including the fast departure to the airport. Stick had never suggested the possibility that Tam Li was gone forever, so Blanche reserved comment on that grim detail and her hopes that Tam Li was still alive. They would trudge on. Stick smothered them in a hug. "You all right, you two?"

"Spec so," said Blanche.

"Let's sit. You must be thirsty." He signaled for a round of beers without waiting for an answer and corralled them toward the booth. "I've got some killer shrimp stir-fry and rice and noodles in the kitchen. Kim can bring it around."

They all sat in the booth, heads together, over Saigon Specials. Kim followed up with bowls of rice and noodles. "They don't want us looking for Jean's mom and we don't know why," said Blanche.

"Their methods of talking us out of it involved assault and pepper spray," said Jean.

Stick's jaw tightened. "Are you sure you're OK? Do ya need a medic?"

"No," said Blanche, checking Jean for confirmation. She picked at the bandage on her hand. "We'll live. I'm angry more than hurt."

"We need to report this to the authorities," said Stick. "On second thought, don't know what good it'll do. But they can't get away with it."

Blanche gave him a quizzical look. "Any ideas?"

"I'm thinking." He scratched his chin.

"Something funny going on with these people," said Blanche. "Why don't they want us to find Jean's mom?"

Stick leaned back in the booth and fixed his gaze on the spinning disco ball. "This has to have something to do with money. Follow that trail." He swung around to Blanche and Jean and hunched his shoulders. "It has to."

"The money trail?" Blanche tapped her beer bottle up and down until Jean put a hand on her arm.

Now Stick was full of questions. "You say Marie got part of the property? The old mother said Tam Li's name when she saw Jean?"

"Yup." They replied in unison.

Blanche took a good glug of the *bia* and diddled over the noodles with chopsticks. She almost conquered it, shrimp and all, but gave up. "We need to get down to Can Tho, Stick. I'll just bet Marie's old mother, Hoa, was right. She had that one blast of coherence. She remembered *something,* if only the name of a town."

"Your Army division was stationed near Can Tho. You know that whole area, don't you," said Jean. It was not a question.

"I do." Stick grinned, his eyes crinkling at the corners. "Deebs! Will you come over here?"

The boy was sitting nearby at a low table playing with pencils and paper. He looked up at Stick, came near, and leaned on his arm. Serious and sweet, the boy was thin and wiry. It was hard to tell his age. His arms and neck were spindly, his narrow face covered in a mop of shiny black hair.

"This is my Can Tho. Deebs is from there," said Stick. "My base was nearby during the war. I went back in '98, and there he was, this little guy. Skinny as an eel. He just kinda stuck. Right, Deebs?" He tousled the boy's hair, and Blanche saw the deep brown eyes. They'd seen a lot, but now those eyes were full of love and admiration. "Things are better now, but there's a lot of poverty there."

"I was wondering about the little guy," Blanche said.

"He took a hankering to me, followed me everywhere." Stick put a finger up to his lips, led Deebs over to a small cot, and returned to the booth. "He doesn't talk, but there's nothin' wrong with his ears. Don't need to pile it on here.

"His digs outside the base was a shambles. They was all livin' in cardboard boxes. Rags on his little body, no food to speak of.

I've seen worse but I don't know where. Done what I can, but it's never enough. I'm still searching for his family, but no luck so far." Stick's thumbnail had worked the labels off three beer bottles by now, his eyebrows furrowed in thought. "Dead. They dead, gone, missing. Hundreds of thousands from all over Vietnam left from Can Tho. It was a jumping off place to escape Vietnam, all the way down the Mekong and into the sea. For years after the war." He hesitated then, and his eyes slid sympathetically toward Jean. Was he warning her? Preparing her for the worst? Blanche felt a lump in her throat. She swallowed half her *bia*.

Jean slumped lower in the booth. "All those families. Taking off into the China Sea."

Blanche shook her head and aimlessly attacked the noodles and shrimp. Her thoughts floated off on some faraway boat of her imagination. She glanced at Jean, unable to shake the possibility that her mother might have been among those fleeing.

Deebs returned and snuggled up to Stick. He deftly began slipping noodles into his mouth with chopsticks. Totally absorbed. "What do you think, Deebs?" Jean asked quietly.

Stick gave him a gentle poke in the arm. "We communicate. He understands me, and me, him. He doesn't need to talk, not if he doesn't want to. Right, Deebs?" Then he leaned over and whispered, "What he's seen shouldn't be repeated anyway."

The laughter of young Vietnamese in Levi's exploded in the background. The band rocked, the young people drank beer and danced to the Stones—far away from the ghosts of war. Living the new life of an evolving Communist party. Did they have to go through all *that* to get to *this*? The clash between new and old was disorienting. Blanche grabbed her beer.

She tapped Stick on the arm. "Will you go with us to Can Tho? It's a lot to ask, but we keep asking."

"Right on. Sure, I'll go. We'll head down there together. Whenever you want."

"I'll ask Thuy to get us a driver," said Jean.

"I've got a car. I'll drive," he said.

Blanche and Jean exchanged a look. "Well…"

"No motorcycle?"

"NO!" Jean and Blanche were in perfect, loud agreement. Stick laughed.

―∿∿―

Early next morning, Stick drove around to the Caravelle and picked up Jean and Blanche. They stood out in front under the canopy with hats on, carrying small backpacks full of water and baguettes, cameras, extra shoes, underwear, and toothbrushes. They were going to make a day or two of it, depending on what—or whom—turned up.

Stick's ride was an ancient Citroen, faded green, pockmarked with dents and skirted all around with rust. It defied the color green in a land of so many green rice paddies, grasses, and trees; this was a shade of Vietnam all its own. An ornament of Nike wobbled on the hood, the mud flaps had pictures of hula girls, and the roof had a crater in it—like something untoward had dropped from the sky determined to do it in. Despite its wear, the car looked sturdy enough. Sturdy as an old water buffalo in a field of goats. Stick threw the door open and it creaked a welcome.

Blanche glanced at Jean and murmured. "Part of the adventure. At least it's got four wheels instead of two."

The front seat was like a couch, so wide they all fit comfortably. Stick, or someone, had scrubbed the scratchy upholstery and carpeting. It smelled of bleach and oranges. Blanche hadn't been carsick in twenty years, and she didn't want to go there now. She rolled down the window and hot, humid air whooshed in.

"Where the heck did you find this car, Stick?" Jean asked.

He draped a wrist over the worn padded steering wheel. "Bought it off a French cav officer on his way out. Running, you might say. He was shedding things and people faster than you could say *moi aussi, touché toute de wa*."

"What does that mean?" Blanche asked.

"Not sure. He didn't speak much English, and the car was a bargain. He handed over the keys, saluted me, and skipped."

The windshield wrapped around, giving them a panorama of motorbikes, waiters carrying trays across the street—and not looking where they were going—skinny dogs yelping, pedestrians scurrying in and out of traffic. Blanche winced and said a prayer. The last outing they had with Stick at the wheel hadn't ended so well. "Awful nice of you to do this, Stick," she said, tentatively.

"I can be nice." His smile revealed a row of brilliant chompers. Today he wore a bright pink Lacoste golf shirt and jeans. His footwear appeared to be made out of old tires. "I want to help. And I'm curious as all get out. Why would the old mama in Hoi An—Hoa—tell you to go to Can Tho?"

"We don't have much to go on. Just a burst of her recollection, and Marie's reticence to get into it further. When Hoa yelled out 'Can Tho,' Marie shut it down," said Blanche.

Jean turned in her seat. "Really? I didn't catch that. Although, given her odd behavior, I guess it does make sense." She folded her arms, set her lips firmly. "No, none of this makes sense."

"If you ask me, it's all pretty strange."

"Where do you want to begin?" Stick shifted and put the thing into high gear. They sped out of Saigon and headed south past rice paddies and hovels.

"I've got a vague idea," said Blanche. "I had a chat with the concierge about Can Tho. It's the biggest city in the Delta. We should check out the business district, definitely. I even had her try to trace the name Dang, but no luck. Nothing fit." Blanche shot a quick glance at Jean. Fortunately, she was staring out the window and didn't seem to hear the comment about the Dangs. They would just have to go and have a look-see.

"City's not so huge." Stick's wrist steered the wheel. His long hair blew wildly off his large dome. "Pretty hard to get lost. We'll do a canvas. I'll ask around to some buddies there."

"If Tam Li settled in with her business skills, maybe we'll find her that way. Maybe as an accountant? Working in a hotel? Or a store?"

"You got it, Blanche. But we'll follow up, like the old mama say to," said Stick. "We won't give up 'til we run outta road, and that's just not gonna happen."

"Oh, Stick." Jean turned and reached over. She squeezed Stick's arm, which was a bit like squeezing a tree trunk. "You make me think of what my dad used to say: 'Your place will be higher in the kingdom of heaven.'"

"Well, not yet," he said. "I hope."

———

They were about forty miles south of Saigon, headed toward the Delta and into its web of canals from the great Mekong River—a 2,700-mile stretch from Tibet across Laos and Cambodia and Vietnam and into the China Sea. The length and breadth of it were daunting, but Blanche was confident in Stick's knowledge. His driving skills were another concern, but she tried not to think about it. At least they seemed headed in the right direction. He passed My Tho outside of Saigon and pulled off the highway.

"My Tho? I thought we were going to *Can* Tho," said Blanche.

"Wasn't sure what kind of time we'd make, but we're doin' good. I want to drop this baby off with my mechanic for a tune up, and I want a word with him," said Stick. "Then I have a little surprise for you." He pulled up to a dock in a village. "We're gonna board the beast and take her into Can Tho from here. You're gonna love it."

Jean sank down in the seat. "The beast?" Blanche looked doubtful.

"Yeah, the hydrofoil. Best way to get to Can Tho from My Tho. I'm tellin' ya, you're just gonna love it."

"That's the second time you said that," said Jean with a rueful glance. "I believe you."

Stick pulled into the drive of a tiny hovel off the highway and turned off the car. He huddled with the mechanic and then waved Blanche and Jean down a slope toward the dock. The hydrofoil looked pretty desolate—an enormous gray rust bucket with Russian lettering on its side bobbing at the end of a length of rickety boards. A group of tourists arrived out of nowhere and they all boarded the clunky boat together. It roared convincingly, chugged away from the dock, and lifted itself smoothly off the mirror surface of the river. They sat on benches, Stick with his hands behind his head, face to the sun. He turned. "Nice, huh?"

It was, but the day was turning hot and humid, although less so as the craft picked up speed. The smell of fish and vegetation and the hint of raw sewage hit Blanche, but somehow the mix came across as exotic. The shoreline was dense with bamboo and lotus and mangrove, the water a brownish red. A French villa crumbled at the edge of the river, about to fall into the drink, another one next to it, grandly and miraculously restored to red brick with white satin trim and topiary on the stone steps—a manicured lawn in the jungle. A girl in a sampan stood up and rowed quietly along the ragged shore, thick with palms. As they skimmed along toward Can Tho, farmers in long boats signaled their produce for sale with samples tied to poles—pineapples, grapes, longan, sopapilla—dozens of other fruits Blanche was just learning existed. Along the banks, the merchants of noodles, fish, rice, and other food stuffs hawked and maneuvered their floating stalls. The panorama of the market was a diversion that served to put Blanche off track. She buried her worries and doubts; it would do no good to bring that negativity to the surface and spoil the moment.

A vendor with a basket of beers approached Stick and he scooped up several. He handed around cans of Phong Dinh. "Here's to ya. Best way to travel in the Delta—the hydrofoil, and *bia*."

Blanche opened the beer while she eyed the churning wake. She lifted the can in a salute. "I guess you'd know. This is all your stomping and sailing ground, so to speak.".

"Yup. But we was on tango boats. The Riverines ran out of ports along the Delta with the South Vietnamese. Rained so much May to September we could hardly see what we's doin'. But the ARVN knew these canals and shores, and some of them were fine allies. It was a good run. We even had detail on motorcycles."

"How'd you do on the motorcycle? Betcha you're better on water." Blanche laughed.

"Aw, right." Stick grinned. He jumped up, stretched his legs, and cracked his neck. "Yeah, we did aw right. The 'rollin' donut' was a kinda hippie bunch, we done our own thing, the right thing. The VC was thick down here. Dense pockets. We was fast, them Southies were loyal, to each other and to us."

The Southies were good to us. Blanche thought again of the luck of running into Stick. He had contacts. He certainly tended toward adventure.

"Isn't it a lot different now?" Jean squinted at the bustling river traffic, swirling around a small island up ahead. The fishermen stood straight in their long narrow boats.

"You bet," he said. "Peaceful now. No such thing with the war and then near thirty years ago with the Commies taking over the South and thousands trying to get out of here. Had to look over your shoulder every second. Lot of good that did."

Stick and Blanche moved to the rail on the deck and watched the water roil alongside. Jean went off to look for a restroom.

Blanche could barely hear Stick above the roar, but the wistful, contented look said it all. "You really like it here, don't you?" said Blanche.

"The people. That's what makes it. And who doesn't like rice and beer? Can't beat it."

"But you fought them. You almost got killed because of them," said Blanche. She stared over the tops of the jungle. The boat had slowed in the narrow channel to navigate around the island.

"They won. It's their country." Stick's words had a blunt edge. "And they lost three million people between the time the French left in '54 and '75 when we finally got out. I'm not going to say we made a horrible mistake because we did what we thought was right at the time. It just didn't work out." Blanche got the feeling that he'd tried to explain himself more than once.

"Three million?"

"Yeah. We lost at least 55,000. Enough misery to go around for everybody."

"You seem to cope, Stick. How do you live here, in a Communist country?"

"I stay away from the 'crats. The po-po. All those people in uniform. A little bit of power corrupts, and so does a lot of it. Don't know what's worse—a little or a lot."

"And you have a business here."

"Took forever to get the bar up and running, but it's going. I get along. Made a lot of friends here."

According to Thuy, and what Blanche could piece together, that meant helping the Vietnamese. Stick seemed torn, but he really wasn't. He'd fought them, now he helped them. It was clear as that. Still, Blanche couldn't help thinking: *a rip in the fabric can be mended, but it's never the same.*

"I wish my dad hadn't gone to war." Bitterness seeped into her voice.

The hydrofoil revved. Stick's eyebrows shot up. His hand gripped the rail as he turned to her. "Now where did that come from?"

"I don't know. It's this nagging thing, that all of it was for nothing. And then, I never got to know him. There's that. And ya know, Stick? I just wish he'd gotten out of it somehow." Blanche could feel the weight of it. A thought was such a little thing, but it was heavy.

Stick's expression softened. He rested a hand on her shoulder. "But he did go. And he did the honorable thing. He done right by his country. And, I have to say, he left a great little daughter. He's lucky like that."

Blanche couldn't help the tightness in her throat, like she was choking. "Thanks, Stick. I guess I have to love it here. No choice." Her face crumpled. "He is part of it."

"Yes, he is." Stick put his arm around her and shook her gently. "With about two thousand brothers. Out there. Still."

Twenty-Eight
I Spy

"GOT A BUDDY RUNS A LITTLE TIRE SHOP on Khung Lo Street," Stick called out to Blanche and Jean, who hurried along the packed-dirt road near the dock in Can Tho. Blanche stopped to pick up an intricately woven cloth, crammed among racks of linens and stacks of reed mats, and when she turned around, she saw everything in the world for sale here, like a whirling kaleidoscope. Watches and clocks from Japan, treadmills and dumb bells, blenders and flashlights, kites, rugs, sandals, hats, and sunglasses from Thailand. Baskets and buckets of shrimp and eels and lobster and fish the size of Blanche, much of it still wriggling. The stalls were packed together tightly on the road. They spilled over into houseboats, long boats, and simple platforms that extended the river bank and provided floating bases of operation. The smell of the sea and spice and broth was intoxicating.

Blanche and Jean caught up to Stick, all the while gawking. A row of silk dresses lifted in the breeze from a shop stall like bright, dancing ghosts. Lanterns hung along the storefronts and over the low plastic tables where diners shook the pungent fish sauce into bowls of soupy rice. A woman served up a steaming, colorful mix from a wok on a cart.

"Ummm, I'm getting hungry," said Jean, but clearly there were other forces at work. She looked around distractedly while she handed some dong to a vendor for a couple of baguettes. She thrust one at Blanche. "Stick? Want some bread?"

Jean tore at the crusty loaf. Her eyes darted to every passerby.

"Nah, thanks," said Stick. "Save some room. Gonna take you to one of my favorite restaurants after we do some business. First, we need to see Phram. He knows everyone."

Phram Lon So was standing in the middle of an open-air shop surrounded by columns of tires almost a story high. His eyes lit up when he saw Stick. "You come back! Mr. Stick!" The flimsy, makeshift walls looked like a good wind would knock them down, but apparently the tires held them up. A litter of kittens mewled and tumbled in and out among the tools and small wheeled vehicles. The mother was curled up on a pile of tires, eyeing visitors.

Stick grabbed Phram's hand and shook it until the man's teeth rattled. He seemed to enjoy it. "You know I can't stay away. Phram, meet my friends."

Blanche and Jean smiled. They both bowed slightly, as seemed to be the custom. Blanche was never sure what to do. The Vietnamese were friendly, but the idea of touching and shaking hands had vague boundary lines. *When in Vietnam, do as the Vietnamese do. That little bow, maybe a light touch on the arm.*

Phram and Stick carried on in a mix of language and a good bit of laughing, guffawing, and nodding. Phram's English was weak. Stick's Vietnamese was not much better, but they seemed to be communicating.

Finally, Stick said, "He doesn't know a Tam Li of the family Dang. But he says a number of Vietnamese who fled farther south from areas up north settled to the east, right on the edge of the city. There are some businesses on the outskirts we should check out. Brickyards and bottling plants mostly. Whadaya say?"

"I say, thank you," said Blanche. "*Cam un.*"

Jean grinned. "Me, too."

Phram cracked a smile. "Good luck. To find mother." He bowed to each of them, his hands clapped together in a prayer.

—————

"Let's quick grab somethin' to eat," said Stick. "Get your strength up."

Jean was tense. They all were, but they were starving. The trip on the hydrofoil had stirred up an appetite.

"I hate to put off this latest lead, but some noodles sound good..." Blanche eyed Jean, then the vendors stirring woks of seafood. Stick walked ahead briskly.

"Strength is good," said Jean.

The Lemongrass restaurant was crowded. The menu chalked on a board above a long wooden bar was unreadable, but the smells coming from the kitchen were delectable. Round tables dotted the room. There was an animal theme here, with pictures of leopards, goats, tigers, water buffalo, and dogs haphazardly hung on the wide-planked walls. A large lizard skittered around in a tank full of rocks and bonsai with a snake curled in the middle like the king of a mini-jungle.

Blanche hurried past the poster of a tiger jumping out of the bush and toward a chair with her back to the wall of wild animals. Her insides constricted. *One bia coming up quick, please.*

Jean suddenly began waving a menu at her. "Blanche, look at this selection!" Blanche was acutely aware of how much they could read each other, and she was grateful for Jean's sensitivity. She checked that one off to their Irish intuition, but the picture of a tiger would forever hang in her brain. A powerful, hurtful reminder.

A delighted waiter held out his hands to greet Stick. "Nice see you again," he said, bowing. He scooted away and promptly returned with bottles of Perrier and 333 beer.

"Gee, Stick. Do you know everyone in South Vietnam?" Blanche sipped her beer.

"Pretty much."

"I hope so," said Jean, her shoulders slumped. Again, this rollercoaster of emotions. Jean seemed up, and then down, in a flash.

Blanche nudged Jean. "I hope that guy's *not* on the menu," she said, indicating the giant lizard in the tank.

"You know you like lizard burgers." Jean perked up. Despite the zoo-like atmosphere, the place smelled of delicious dumplings and ginger and spices. "Hope that's regular old chicken or pork coming out of the kitchen."

"Might be a little snake, but ya don't have to order that," said Stick. "Very popular with the Vietnamese. Tastes like tough chicken. Think I'll get me some."

Jean gulped. Blanche winced. Some things she just wasn't ready to try, though the food so far had been the best she'd ever eaten—she'd said the same after her trip to Mexico City when her cousin Haasi had taught her to appreciate her taste buds.

"You ought to try the *bun cha*. Grilled pork meatballs, best in the world," said Stick. He snapped his napkin open and tucked it into the neck of his polo. "Hate to get snake on my shirt."

Blanche ordered the meatballs with a side of broken rice and veggies. Stick's idea of "grabbing" something was a two-*bia*-a-piece lunch. To accompany his snake course, he ordered scallops served in the shell, sauteed in butter and garlic for a sampling all around. Jean ordered elephant-ear fish that arrived with a crusty coat, standing on its side in a metal rack. (It was bad luck to serve the fish lying down, Stick said). She removed it from its little metal stand and deboned it deftly. They ate white, red, and brown rice, hearty and chewy as barley. A plate of grapefruit and orange slices with hot, salty chili powder. A wreath of radishes, onions, small tomatoes, peppers and watercress with a dressing of lemon and sugar.

"How am I going to go back to eating Minute Rice?" Blanche was on her second helping of heavenly rice. "And how do they know to put all these things together?"

"Thousands of years of practice," said Stick, waving his fork. "Mixing up Asian, French, Chinese, Portuguese, Japanese. Even American. They kicked most of these people out, but they kept their food and came up with this. You like?"

"Very much," said Blanche, finishing off her rice.

Stick was well into a plate of cobra in spicy oyster sauce and sautéed greens. He offered to share a chunk of snake, but they both passed. "Should have taken you to that snake farm outside My Tho. Big attraction for the family weekend outing. I don't know how they do it, poking them cobras with sticks, but no one's been bit yet—that I know of."

"No, thanks," said Blanche. "Creepy enough to see the thing staring at me from the bottom of a wine bottle."

Stick laughed and polished off his beer. "You wouldn't like that snake wine anyway. Tastes terrible." His brows knit together. "Stuff has a bad bite."

Blanche groaned.

Jean was unusually quiet, again, frequently looking out the window, glancing at every face that came by. "My mother might be walking past. Right now."

Stick's distraction with an array of lunch dishes had worked— to a point. He winked and excused himself. He headed toward the kitchen. "Be right back."

Blanche watched him lope off and chat up the chef. She turned back to Jean. "Wouldn't that be something, if your mother just popped in?"

Jean crossed her arms on the tabletop, her mind clearly elsewhere. She'd hardly touched her food. Blanche shook her head.

"What are you doing, Jean?"

"Just watching, I guess." She looked up quickly as Stick walked toward them. "Shouldn't we be getting on?"

It was a letdown to think they were close, but maybe far off. Finding Tam Li wasn't impossible, was it? Blanche cheered herself, even though the cheers were now ragged.

Then there were the questions: would Tam Li willingly recognize Jean? Would she want to? Jean didn't have a recent picture of Tam Li, except for Jean's mementos—and her resemblance to her mother, according to Sister Joseph and Marie.

Blanche drew Jean's attention from the window. "If you see her, we could bring her in here and feed her. Just look at all these goodies." But Jean was off in another world. She'd been anxious since they landed. "We're close, I just know it," Blanche added.

"I wonder what she'd say." Jean picked up her fork and idly cut her shrimp into bits.

"You mean, you wonder what she *will* say. She'll dance you around the block, hug the life out of you. She *will*. Jean, she'll be so grateful you found her, and think how it will change both your lives..."

"Just hope she wants to start that new chapter."

Blanche's exhilaration flagged. Regret tugged at her—what she wouldn't give to start a new chapter with Rose! "Jean, your mother's waiting..."

"You never let me down, Blanche, and you don't deserve all my annoying anxious moments. You're really the best. But I feel like I oughta prepare for the worst."

"How about *not*." The milling crowd hurried past the window, and Blanche's eyes followed the scurrying residents of Can Tho. A woman carried a long pole with baskets attached to either end.

A cyclo scurried by with a fat passenger. A young girl balanced a tray full of fruit on her head. It wasn't anything like Tampa, Florida. *How is this going to work?*

Stick resumed his seat. He looked like he'd swallowed a snake whole. Blanche wondered about that look, but she held back.

"For people so tiny, they sure know how to eat," Jean said quietly. Her eyes were bright and calm now … resigned? She picked up a bottle of fish sauce and sniffed it. "Takes some getting used to, but it's good. Think it's the anchovy. Stick, didn't you say they make this stuff here?"

"Sure do, and guess what: a bottling plant is on our itinerary. Next."

Jean set the bottle on the table with a definitive tap. "Do you think maybe…? What did Phram say?"

Stick speared the last dumpling and chewed thoughtfully. "Best food in Southeast Asia, no contest." He averted his face and wiped off his chin. Folded the napkin carefully. But he couldn't resist Blanche and Jean's stares for long. "I didn't want to say anything."

"Well, do tell," said Blanche, leaning over the table. "You know something, don't you? Besides the best stuff to eat in Vietnam."

Stick played with his fork. "Look, I don't want to get your hopes up and all. Phram was excited, all right, and not because you two are the most gorgeous gals in town. He said, Jean, you look awful familiar. And I just had a little chat with the chef and Vi, the waiter who was here."

Jean shook the bottle of fish sauce.

Blanche wondered if, indeed, Tam Li might be strolling by that restaurant window. Strange things had been happening. They might just chalk up one more. Blanche looked out at the passersby and she stiffened. Now she squeezed Jean's arm so hard the girl squeaked.

"Jeez, Blanche. What's wrong? You look like you just saw a ghost," said Jean.

Blanche shot upright. "Worse. I swear I saw that scumbag who jumped us at the hotel. He's out there on the street. Spying on us."

Jean and Stick turned toward the window. Indeed, a man leaned against a tilting light standard, smoking a cigarette. He jerked away. He was dressed in black top and trousers and a cap pulled low on his forehead.

"That's him, gotta be," said Blanche. "He's even wearing the same outfit." She stood up, fists clenched.

"Slow down, Blanche. Lotsa people wear those clothes. Pretty standard issue. What are you gonna do? Go out there and beat him up?" The way Jean said it, it was almost an invitation.

"I want to talk to him."

Stick narrowed his eyes. He was already headed toward the door.

Jean said, "You told me you couldn't place the guy who jumped us." She craned her neck. "You thought maybe it was that guard..."

"Well, I'm getting flashes of recognition." *Will I ever get that night out of my head?* "Why the hell would he be *here*?"

By the time Stick reached the door, yanked it open, and took a couple of strides toward the light pole, the man had vanished.

"Let's go!" Stick waved them down the street to a pack of cyclos waiting by the river. Blanche's eyes darted everywhere, looking for the thug who had been lounging by the light pole. Every man in black was suspect. Her nerves were keyed up.

They hurried to catch up to Stick. "Listen, Jean, let's not worry about it," said Blanche, worrying plenty. "Why would someone follow us all the way to Can Tho? Just to spy on us?" Her misgivings were multiplying.

"I have no idea, Blanche." The tone of her voice said otherwise.

"The long arm of Marie?" The idea was unsettling. Blanche didn't want to give it credence, but she was thinking it: *Someone does not want us to find Tam Li.*

Jean said it. "They don't want us to find her."

"We'll push ahead. And, really, I don't know why anyone would want to mess with Stick. That would be pretty stupid."

"We're not dealing with geniuses here, that's for sure. They're dangerous low-lifes."

"Let's see if Phram's hunch is right. Wouldn't it be nice to wrap this all up … in a bow."

Stick was chatting with the driver of a cyclo, a sort of tricycle with the seat in front and bench behind. He helped Blanche and Jean climb up, and Stick took over a second cyclo. They headed in tandem over a rough road out of town to check out the bottling plant. The driver hopped the ruts, skimmed over the smooth spots. Blanche figured she and Jean were fairly lightweight passengers. Even so, they were a cargo of two adults. The driver held a steady pace, weaving around stray dogs and people. Blanche stared ahead and prayed they were on the right track— that it would *all* be smooth from here on out.

Stick encouraged his driver in a continuous patter of half English, half French as he breezed ahead of Jean and Blanche like he was carrying a feather. *Some feather.* Blanche's cyclist pulled alongside Stick. He gave them a thumbs up, his blond ponytail a mess. "How ya doin', ladies?"

They nodded, though Blanche ground her teeth.

"The whole business is nerve-wracking." Jean turned to Blanche. "But he sure has the right attitude."

"Couldn't be more positive. He's a walking adventure of a lifetime."

"It *is* a good one. Even if we don't… But Stick? Wonder why he's … Stick."

"I don't know. Just seems to be the type who likes to help. Thank heavens."

"And thank you, Dad. Sometimes I feel like he's there. *Wherever.*"

"Yes, thank you, Hank *and* Thomas."

They pulled up in the red dust outside a brick building near a river channel. The sign over the door read "Can Tho Moi." The place looked deserted, but Blanche could hear the faint grinding of gears and buzz of industry. The sounds of glass and metal clinked deep inside the building. On the top floor, two windows were dark.

Stick and the drivers climbed down and he paid them. They repeated *cam un* and *merci* and thank you at least a dozen times. Stick talked them into waiting. They seemed reticent until he flapped his arms and drove his point home. They shuffled back into their seats, smiling at the extra tip.

Blanche glanced up at the windows again as she climbed out of the cyclo. A face appeared in one of the panes and then withdrew quickly. She steeled herself. Jean had missed it.

Twenty-Nine

Step Into the Sun

STICK KNOCKED ON THE DOOR. They waited. "Hello! *S'il vous plait!*" Then he banged it a good one and called again. Nothing. He stood back and looked up at the windows. "We see you in there!"

"The direct approach," Jean murmured. "Do you see anything?"

"Maybe a face? Gone now."

Stick turned to them and grinned. "Sometimes they're a little hard of hearing."

The door opened a crack. "What you want?" The woman looked up at Stick, and without the slightest hesitation, said, "Go away. *Dee-dee.*" Her hair was in a tight bun and her immaculate apron fit snugly.

"Sorry to bother you. We're looking for the family Dang. Do you know anybody by that name?"

"Many Dang. Who you want?"

"Tam Li?"

"No."

Stick had managed to get his foot over the threshold, and now he had a hand on the door. She wrenched it out of his grasp and was about to slam it shut. From the recesses behind her, a man hollered at the woman. Something unintelligible. But the woman froze.

He came up to the door and stood in front of the woman—a small man with a huge voice. "You look for the family Dang." It was not a question. "They are here near Can Tho. Not in this place." His eyes roved from Stick to Blanche. When he looked at Jean, he visibly sucked in his breath.

There's that reaction again! Blanche's heart fluttered, but she dared not look at Jean. The man had seen Tam Li in the past, and Jean was a dead ringer. Blanche was sure of it.

Blanche stepped forward. "Where are they?"

Jean was walking in circles. She bunched the front of her shirt in her long fingers, her cheeks red splotches. Now Blanche's heart was racing.

"Having small business, and guest house," said the man in the doorway. "Some people bottle special fish sauce." He gestured with his head down the dirt road, a tunnel of growth that led farther out of town.

Stick went back to the cyclo drivers with instructions. They shook their heads vigorously until Stick produced a wad of dong. They immediately changed their minds. He held up one finger. "Wait." He went back to the door and banged on it again. The man appeared. Stick asked, "How far away is the bottling operation?"

The man lifted his hands and held them about a foot apart. "So. Not far."

Jean stood there gawking. Blanche steadied herself and grabbed Jean in a hug. "We're almost there."

"I don't know," said Jean faintly. "Lots of bottling plants with all the fish sauce they eat. And the name. It's like Smith or Brown…"

"C'mon, troops, let's head out," yelled Stick. He chattered at the cyclist and pointed down the road through the trees.

The dirt road in a tunnel of palms and bamboo was well worn, but a few houses and little signs of life marked the route. The cyclos pushed forward for nearly a mile and came into a clearing of rice paddies with crypts of ancestors rising out of the fields. Then, farther along, a low building appeared under a canopy of branches, its portico ablaze with a vine of orange flowers. A white ceramic Buddha in the lotus pose, as big as Stick, guarded the door. She had a red swastika on her chest and a crown of tightly wound hair. No sign of activity came from the property. There were outbuildings in back and the brush had been cut away and pruned. Someone was taking care of this little corner of the jungle. There wasn't a sound except for the crackling of palms and the occasional call of an animal.

The tension weighed on them, the air heavy and humid. It was hard to breathe.

"Stop here!" shouted Stick. "We'll have a look." Wheels and feet ground to a stop on the dirt path.

Blanche's cyclo pulled up next to Stick's. "But this doesn't look like a business, Stick. It looks more like a house. Kinda like Uncle Five's place." Blanche hoped she was wrong.

"Still worth a look. They do business out of pretty surprising places."

Before they climbed down, the heavy carved-wood door creaked open, and a woman in a white *ao dai* stepped into the sunlight. She hesitated, an apparition in black and white, her high forehead so like Jean's that the resemblance made Blanche gasp. The woman stared at them, and then extended a slim arm and waved, slowly.

Jean needed no invitation. She stumbled out of her seat and ran up the path right into Tam Li's arms. Stick's bellowing was louder than a water buffalo. Blanche sat on the narrow little bench, unable to move, shivering although the afternoon was hot and steamy. She locked in the moment, one she never wanted to forget. Mother and daughter embracing in a pool of sunshine.

"Well, by golly jeez. If that don't beat all," said Stick. "Mommy."

Jean and Tam Li drew apart. They looked so much alike Blanche did a double-take: *twins!* She leaned closer for a look. Both with the same long, black hair. They were even the same height and weight. Tam Li bore faint creases around her eyes— the same shade and lovely almond shape as Jean's. Their clothes were a snapshot of two worlds, but the smiles were the same. Blanche strained to hear Tam Li's voice for the first time. "My heart is whole again," she whispered, holding Jean's face in her hands. "*Thao.*"

Jean looked in her mother's eyes. "*Thao?*"

"Your Vietnamese name: kind and sweet, obedient to parents."

Blanche was speechless. *How did they know?*

Stick sent the cyclos rumbling off to Can Tho, and the four gathered under the portico. "Guess we'll be here for a spell. We'll deal with transport later," said Stick, but nobody seemed to notice in the middle of all the hugging and tears.

Blanche approached and stuck out her hand. "Madame Tam Li, it is a *pleasure!*"

She pulled Blanche toward her. "Now who is this little girl, *Thao?* A sister?"

"Yes, a sister!" Jean held her mother's hand, tightly, and Blanche's, the three of them drawn together. Stick, with his arms behind his back, rocking heel to toe as if he were presiding at a ceremony. "This here's one fine day," he boomed.

"Mother, they helped me ... find you..." Jean's tears drowned out her words. "Blanche Murninghan and Stick Dahlkamp."

"Blanche?" Tam Li looked confused.

"Her father, Thomas, and Hank were close ... during the war. If it weren't for Blanche, and Stick, I wouldn't be here."

"Now, I don't know about that." Stick set his sandals far apart. "I'd say this moment is meant to be. No matter what, or who."

Blanche wanted to laugh, and shout. *Tam Li is ecstatic to see Jean! No doubt about that! Thank you, heaven!*

"You've come so far," said Tam Li.

"Yes, but finally, " said Jean.

Right then, Blanche knew Jean had left the West and rejoined the Southeast. The world had opened wide for her sister friend.

"I know Hank wanted you to come," said Tam Li. "I hoped it would happen one day. It wasn't easy, was it? Ever. Is he…?"

Jean put her fingers to her throat, but she didn't speak. Blanche held her breath, and her tongue. She stepped closer to Stick.

Tam Li's face fell, the sudden ghost of age shadowing her expression. "I'm sorry."

"We have a lot to talk about," Jean spoke softly, but Blanche could hear a spark of determination—to erase the past and live now?

More than twenty-five years of talking." Tam Li straightened up with a presence Blanche recognized in Jean. "You must all be tired. Come in and sit. Tea?"

Tea. Blanche was ready for a bottle of that snake wine or something stronger. She couldn't remember being so happy—and relieved—in a long time. Jean and Tam Li walked through the door, their heads together, like they'd never been separated. The buzz of their voices was music to Blanche.

Stick kept up the litany, "Well, I'll be a son of a gun … a monkey's uncle … I'll be dipped and fried."

Blanche nudged him. "Stick, you're just … the best."

The door opened to a dim lobby—bare except for a spray of yellow gladiolas on a low table and a thick Oriental runner down a hallway that separated rooms on either side. The space fanned out from there and it looked every inch a business. Blanche peeked into a tidy office with wire baskets of papers, comfortable chairs, and bookshelves. The sound of a fax machine clacked away in a far nook. An enormous commercial kitchen was tucked in the back. Steam rose from vats on large stoves. Workers bent over high butcher-block tables, others hurried around the kitchen.

"They're preparing the fish in barrels for fermentation. Later it'll be pressed for the sauce," said Tam Li.

Fish sauce. The lifeblood of Vietnam. "Smells … intense," said Blanche.

"Yes, that is Vietnam."

Reeds covered the floor. The walls were tiled white. It was pleasant, busy, heads down and arms bending to the work. No one looked up at the visitors standing in the doorway.

Tam Li pointed at the stove and all along the counter where bottles were lined up. "My special recipes. For the anchovy sauce. Barbecue sauce. Ginger-chile. You know how we love our rice, and we like to dress it up." She looped her arm through Jean's and hugged her again. She pointed past the doorway and out to the back where palm trees shaded several tables on a brick patio.

Impeccable, all of it seemingly at the hand of Madame Tam Li.

"You don't live here, mother? It looks like this is all business."

Tam Li laughed. "Yes, all business. My home is a short distance away, just down the path. An old French mansion on the river … in need of repair, I'm afraid, but it's comfortable."

Blanche and Jean looked at each other, and in unison: "Wow!"

"We might have seen it from the river," said Blanche.

"Maybe. But it's doubtful," said Stick. "There are a number of the old places along here, some in pretty good shape. Most of them not so much. They need a lot of upkeep."

"Yes, doubtful you saw it. It's somewhat … hidden," she said quickly. "Fortunately, I have Ngo and Bu to help. They're a couple who fled with me to the south. They do repairs and cook, but they are on holiday now. They have been my family. But now my family is here. Complete." She squeezed Jean's hand. "I feel like I was always waiting for you. I knew Hank would send you. I hoped and prayed…."

"You did?" Jean seemed incredulous. "We tried so many times to reach you, mother."

"It is a long story. You're here, and now that's all that matters. You must tell me more about your father." She spoke rapidly as if she'd remembered something she had to do. "Why don't we walk over to the house and have tea there?" Tam Li was already out the door, the tails of her *ao dai* lifting with her brisk steps. She wore black satin slippers on narrow little feet.

Tam Li hurried along, mother and daughter hanging on to each other. The years of pain seemed to melt away; the fear and anxiety were gone. The dream of finding mom had come true, and it was all worth it. Jean clutched Tam Li's hand. There again, she looked over her shoulder.

Blanche denied the nagging thought that things were left undone. She told herself that the adventure was coming to an end nicely.

Or is it?

Blanche peered into the brush, but all she saw was impenetrable growth. Leaves the size of platters, vines strangling the trees. All quiet, for now.

Thirty

Clunk

BLANCHE AND STICK FOLLOWED Tam Li and Jean down a wide path cut through the jungle. Mother and daughter had hardly let go of each other since their meeting. They leaned in together, one completing the other's remarks like they'd never been separated.

Blanche watched them walk ahead and felt a twinge of pain—and envy. It had been a long time since her mother died. All along the way, Gran had kept Rose alive. They'd almost hit the mark. Gran had convinced Blanche that Rose was watching over her, especially in the worst of times, and there had been some doozies. Blanche always dreamed of her mother, and this was one dream come true. For Jean.

The path ended abruptly near the river. A large cream-colored mansion with a red-tile roof perched close to the bank, like a lady about to dip her toes in the water. Half a dozen high narrow windows cut into the pale brick, and a black filigreed balcony on the second level created a roof for the front porch entry. The house sat above ground at least half a dozen steps, which ascended on both sides of the raised porch. A filigreed railing enclosed the steps and porch and matched the balcony above. It had a classic balance, a faded colonial appeal. An *old* lady who had not quite lost her looks.

Inside, past the entrance, large windows in the back gave the house a lot of light. The space seemed smaller than it appeared on the outside. Blanche's sandals flapped over the worn tile floor with a pattern of fleur-de-lis. She caught a view of the river. The living room was lime green, market vases covered with trays served as small tables, and a tufted sofa matched the walls. Regency armchairs finished the seating area. Very spare and bright. Blanche had an urge to say, *I love what you've done with the place.* Jean glanced contentedly around the room and smiled at Blanche before resuming her chat with Tam Li.

Stick walked over to a long table under a window and became absorbed in a collection of tools—or weapons. Tam Li and Jean sat down on the lime green sofa. Blanche wished she had a picture of *that!*

But now, she was feeling the whole experience. A lump caught in her middle. She needed to get away for a moment. Decompress, collect herself. She immediately was drawn through the house and out the back door toward the water. She was sure she had gills and fins somewhere in her constitution. She couldn't resist lapping waves or the flat gleaming surface of a river. In this case, a tributary of the Mekong. She was overcome with the grandeur of it, so calm and vast. The channel seemed to stretch wide for as far as the eye could see and fall off the earth. The mangrove hugged the shore, keeping the land intact and giving privacy. The palms leaned over the water and crackled softly. She wasn't alone out there. Storks and egrets pecked and dipped on a small islet in the river, the only companions in Blanche's idyll.

She sat down on a wooden bench and sighed. *Guess it's mission accomplished. So happy for Jean! So sorry, Dad, never did hear more...*

—⁓—

A scream pierced the quiet on the riverbank.

Jean! Or Tam Li? High pitched, a female scream.

Blanche didn't move. She sat rooted to the bench and then slid toward the ground, crouching lower and listening.

Listen and silent. Same letters–close sisters, Blanche. She could hear her cousin Haasi warning her.

She crept off across the lawn toward the house and hunched her shoulders, reflexively, as if to ward off possible danger. She moved slowly, from tree to tree. She made it, undisturbed, to the house and hid in a clump of bushes under a window. She waited. All was quiet. She rose and looked through the glass pane into the living room.

Stick! He was lying flat out on the floor. Twitching. Groaning? She couldn't hear him, but she could see him, and he was alive! He hadn't screamed. She swore it was a woman who had screamed.

Out of the corner of her eye, beyond Stick, a wisp of white disappeared through a door. A curtain? An *ao dai*? It may have been wishful thinking; Blanche willed them to be safe, to suddenly walk back into the room and make it all right. But Jean was missing from this picture, and so was Tam Li. There was not a sound except for the chittering of birds and insects in the swamp.

Why can't we get on with it and have a nice, uneventful end of tour? It wasn't going to happen like that, and Blanche knew it. Here was another hurdle—another pothole tripping them up on the way to happily ever after. It wasn't fair, and Blanche didn't like it one bit.

Her one main, nagging fear, the one she kept burying, was that the goons had found them. Again.

She backed away from the window and crept around to the door into the living room. She peeked inside. Stick was not moving, and worry swept over her. She came closer. His chest rose and fell with shallow breaths. She didn't see any evidence of wounds. She put her hand on his forehead, cool and damp, and his color was all right. She tapped his cheek lightly, but he didn't come to. Out cold.

"Jean! Tam Li!" Blanche looked around and whispered hoarsely. There was no answer from either mother or daughter.

Blanche kicked off her sandals. They'd made a flappy sound on the tile, and she needed stealth. Keeping a low profile, she sidled along the wall. The room bore signs of a scuffle. Pillows were thrown about, a chair overturned, a lamp on its side. All this confusion, but the place was deathly still. She hadn't heard a thing, except for that scream.

Where are Jean and Tam Li?

The table of implements Stick had been examining was neatly arranged. Blanche squinted at the array, obviously antique. Some polished, some old and rusty, others a beaten patina of silvery metal. Spikey, round, lethal-looking discs, chisels, short pokers, and mallets. *Mallets!*

Blanche had a deep aversion to violence even while she routinely got sucked into it. Her anger often gave her nerve, and a survival instinct kicked in, like now. No one was going to take advantage of her, or Jean, or anyone close to her. Someone had knocked out Stick. It made her burn.

She lifted the mallet off the table. It was heavy, more than the average hammer, and the handle was smooth and well-worn—a tool of many uses. *Oh, Lord, I hope I don't have to use it for what I think I'm going to have to use it for.*

Blanche headed toward the door where she'd caught that white wisp. She crept along the wall and listened for some sign of life.

A muffled sound, then scraping, and a thud came from another room. Blanche stuck her head through the doorway. A long dim hallway. She waited. Those sounds again.

She clutched the mallet with both hands and raised it to her chest, the adrenalin kicking in. She moved along the wall toward an open door. A shaft of sunlight poured out into the hall. She stepped closer and peered inside. Jean and Tam Li were tied back-to-back in rough wooden chairs, masking tape over their mouths.

Jean's eyes reflected terror. She shook her head fiercely, and Blanche mouthed, *What?* Tam Li was no help. She looked straight ahead at the fronds of a palm tree slapping the window. She sat stiffly, a look of resignation—or stoicism?—on her face.

Blanche hesitated, ducked back in the hallway, and rested her head against the dark wood paneling. She shuddered. *What do I do now?* She gripped the mallet. It was an unwieldy thing, and she was not used to handling tools. She hefted it up and down, getting the feel of it. How was she going to use it to her advantage? She shut her eyes tight and willed herself some muscle—and a whole heck of a lot of nerve.

Blanche stepped back into the room. Jean caught sight of the mallet, and relief lifted her expression. She pointed toward a far door with her chin.

Blanche hunched down and skirted the room toward the women, removing the tape and starting on the ties. "No, Blanche, get over to the door with that thing! And see what they're saying," said Jean. "I'll work on this rope."

Blanche moved to the far door. She pinned an ear to the wall. Now she heard it. Men, talking. She was sure it was more than one male voice. They were arguing in Vietnamese, and not a single intelligible word stuck out. Garbled, but there was no doubt: they were angry about something or someone.

Tam Li still had not moved. She sat like stone, her face pale and blank. "Psst, Madame Tam, what happened here?" Blanche didn't expect an answer, but out of confusion, she had to ask.

Tam Li smiled sadly and shook her head. "Go, Blanche. Leave here. We will fix…."

"Leave? Now? How am I—or we—going to manage that? And tell me, how are you going to fix anything? You're tied up."

Blanche was crouched next to the door, the frustration building. She held the mallet tightly.

Tam Li looked at the tool. "You may have to use that."

The two men were still arguing in the adjoining room, but then they broke apart. They paced, their footwear clicking on the tile floor. A kitchen? Greenhouse? Porch? One of them stomped toward the doorway where Blanche stood up against the wall. She steeled herself, all of her muscles contracting. She held the mallet in her fists and waited.

She heard them now, something in French, repeating it. "…*nous tuerons…*" Blanche was something of a student of languages. "…we will kill…" He said it again, loudly, to his partner whose voice faded off.

Her fury spiked. The guy stuck his head through the doorway, and Blanche let him have it. All the pent-up anger came down with that mallet. Her aim was on target, and he fell face down at her feet, half in and half out of the room. She dragged him in, peeked around the corner. Empty. She closed the door.

Jean was grunting in a frenzy over the ropes. Blanche leapt across the room to help, then fumbled with the ropes that bound Tam Li to the chair.

"Hurry, Blanche. That other guy will be back, you just know he will… They want to kill us!" Tam Li's urgent warning gave Blanche a second to retrieve the mallet and get back to the doorway. They could hear the man outside yelling into a phone—an insane rant that was frightening. His footsteps pounded toward them.

He bounded into the room, but he didn't see Blanche raising the mallet, Jean at her back. He tripped over his partner and Blanche clunked him a good one. He ended up spread-eagle on top of his friend. The two, a perfect sandwich of depravity.

Here he is again! Marie's buddy, the watcher. The one who'd jumped them in the hotel room.

"Enough already," the man said. He started to get up and now Blanche gave him another whack on the back of the head.

"Well, I guess you're not interested in hearing his side… Good thing," said Jean. She rubbed her wrists. Tam Li seemed to be coming around slowly, but she was in a daze.

Jean took Tam Li's arm and the three stood over the two men, knocked out cold. "Wow, my friend, Bang."

"Or Clunk? They should be glad I don't have a gun," Blanche said. Her eyes were on fire, her scalp electrified. She still held the mallet with both hands and was ready to swing it again.

"How does someone so small do so much damage?" Tam Li went for the rope. "Quick. We need to tie them up and get out of here."

"And get Stick," said Blanche.

Tam Li wrapped the four ankles together with remarkably strong hands. "We have to go. *Now.*" She sounded urgent. "Get Mr. Stick in the other room. Did they tie him up, too?"

Stick hovered in the doorway, rubbing the top of his head. "What the hell?"

"Exactly. Come on, Stick, give me a hand," said Blanche. "It's time to hit the road."

Thirty-One

She's Got Mail

"OKAY, MOM, START TALKING," said Jean. Blanche peeped over the front seat at Jean and Tam Li. The years fell away, and a mother-daughter quarrel started up that defied their time of separation. Blanche saw the blood boil faster than a pot of water set on high. Jean was, indeed, hot.

"Let me catch my breath." Tam Li wrapped the shawl tightly over her *ao dai* and stared straight ahead as Stick jammed Tam Li's old Japanese car into gear down the rutty road. It bucked and chugged, but they were safely on their way.

"And what about all the people back there at your little factory, making that sauce, bottling it up? You just going to leave them to those thugs?" Jean sounded desperate, explosive. "*What is going on, Mother?*"

Blanche froze. She turned back to the road with a quick grateful glance at Stick, keeping her eyes riveted on the tunnel of trees ahead.

Tam Li's voice was tinny, desperate. "Ngo and Bu, my wonderful staff, are away, and the workers are fine... They don't know about any trouble, and they're not involved. It is all me." She shrank down in the back seat, her face silver white. "I need to explain. I will tell you everything."

Jean glared at her mother, her fists clenched in frustration. She looked about to burst into tears. Stick concentrated on the driving, and Blanche assumed her position after taking another peek at the passengers in back. She couldn't resist throwing a word or two over her shoulder. She was eager to shed some light, which she sensed she was failing at, miserably: "That one. He was the guy who jumped us back in Hoi An. The guy in cahoots with Marie. I'm sure of it. What does he have to do with this latest … assault?"

Tam Li's composure crumbled. She shook her head and reached for her daughter. "They show up, and then silence. It's torture, this not knowing, the demands."

"Tell me," said Jean.

"Wait," said Stick. "Let's secure the troops. We're almost to Loan's. We'll be safe there. Does this road lead to Puquot, Madame Tam? Seems like…"

Tam Li sat up straight. She seemed eager to be useful. "Oh, yes, Mr. Stick. You are doing very well … on navigation."

He grinned. "Do need some help now and then. We all do. We'll be at Loan's soon, then you can spill. We can make a plan. Sounds like we definitely need a plan."

Tam Li sat back in the seat. She started to fade, a whisper of a woman with a delicate voice.

Purposely so? Blanche gave her the eyeball. Something was not adding up.

"I am so sorry," said Tam Li. "I never meant for any harm to come to you. It's why I sent you away in the first place. To *not* have you exposed to such … evil."

"What, mother? The war and all that chaos has been over for a long time." Jean's anger and annoyance collapsed. She held her mother at arm's length, her gesture suddenly tender.

"There can't be secrets," said Tam Li. "We're family, we're together, and I'm never going to let you go."

"I believe that. I know you mean well, but there are secrets. I'm here now, and I need to know everything."

Tam Li's lips were set at no, but her eyes said yes.

"You must have known I would come," said Jean. "Someday."

"I hoped, yes. Hank promised, and if he didn't send you, I would find you. I didn't know *how*." Tam Li looked out the back of the car at the road behind them. "I wanted to join you in America, but it was *impossible*."

"Like I said, you need to start talking, Mom."

"Where do I start…"

Jean tapped Stick on the shoulder. "How far?"

He waved in the direction of a road surrounded by thick jungle. "There, in the bush. Madame's directions, perfect. They won't find us there."

—*⁓*—

"You're all troopers, gotta say." Stick wrestled the car over the uneven road, the palms slapping the windshield. "But we need to hole up for a bit. At Loan's. He's my friend."

"Who isn't?" Blanche murmured. It seemed Stick's network of friends and "family" was wider than Blanche had imagined, and she was becoming evermore grateful for it. She was also dismayed at how deeply they seemed to be sinking into trouble and needing help. It was a beautiful country with lovely people, but there was a seedy underside that kept blindsiding them. She hadn't found out anything more about her dad, and, at this point, she didn't think she would. Blanche was done with the scene. She longed to put an end to this misadventure and get back to the island. In one piece.

Blanche craned her neck at her surroundings, the vines so dense they formed a green wall. Stick pulled into a narrow road that led to Loan Bac Tao's house two hours outside of Can Tho in the village of Puquot. It was almost dark, but it didn't dim their host's hospitality. At the sound of wheels crunching on his driveway, he came running down the steps, his arms open wide. His home was a simple thatched structure: large, long, and elevated, with a yard full of chickens, dogs, and small pigs grazing and leaping about near the front door. A curtain covered the opening. The windows were holes in the walls.

Loan grabbed Stick's hand and ushered them all up the steps. His smile lit up the place as he led them to a back room nearly the width of the house.

"Loan, my friend, brother, we don't want to trouble you. We're only stopping briefly."

"Mr. Stick, you no brief about anything," said Mr. Loan. "You the long shot."

Stick laughed. Blanche, Jean, and Tam Li smiled anxiously.

"It is very kind of you, Mr. Loan," said Blanche, after introductions all around. "We won't stay long. We were just…"

Jean looped her arm through Blanche's and tugged.

"We were just out for a drive," said Blanche. They were bedraggled, smudges and wrinkles everywhere, tension etched on each face.

Loan looked them up and down, hands clasped over his immaculate top. "Hmmm. No such thing," he said. "Where Mr. Stick is, is always more to story."

"You know me too well," said Stick, with a gritty edge.

"Yes," said Loan, now suddenly solemn. "You rest now. I bring you spring roll and *bia*. Mr. Stick favorite."

"I will catch you next time, Loan."

"Ah. You always catch me, Mr. Stick."

The back of the house was surprisingly comfortable with reed mats on the floor and pillows, and built-in seating lining the walls. Low tables and candles. The ever-present Buddha in a corner. The windows—rather, the openings in the walls—looked out on the dark shapes of bamboo and fruit trees. Something was blooming; the wind blew the fragrance into the large space. Chickens and roosters pecked in the backyard. A dog howled.

They sat together, away from the windows. Loan went off for refreshments.

"We're safe now, so, if ya don't mind, I'm gonna get some shut-eye. That hit on the head warnt good for this ol' bean," said Stick, tapping himself on the temple. "Got a terrific pounding up here, but when I get up, we gonna sort this whole thing out. Them hounds that was after ya, gotta stop that business. Prontito." He was sitting, elbows on knees, his pallor pasty. His hair hung down in lanky, white strands. He went to the far end of the room, lay down, and was snoring in a minute.

"Hope he's all right," said Blanche. "Certainly hasn't been an easy time for him since he met us." She bent over him, shaking her head. She put a cotton throw over his huge frame. He groaned and resumed snoring.

"How did you ever find him?" asked Tam Li. She sat primly, almost defensively, knees together.

"Luck," said Jean.

Blanche nodded. "Good thing we like to have a cocktail now and again. He owns a bar in Saigon. We wandered in—what? Seems like weeks ago, and it's only been *days*. The rest is history. He knows everyone in South Vietnam. He's been an enormous help."

Tam Li relaxed and took Jean's hand. "You've both been through so much."

"Yeah, we have, Ma, and so have you," said Jean, now soothing, coaxing. "I need to hear what's going on. *Please.*"

"For twenty-five years?" She looked away and smiled A private, sad smile.

"You can start where you like, but for all intents and purposes, I want to hear about *lately*...."

Tam Li took a deep breath. "I have been blackmailed. Not just lately. But for many years." The news lay like a hot grenade thrown into their little camp.

Blanche was speechless. Jean demanded: "You *what? Why?*"

"I hoped they'd go away, lose interest. But it got worse, all through the years of the war and afterward. We were afraid of not going along with the Communists—bowing to their extortion to join the party and their methods to bend us. You must understand. Fear rules. I was *afraid*. I ran, but they found me, and it all began again."

"*It?*" Jean was incredulous.

"What do they have on you?" asked Blanche. "Why didn't you turn them in to authorities?"

"Who's the authority? Easy to say, not easy to do. These bad people pay off key officials. It's been going on forever."

Blanche began pacing. She was furious. *Someone has got to help. They can't get away with it.*

Jean looked from her mother to Blanche, desperately.

Tam Li continued in a dead-tired tone. She seemed resigned. "When the Communists took over, it was obvious I fell into that hated group of bourgeois. I had to hide and pretend to be a poor woman without resources. A refugee fleeing south. But I had to be careful. If I didn't, the whole family would be sent to the re-education camps or killed." She shook her head. "Look how that turned out."

"Were they? Were *you*? Sent to the camps? Any of the family killed?" Jean held her mother's hands, leaning close to her face.

"No, no. We were lucky there. But not completely."

"And the hotel? The family ran the hotel after the war," said Blanche.

"For a short time, and then we paid. Dearly," said Tam Li. "We kept the business small, but they found a way to take advantage of us."

"You were *robbed*." Jean nearly shouted it.

"Yes, and it doesn't stop."

Blanche stomped around the room, hands on hips. "We have to *do* something."

"*Do?*"

"Yes. Do," said Tam Li, but her tone was frazzled. "I have to be done with this bad business. I don't want them near either one of you. It's why I played the game. I was very afraid they would find you and involve you in their schemes. It's all bad and complicated."

"What do you suggest we do?" Blanche threw herself on the cushioned banquet, her eyes fixed on Tam Li.

"I don't know. It's different now. Things are changing. Back then, we—how do you say it—we kept a low profile managing the business. My parents were old. We maintained what was left of the property in Hoi An, and it went on for a while. But we ended up with little, selling off bits and pieces quietly. And now this." Her face constricted.

"You have always been successful, Tam Li. And you are now," said Blanche, elbows on knees, hands clasped resolutely.

"Success. What a strange word," said Tam Li. "We finally sold off everything, but Marie...." Here Tam Li stopped. She appeared to be tasting something bitter. "Marie and her henchman took what was left of the assets." Her voice drifted away, leaving it there. "They've told me repeatedly they would turn me into authorities if I complained. Tell them I was a wealthy business owner with past allegiance to the ... invaders. I'm vulnerable. They demand payment for silence. I don't have any idea what they are capable of doing. To me, or you." Her disgust was palpable. "At all cost, I couldn't let them ever find you."

"Fear. Ugh," said Blanche. "It rules."

"*They* should be turned into the authorities," said Jean. Her disgust matched her mother's. Blanche was surprised at the resemblance of the two women in every way. Even their feelings seemed to mirror each other.

"Now it has reached a point," said Tam Li.

"Mother, this blackmailing began so many years ago. The camps have been closed. How can they continue to do this?"

"They lied then, and now they make up more lies. I trust few people. I've been so afraid of what their lies might do. You know, part of fear is the not knowing. I have to pay bribes to the blackmailers, or I will end up paying off the officials, these thugs tell me," said Tam Li. "*How can this be?* I put them off with small payments, pleading start-up costs for the new business, but that excuse ran out. Now they are stepping up, threatening to frame me for corruption and other fake claims. Old ones, and made-up new ones. They are making it very difficult to make fish sauce if they don't get their way."

"That's just stupid. Cutting off their nose. Killing the golden goose...." Blanche's felt her temperature rising. "What sense does this make?"

"Ha! No sense. None of it!" Tam Li threw her hands up. "They'll take the business, the work that I've built. It's thriving. It'll be for them, too."

"I stirred things up by coming here," Jean said, barely above a whisper. "And dragged you into it, Blanche." She lowered her head, put her face in her hands.

Tam Li stroked Jean's arm. Her face resumed that stony stare of earlier in the day when she was tied up by thugs in her own house. "I will kill them." Steel in her tone. "They won't harm you. I won't let them."

"Whoa. I'm all for some maintenance. God knows I've tried. We have enough of this type back in the good old USA." Blanche jumped up and started pacing again. "I clunked those two on the head. But kill them? Can't we just report them? Get them locked up?"

"This is a Communist country. Marie has connections to officials. It is all about the bribe." Tam Li hammered down the facts.

"We can still report them. There are police here, mother," said Jean. "Don't you have records of these blackmail payments? Letters? Emails?"

"Records? You know the history of those who've kept records. It's a way to trace people who cooperate with the allies and those outside the Party. I've had to be careful. These blackmailers are careful. They leave no paper trail."

Tam Li sank into the cushion—worn down, yet at times her strength flared.

Blanche wanted to hear more. *There is more, I'm sure of it...*

Loan shuffled into the room with a tray of tea and *bia*. A girl of ten or so, huge friendly eyes and a sweet expression, followed him with bowls of steaming dumplings, rolls, and a large basket of fruit. They placed the food and drinks on a low table.

Loan straightened up and clasped his hands with a good deal of authority. "Ah, I see Mr. Stick, how you say, tuckered." He bowed toward his reclining, snoring friend. "We are happy you are here," Loan continued. "My daughter, Hyunh. 'Golden.' She will help you if you need anything." The little girl smiled shyly, fussing with her long black braid.

Loan resumed his greeting. "Over the years, he come to me, I go to him. Now you enjoy. Please." The matter seemed settled— an understanding between friends. Once again, Blanche was surprised at the ability of so many of their hosts to be so pleasant and warm, excluding a few bad blokes.

Loan nodded at the women. "You will take all the time you need now. I am here to help you. Rest, eat, and drink. Sleep." Hyunh produced several blankets from a large hamper in the corner.

Blanche could not say no to any of this. Yet, she was disturbed at Tam Li's news and could not contain her anxiety. They needed to figure out their next move. In the meantime, she eyed the dumplings and fish sauce. She needed to eat something. She realized she was starving. They were safe, for now, but who could tell about tomorrow? Stick snored on. She hated to keep leaning on him, but they had to get out of this mess, and Stick knew the territory. She had the inkling of a plan, and when he woke up, she'd try to convince him to consider it.

She looked out the window into the darkness. *They're still out there, that bunch of thugs.* It was unnerving to think one or more of them might pop up out of nowhere, as they'd done again and again in the most unlikely places.

Loan finished setting up the small plates and teacups and helped his daughter with the bedding. He peeked at Stick. "All good for now."

Blanche had been watching their host. She had a sudden urge to throw her arms around him, but, in a rare show of reserve, she bowed instead. "You are so kind, Mr. Loan. I—we—can't thank you enough."

"You are guest. We are friends, and friends help each other."

He left the room. Blanche felt drained. She took a sip of tea; she wished she could read the leaves in the bottom of the cup. Tam Li and Jean huddled together, exhaustion etched on their faces.

"We need a plan," Blanche mumbled as she draped a light blanket over her shoulders and sank back into the banquette.

Jean looked up. "Don't we, though."

Thirty-Two

Hideout in Chinatown

IT WAS MORNING. Blanche sprang up, totally awake. It had been a hard resting spot on the narrow cushion, but she felt fine, even good. The sun beamed through the opening in the wall. A rooster crowed.

Day Nine! Blanche was feeling the rhythm of the new country. The food and people, and the crazy ups and downs. In a week, they'd found Tam Li, but now the business of the blackmailers weighed heavily. They needed to extricate Tam Li from that mess and secure the team of mother and daughter. *What's it going to take? Another invasion?*

Blanche looked across the room. Stick was gone, Jean and Tam Li were still asleep—or at least curled up in oblivion on thin mattresses in a far corner.

Rested but in a sweat, Blanche worried. *What do we do now?* She hung out the window, checking for a lurking goon in a black mask and trousers. It was wearing her down, this constant looking over her shoulder. She breathed in the green air, and it worked— the perfect stillness, orchids trailing up the outside wall, and the chittering of insects and birds.

Loan startled her, moving soundlessly into the room with a large basin of water. "Good morning, lady. You may wash. Latrine out in back. Hyunh help, if you wish."

"Thank you, Loan." She smiled, grateful for the hospitality and the sweet scent of fruit trees wafting through the opening. The paddle fan moved lazily above. "Everything good this morning? So nice of you to put up with us." She stood up and folded her blanket.

Loan set the basin down on a low table with a firm tap and a splash. "Oh, yes. It is always good to see Mr. Stick and now friends," he said, bowing. "How you sleep, Miss Blanche?" He eyed the seat under the "window."

"Very well, thank you. It's amazing how restful it is to get away and sleep. In the jungle…"

"Yes, get away," he murmured, adding a thin cotton towel next to the water basin. "That is a good idea. A Mr. Stick idea. He is drinking tea. Outside. You join him soon?"

———

Blanche pulled herself together. She washed her face and found her toothbrush, surprised that she'd had the foresight to guess their outing would take longer than a day. She dabbed at the streaks on her T-shirt. Refreshed was stretching it. Blanche hurried through the house, past silent family members bent over their work. Sweeping, stirring, cleaning vegetables at a wooden table. She found Stick in the backyard, and her immediate focus was to have a *tete-a-tete*. She interrupted him as he peeled a strange-looking, brown prickly thing with a thin knife.

"What're we gonna do, Stick? Those guys are probably out there somewhere, and you know they'll be back."

"Hmmmm," he said, the blade suspended.

Blanche perched on the small wooden chair, not particularly interested in eating. "We need to get on it. They're blackmailing

Tam Li, Stick. You missed it. You passed out before she dropped that little bomb."

He sat back so hard the chair almost tipped over. "So that's it. Had to be some reason those guys keep popping up."

"What's that supposed to mean?"

"Follow the money, Blanche. Always follow the money. This has gotta have something to do with filthy lucre. Crid. *Dong.* You and Jean must be putting a crimp in their style."

"Just off the top of your head?"

"Nah, been pondering this one a-lately. I mighta mentioned it, but now I'm pretty sure that's the case. Why, out of the blue, these thugs just up and appear? And they keep at it."

"But what do we have to do with it?" The thought had crossed her mind, too—as soon as she'd considered that money was involved.

"Jean's mama's girl. Half American. Landing in the middle of their scheme. They don't like that."

Blanche mulled it over. "Maybe we can work that angle: the Americans have landed. Again."

Stick shook his head. "You know what happened the last time. Didn't work out so well for us. This little country kicked our collective asses. Excuse me."

"Well. *What are we gonna do?*" The question was rhetorical. She wanted to grab Jean and Tam Li and get the next plane out. Stick would never budge, a thought that suddenly saddened her. They'd eventually have to say goodbye when all this craziness was over.

He seemed to be studying a distant treetop. The teacup in his enormous hand was almost funny. She would have chuckled, except for that re-occurring spike of fear. He was thinking so hard she could almost see the sparks.

"You okay? How's your head?"

"Hard as a rock." He knock-knocked himself on the forehead. "For good luck."

"I think we're gonna need it." She slumped, elbows on the table, and helped herself to a banana. She eyed the brown thing with its orangey innards that he was slicing. "Ugh, what's that?"

"Sapodilla, I think. Want some?"

"No, thanks. Seems to be no end to the exotica fruits..." said Blanche. "What you thinking now?"

"No end to it," he said, his gaze wandering off again. "We should get back to Saigon. We need to get help." He rubbed his head with the end of the knife. "Loan is good to hide us overnight, but I don't want to put him in danger any more than we might've already. We need to get to the bottom of this blackmail crap."

"Any ideas about where to go for help? It's our word against theirs. Tam Li says there's no paper trail."

"I'm working on it as we speak," said Stick. "We need something ... solid."

"Now you sound like Tam Li," said Blanche. "You're not going to kill anyone. Are you?" She didn't want to go there, but she had to ask. Tam Li has been fierce on the subject of ending the whole thing. Violently. But what they needed was sufficient diversion. More death and killing wasn't going to solve anything in this place that had seen too much of it.

Stick grunted. "Killing. Don't do no damn good. Mostly."

Jean walked unsteadily over the patio stones toward them. She fell into a chair opposite Stick and Blanche. "Good morning. It is, isn't it?" Her eyes were so puffy that they were almost closed, but she was smiling. "How's your head, Stick?"

"Good. How are you? Sapodilla?"

Jean's eyes opened slightly. She shook her head. "I could use some tea bags on my eyes. It was a bad night. Mom woke up mumbling and sweating. She's still asleep."

Blanche passed her a basket of sticky buns and a cup of tea. "We've got problems—especially with what she's been through. And now we're in the mix. We're going to have to think of something." She looked warily at Stick. "Something that doesn't involve murder and more mayhem."

He appeared not to hear her as he piled fruit remnants into a neat little stack.

"I can't think. I'm in a daze," said Jean. She chewed automatically. "I don't know what I'd do without you two."

"Well, here's the deal." Stick stood up abruptly. The chair skidded sharply over the stones, and Blanche winced. "We're gonna head back to Saigon, and all you ladies are gonna bunk at my place. I'm sure Tam Li won't mind a bit if we borrow her car. I can leave mine in My Tho for now. Seriously, we're going to get a handle on this here situation. One way or tuther." He hitched his jeans up and stomped into the house. Presumably to have a word with their host.

Jean looked at Blanche and shrugged, but her lips quivered. "I don't know, Blanche…"

"Another bun?" Her mind was far from buns. Ideas percolated in Blanche's brain. They could run, but it seemed to be getting increasingly difficult to hide. It was time to take this matter in another direction. She was itching to get back to Saigon and find a way out of this mess.

———

Stick lived in Cholon, the Chinatown of Saigon. The buildings seemed to hold each other up, one modern aluminum and brick and plywood job next to an elegant, ancient temple of Chinese design.

Stick's "house" looked like a temple. The Temple of No Apology, Blanche silently named it. It stuck out with its green tile roof, like a wig askew, atop red walls scrolled with dragons and vines, snakes, and floral motifs. Embossed and carved and peeling in red paint. A paneled door gleamed shiny black, its brass hardware polished. The structure tilted precariously, but the door sported a bold, proud entrance.

"Home sweet home," said Stick, pointing the way after ditching the car in a hidden lot at yet another friend's property. He hurried them along the street, all of them checking alleyways and passersby. "You ladies, get inside. Quick."

"And then we'll decide…" said Blanche.

"I sure hope so," said Jean. The dim entry smelled of spicy, musty cooking odors. Blanche also got a good whiff of dog and sandalwood—the origin of which made her wonder about Stick and his neighbors. They ascended another set of steps to Stick's living quarters, a warren of small spare rooms with couches and throws, books, pillows, candles, Buddhas, and several signed footballs and baseballs on pedestals. A counter separated the kitchen area from the living room in the front of the apartment. Antique patterned rugs criss-crossed each other on the wooden floor, swept clean, and the windows front and back let in the soft afternoon light.

"Set yourselves down," Stick said. "*Mi casa es su casa.*" He pointed to the couches and busily turned on floor lamps with rice-paper shades. A glow flooded the large room. Stick's decorating stuck to black and red, mostly. With a large American flag on one wall next to a large brass Buddha. Blanche felt safe here, for now.

He opened a window, and motorbikes beep-beeped … and birds chirp-chirped? Indeed, in one corner, an elaborate white wicker cage was home to two brown-tipped yellow birds that sang their hearts out. "Meet Sig and Martha. Happy to see me, guys?" Stick replaced the newspaper on the bottom of the cage, dumped some seed in a small cup, and poured water in their little trough.

"Are they a happy couple?" Blanche curled up, her legs under her, and pounded a pillow.

"Don't have any idea. Shop owner was fixin' to let them go, and I rescued them. Been here chitterin' and chirpin' nye on five years." He pursed his lips at the birds and cooed.

"Stick. Have you ever been a happy couple?" *Bang Murninghan, at it again. Hope that wasn't too rude.*

"Blanche! What kind of question is that?" Jean's tone was a cross between schoolmarm and affection.

"I'm sorry. Don't mean to be nosy," said Blanche.

"You can be anything you like," said Stick. "I was a couple. Once. My-Kai, my beautiful pearl. Died of the orange...."

He picked up a framed photo and showed them a beautiful young woman, perhaps Vietnamese, hair pulled back, a smile that nearly covered her face. "We had some good years. Great ones..."

"The orange?" But Blanche knew, even as the words escaped.

"Yeah. Agent Orange. Funny, they call it that. Barrels of herbicide with orange markings, but the stuff inside is poison of the worst color. During the drop, it killed everything in its path. Jungle, and people. She'd fled her village and lived here, but the sickness got her." He set the picture back on the narrow bookcase next to a candle and a dish of jewelry. "Was me who killed her. Sure as shootin'," he mumbled.

Blanche uncurled herself and went over to Stick. "You didn't." She reached up and rested her hand on his shoulder. "Remember what you told me? On the boat? I wished my dad had never come here, but you said it was the right thing. At the time. Stick, you always seem to do the right thing."

He hunched his shoulders and shook his head. Blanche barely came up past his chest. She patted his arm. The late sun burst into the room, the dust shifting in the light.

"You've done so much," she said. "No, you *do* so much." Tam Li and Jean nodded vigorously.

"Caint be 'nuff."

Blanche paced to the window and back to the bookcase, where Stick moved around the candle and a bunch of dried roses. "Seems you've had enough, or at least enough of this crew," she said. "Where's it all gonna end?"

He grinned then—with a touch of irritation. "We're not done with this little adventure. Gotta find those dudes who're causing all the trouble and finish it off. Won't be no peace 'til we do."

Blanche plunked down on the couch next to Jean. "Well, that's true."

"Yo daddy would be proud," he said, but his mood was somber.

She looked up at him quickly. "Ya think? What would *he* do?"

"Same as any old grunt. Get out there and get 'er done." He twirled a key ring and checked around the room. "You ladies gonna be comfy here for a while?"

"Couldn't be better." Jean chimed in. "You going somewhere?"

"Steppin' out. Shortly, not just now."

"I'm sorry about all this, Mr. Stick," said Tam Li. She wrapped her arm around her daughter and shook her head.

"Let 'em keep a-comin'. Ducks and creepers. And blackmailers?" Stick seemed to make the impossible manageable. He'd been their savior and the perfect guide—and so had Thuy, who had taken off to see her family in Pleiku. He walked into the kitchen area and set a pot on the element. "Tea?" he called out. "Our answer to everything. And maybe a shot or two of whiskey." He set a tray on the counter and loaded it with cups, glasses, and a bottle.

His determination was contagious. Blanche focused on that. She got up and started pacing again. "I've got an idea."

"I'll bet." He came into the living room with the tray and set it down.

"We need to get out of here. Get ahead of them."

Stick shook his head. "Seems they been ahead of us."

"No more."

"What you got?"

"There are authorities, Stick. If not the Officer Bungs of the world, maybe someone at the consulate can help us out."

Stick sat across from them and raked his scraggly beard. "I don't know. Maybe. We can check it out. Right now, best you just sit tight. Nothing doing tonight anyways."

Blanche poured whiskey into the sugary tea and sniffed the heady aroma. The alcohol did its strange, contradictory work, but Blanche, after all, was beginning to wonder if there was a future in it. She was relaxed and anxious at once. "Tomorrow, for sure."

"We'll talk." He put the keys on his belt. "Promise you won't go running off? Consulate closed now, and there's no place to run. Do *not* call Officer Bung."

"No kidding," she mumbled.

"I'll be back soon," he said. He went over and peered down into the street. He locked the window and turned on an overhead fan. "Kim's bringin' rice and things over. He be here soon. And he can get in. Don't let nobody else up here, ain't expecting nobody." He stacked some newspapers, picked up his cup and saucer, and slid them onto the counter. He winked and headed for the door.

"Stick!" Blanche called after him. But he was gone. Blanche set the cup down and frowned.

Tam Li, clearly, was fretting. "Blanche, what are we going to do? I'm sure Hank had no idea this would be...." She looked at Jean for reassurance, but Jean looked away. "What is it, Jean?"

"Dad meant well, about a lot of things. He cared about us. You, too, Blanche, and he didn't even know you. That's about all I can say."

"Hank knew Thomas. We're sort of ... one big family, I guess, and families stick together," said Blanche. "It'll be all right." She was shaky on the details of how that would happen, but it would happen. "We'll do it. Like Stick says, we'll get 'er done." *Or die trying.*

Thirty-Three
What's Old Is News

KIM SET BOXES OF COOKED RICE, spring rolls, and shredded pork and vegetables on the kitchen counter. "From Mr. Stick and The Follies. *Bon appetit*," he said. He spooned the rice into small bowls and produced sets of chopsticks.

"So kind of you, Kim, to come out at this hour," said Blanche, realizing she'd lost track of time. It had to be close to midnight. She reached for the chopsticks, determined to conquer *something*. "Do you know where Stick went?"

"Mr. Stick be back soon," said Kim. "He say, no worry."

Well, that's easier said. Blanche chomped into the pork and veggies and sprinkled the rice liberally with fish sauce. She was getting used to the pungent anchovy-based *nuoc mam*.

They ate, drank, and settled restlessly around the room, reading old *Stars & Stripes*. Blanche had found a copy of *Heart of Darkness* but didn't have the heart to keep reading. She couldn't sit still anyway. She found Stick's closet of whiskey and refortified herself. It was a bad idea. She made herself close her eyes, but she was soon up pacing the room.

Footsteps stomped up the stairs. "Al-lo!"

"Stick?" Blanche looked toward the doors and windows front and back for an exit, just in case.

Loud voices. Excited French, English, and Vietnamese, yelling over each other. The racket echoed in the stairwell. Whoever was out there paused. Kim dropped a roll on the counter and pulled a gun from his belt. Pointed it at the door.

"No! Kim!" Blanche leapt to the side of the door and yanked an umbrella out of a bucket of walking sticks.

"What is going on?" hissed Jean. Tam Li cowered into a bank of pillows.

"Have no idea."

"You're getting good at that, Bang," Jean said, eyeing the makeshift weapon. "Drop it and get over here. *Now*." She pulled at her mother's arm and scooted over on the banquette.

The door flew open, and so did the umbrella as Stick bounded into the room. He fought the voluminous blue nylon and pointy spokes. "What are you doing?" He emerged. "Blanche, that's bad luck!"

She wrestled the umbrella closed and stashed it in the bucket. "Sorry, Stick. I'm getting so jumpy."

"I guess," he said, nodding at Kim, hitching up his keys.

Kim was still at his post with the gun drawn. He lowered it, recognition flickering across his face, and he holstered it casually. He and Stick went through a complicated series of fist bumps, finger signs, and chest thumps.

"Who you talkin' to out there?" Blanche drew her hands over her face.

"The neighbors. Askin', they see anyone funny, and the answer is 'no,'" Stick said. "But I'm not feeling good about any of this. I'm gonna see about a bodyguard for y'all."

Blanche's face felt hot; she raked her fingers through her hair, now a mass of springs. The booze had worn off, and she was feeling quite ragged. "Why do we need a bodyguard?"

Jean crossed her arms and huffed loudly. "When do we *not* need one…".

"What's the game plan, Stick? The more I think about it … we need to get help. We should go to the American authorities. What do you say?" she said.

"Girl, what authority you talkin' 'bout? This here's a Communist country. Ain't Tampa, or that little old island of yours."

Blanche flopped down on the cushion, her brain working itself into a frenzy. "We can't let this go, Stick. They're out there."

"I know, I know. We caint do anything now. Look, Blanche, it's dark, it's late! For now, just sit tight."

She was off walking in circles, the empty teacup in her hand.

Stick shook his head. "You're safe here. Kim's gonna hang around," he said. Kim acknowledged with a nod. "You ladies bed down. I got plenty of cots and blankets. Some T-shirts in the drawers." He beckoned them toward a couple of back rooms. "Kim's gotta gun, and *nobody* gets past Kim."

Kim stood like a sentry at the kitchen counter. The gun was out of sight, but the robotic movement of the teacup to his lips and the stony look on his face was only minimally reassuring. He wasn't much taller than Blanche, and he wasn't all that scary except for the expression. Blanche would not want to wrangle with him.

The door banged shut behind Stick. Blanche followed Jean and Tam Li to the back of the apartment. She put on one of Stick's T-shirts, which was like wearing a tent, and crept under the cover of an old Army blanket in the den. Jean and Tam Li took the other room. Blanche didn't think she'd fall asleep, but in no time, it was lights out.

———

Blanche was wide awake the next morning at seven. Kim had gone sometime in the wee hours, leaving a scribbled message that said the "base camp" was secure. *Stick must have sat in on that English lesson.*

She made herself some tea and chewed on a leftover dumpling.

An hour until the consulate opened.

Jean emerged from the back of the apartment. Her bale of long black hair framed her face, and her T-shirt was askew. "Mornin'," she said and gave Blanche a peremptory hug. "Got any more of those dumplings?"

Blanche handed her the paper tray and a bottle of fish sauce. "Should we get dressed? Same old thing? I guess we've done that. Three days ago. We need to get over to the Caravelle and change—and we need to see Rob."

Jean plopped on a kitchen stool, a half-eaten dumpling, neglected. "How did it come to this, Blanche?"

"Cheer up. We have Mom, and we're not gonna lose her now!"

At that, Tam Li called out, "Good morning!"

"Look, it's been *hours* since Stick left," said Blanche. "We have to make a move. Can't just sit here." She stood up abruptly, tea sloshing out of her cup.

Tam Li joined them and sat down next to Jean on the couch. They'd all gotten into Stick's stash of T-shirts for the night, and now the three of them read:

"Butter Up and Pucker Up. I'm comin' for Yooooou."

"I Cain't Give You Nothin' But Love, BAAAABY."

"Spinach Is My Middle Name."

Jean looked down at her "butter" shirt. "Well, at least he more or less has the punctuation...."

"I care less about his editing skills and more about where the heck he went," said Blanche. Her T-shirt nearly brushed the floor. It was a 4X; Blanche was a child's fourteen.

Jean pulled her knees up into a ball under her shirt. "You wanna leave? Now? Shouldn't we wait for him? He said he'd be back soon."

"*Soon* has come and gone," said Blanche. "Let's get out of here. I'll leave him a note."

—⁓—

Rob greeted them at the door of the consulate. Animated and taller than Blanche remembered. He still had a stain on his shirt front, but the rest of him was reasonably neat. He reached for Blanche's hand and pumped it up and down, smiling and nodding at his trio of visitors.

Rob's enthusiastic greeting eclipsed all complaints of thugs and blackmail. He shook Tam Li's hand warmly.

"Bet I know who *this* is!" He smiled broadly, still holding on to Tam Li, his gaze shifting from her to Jean and back. "So happy you found each other…."

"How did you know?" Jean stood arm in arm with her mother. The two beamed with happiness.

"Well, all I need to do is look at you two!" His face lit up. "And Sister Joseph at the Tu Do. We did some calling around, and she got back to us. She'd gone through some old records and traced a donation from the Dangs. She had a good idea you were on the right track, and I was just waiting to hear. Now I see for myself!"

"We supported the hospital for many years," said Tam Li. "Most of those donations were anonymous, but we could not forget her kindness. I'm surprised she had any record."

"Just some old notes. She took a chance because if the authorities had found out, it would have been bad for Tu Do. But thank heavens!" He laughed and rolled his eyes. "I just heard and haven't been able to reach you for an update. Sister could not reach you either. Miss Blanche, aren't you all at the Caravelle?"

"Yes, we were … and are. But we went off to look for Tam Li. And our friend, Stick, knows so many people…."

"That's it, follow every lead. Shoe leather, like Kathy said." He cleared his throat and tugged at the knot in his tie. "Very well." He lowered his voice, and his eyebrows drew together. His total focus was on Blanche. "I have other news." He motioned for them to follow him into the lounge. Blanche began to sweat. She didn't know why, except that something crept over her. An eerie feeling of light and shadow. She wanted to let go and begin blabbering, but she didn't. Couldn't.

"What is it." It was not a question. Blanche's stomach dropped. She wouldn't give in to the premonition. She would go along and *listen* and somehow contain the wobbling in her legs.

"Let's sit down over here," he said, pointing to some chairs in the corner of the lounge.

Once seated but hardly settled, Blanche burst out. "News, you say?"

He leaned forward and took her hands. Then he let her have it. "It's your father," he said. "Specialist Thomas Xavier Fox. We found him."

Thirty-Four

Magic Cup

IT IS A GOOD THING I'M SITTING.

Blanche held the edges of her chair for dear life. She could feel a lightness in her head, and the walls were closing in… Was that a ringing in her ears? Jean was talking to her, Tam Li was … cooing? A male voice. Rob. Then Kathy Martell rushed down the hallway toward her and handed her a glass of water. The world slowly began to come back, a world that included her father. She didn't want to talk; she just wanted to sit and hear again Rob's words: "We found him."

She drank off half the water. Chairs glided over the carpet closer to her. Smiling people surrounded her. Someone patted her hand. Rob had gone away, and now he was walking back, flipping through a folder. He sat, tilted his head at Blanche, and waited. Several heartbeats. Blanche stared at the folder.

He held it open. "They found remains," he said gently. "There was not much evidence at the site, but what was recovered has been positively identified as the remains of Thomas X. Fox." He bent over a page and read: "Dog tags with a p-38 attached, several bone fragments, femur, etc., fabric remnants…." He looked up then. "And a coffee cup. Definitely your dad's."

"Coffee cup?"

"Yes, fashioned distinctly, according to reports."

"Reports? But how?"

"Witnesses filed details." Here he nodded at Jean. "The Defense Department uses this type of thing, of course, and they have teams that go out regularly to scour the jungle and other sites for those missing in action. We don't stop."

"Almost thirty years later...."

"Doesn't matter. We keep on until we find them."

Blanche sat back. There were so many questions that buzzed around in her head, but for now, she let him talk of reports and findings and coordinates and teams. It was a blur, but she was glad, a warm spot widening and taking over, filling her up.

Jean had been sitting quietly, her eyes down. Her fingers worked nervously in her lap. "It's time. For more."

"What now?" Blanche could feel herself coming to, her temperature rising. She didn't want the glow to leave, but what was this? Was Jean holding back? *Again?* They had been down that road before, and it had been bumpy.

"Wait! Don't get mad, Blanche, and run off or something." Jean half stood, her eyes unusually bright. "I hoped this day would come and, oh, how my dad hoped for it. I wish he could know... But there was never any point in counting on it." She sat down. "Rob? Please. Help."

"Jean's father? Henry McMahon?" He looked at Blanche, his demeanor business-like. "You know he was there when your father disappeared. He was a witness on that patrol." He put his elbows on his knees and balanced the open folder in two hands. "Mr. McMahon gave us the coordinates of the incident, and over the years, he wrote and called. He described that day. What he could remember and what came back to him. Over and over again. He contacted us on a regular basis, so much so they tell me that he was on a first-name basis with some in the Defense Department."

The pride in Jean's face, the hint of love in Tam Li's, made Blanche's heart race. "Oh, Jean, you…" Blanche grabbed Jean's hand.

Jean struggled with the words while Blanche held on. Jean drew back and looked Blanche in the eye. "He wouldn't stop. He badgered every department in the government. He wanted you to know—someday. He didn't know when."

"But what about the coffee cup? How do you know it's his?" Blanche's throat caught on the words as Rob opened the folder.

"It's distinctive," he said. "Mr. McMahon described all their gear, including Thomas's coffee cup made out of a fruit can. It was a piece of pride. Hank said he teased him about it, but Thomas had grown fond of his handiwork, the lid peeled back and folded into a handle. It hung from his pack, always, and, fortunately, scavengers didn't care about an empty can. Only weaponry and items they could sell off. The details are in this report." He paged through the folder. "And something else. A bit unusual. Your father filed identifying papers and an 'acknowledgment of paternity' with Rose Murninghan's name and dates of expected delivery." He looked up at Blanche. "You."

Blanche choked. "Then why didn't they find me?"

"No date of delivery, no address. When the paperwork went through the mill, Thomas Fox's mother, the contact, was deceased. It's one of those bureaucratic … missteps." He stood up abruptly, nervously, righting the papers in the folder, then he sat down again. "Now you're here. We'll finish up the details and get this settled. Right away."

Blanche reached for the folder, and he handed it to her. The black and white forms, the pile of papers, copies of letters, all the words swimming in front of her eyes.

"When do I get his … effects?"

"They are at a processing center and have been there, being cataloged. We didn't have a recent contact for Mr. Fox. We couldn't reach Mr. McMahon. I understand he was quite ill and now has passed away."

"I wish he'd known. I think this search kept him alive longer than the time he had," said Jean. "He just wouldn't give up."

"You didn't either, Jean." Blanche held the folder tightly. She wanted to run away and read every word of it, even the stuff she knew would be indecipherable.

"The items and the remains will be returned to you at the time and place you choose. You may wish to make burial arrangements."

Burial arrangements? All she could think about was a rusty coffee cup that had been her father's and would soon be hers. "The coffee cup. When do I get that?"

"Soon," he said. "It's yours."

"My father's."

—⁓—

"Uh, Rob, we have some other business," said Jean. Tam Li twisted her fingers and looked around the room like she was searching for a place to hide. Blanche still sat with a folder full of details involving her father's recovery. She clutched it to her middle. She was slightly dazed, but now she came to when Jean brought up the "business."

"Yes. Major business," said Blanche.

"My mother has been blackmailed for decades. And we have recently been attacked. In Hoi An, and more recently in Can Tho. We need to do something to call off these people...."

"You've been *attacked*?" His eyes darted over each of them, a look of concern clouding his expression. "Are you all right?"

"Yes, yes." Blanche squeezed Jean's arm. "We're pretty resilient and quick."

"Gotta be," said Jean.

"Did you call the police?"

"Everyone says not to," said Blanche.

"That's true, there are problems. Especially with visitors," said Rob. "We have little recourse. But with proof of what you say, we might be able to do something about it. We could get an investigation started and pursue recovery and protection...."

"I don't care about recovery of anything," said Tam Li fiercely. "But protection, yes, especially for the girls. And I—we—want to move on. I want them to leave me and my daughter and all of us alone so we can live in peace and keep our bottling operation."

"It will be difficult," Rob said firmly. "It's your word against theirs. I'm being the devil's advocate here, but you know they play hardball with outside 'interference,' as many in the Party prefer to call us."

Jean and Blanche deflated like the air had been let out of them, but Tam Li was staunch. "What they do is against the law. All laws. Everywhere."

"There must be a way," said Blanche. "They can't do this."

Rob's demeanor had not changed. He put on the face of the bureaucrat, and it stayed fixed. Then he stood up. "One minute. Please wait here." He strode out of the lounge–Blanche was hoping–to go and perform some diplomatic magic.

Blanche turned to Tam Li. "I know records were destroyed, and you probably didn't keep any. But, *nothing?*"

Tam Li appeared to go into that shell of hers, part fear and part retreat to safety. She held tightly to Jean's hand; her mouth clamped into a tense refusal of reality. Blanche's eyes pleaded with Jean. She shook her head. They looked up to see Rob striding back toward them, riffling through another set of papers.

He scooted the chair close to Tam Li. "Look, like I said, it's your word against theirs. Do you have any proof of these ... transactions?"

"I do not know if this will work." Tam Li looked at Blanche for reassurance. "I am so reluctant..."

"Don't be," urged Blanche. "It's time. If you have anything, it might help."

Tam Li seemed skeptical. The ticking clock was maddening. But then Tam Li whispered, "I have diaries. They are hidden on the property. There is personal information in them. But there are remarks of this business happening. For decades."

Rob shot up, dropped the papers on a table, and turned around, his hands on his head. This was an odd dance for a consulate employee, but Blanche was intrigued and happy to see this version of the Irish jig.

"That's it," he said. "Are the entries dated? Do you have *any* witnesses?"

"Oh, yes, dates, times, places, and I do have my trusted staff. I wanted to track for myself the amounts of money and to whom it went." She frowned and shook her head. "Not that it would ever make any difference."

He grabbed Tam Li's hand and shook it. "It makes a whole lot of difference! I'd like to get it going. I can't guarantee the outcome, but, obviously, with records and the consul's insistence, we should be able to track these people or warn them away. Get you safe and serve some protection from these ... thugs. Catching them might be another matter, but if they find out they've been discovered, a Communist prison may be incentive enough to make them want to change their line of work."

Tam Li scooted her chair back. "No! You can't do that. They're devious. They hide. They may come out and hurt my daughter. And Blanche, and Mr. Stick."

"Mom! Slow down. They aren't going to do a thing to us. Anymore." Her conviction trailed off.

Blanche, still gripping the folder, faced Tam Li. "We need to get to the bottom of this, or they will keep at it. They *will* get to you, and Jean—and me—if we don't get *them*."

"She's right, Mom," said Jean. "We need to pursue this."

"It's a problem, the corruption," said Rob. "One that's not so uncommon."

"You need to do what you can, Tam Li. You have the ammunition," said Blanche quietly. "You need to trust … Rob. And the US government?"

Jean cast Blanche a sideways glance. "Really?"

"They did find Specialist Fox. They help American citizens. And your mother. Come on, Jean."

Tam Li nodded, and so did Jean.

"It's a long shot. Get those diaries and get back to us. We'll get on it," said Rob. "In the meantime, be careful. They're still out there."

Thirty-Five

Four Down

THUY WAS AT THE WHEEL, waiting for them outside the consulate. Blanche walked behind Tam Li and Jean. She hugged the folder Rob had given to her, thinking about her father. He was not forgotten; they had cared about him all these years, and they'd found him. His case had been ongoing with the other MIA's, and thanks to Hank, additional information had been added over the years. It was a great feeling; she was elated, buoyant. *Then why do I feel so spooked? And not in a good way.*

She wanted to see Stick and fill him in on the details. He would understand, not that Jean didn't, but Stick had been there. He'd been *here*. A long time. They'd reached him at home after they finished the business at the consulate, and he'd promised to bring Tam Li's car around to the Caravelle. She needed to get back to Can Tho and pick up her diaries. The matter was more or less settled, with the details to be worked out. But at least it was a start to stopping the blackmailers. *And Marie?* The woman's involvement bugged Blanche. She had to be behind this trouble. Getting the blackmailers, and tying her into it, were steps in the right direction.

Jean and Tam Li climbed into the car. Blanche sat in the front seat. "Hello, Thuy." The guide looked out her window to the left, a short little grunt for hello. She was not her usual ebullient self. Blanche scrunched into the seat and rolled down the window. "Back to the Caravelle, then? We've been in these clothes for three days! Whew!" Thuy gave Blanche a weak smile.

Maybe it's the lack of deodorant … or something else? All Blanche could think about was a warm bath, a clean outfit, maybe a nap. And nailing some thugs in the bargain!

"Yes, we go to hotel. *Tout suite.*" Thuy cut off motorbikes and cyclos that managed to swim around them, avoiding a re-enactment of duck soup. Her driving was brash and brave at once. Blanche looked forward to getting out of the car. Her stomach was doing flip-flops.

Blanche was getting the hang of streets in Saigon by now—after more than a week of sightseeing and mishap. They were now well out of the district of hotels, restaurants, and shops. The streets were desolate, unusually empty for such a bustling city. Then it hit Blanche. *This is not the way to the Caravelle.* She shot Thuy a look. The driver, her head barely clearing the steering wheel, held it at ten and two and careened down an alley.

What now?

Blanche turned in the seat and caught the fright in Jean's eyes. "We certainly are making good time. Maybe too good," said Jean, weakly.

"Yes, need horn, luck, and prayer to drive here. I suggest pray now."

Blanche had a cold feeling. A lump of dread formed in the pit of her stomach, the inevitable tug of being pulled downward. She needed to get hold of this situation. "Why is that, Thuy? *Where are we going?*"

For answer, Thuy yanked the wheel and headed down another side street into an area with warehouses and a large parking lot on the river. "This is not the way to the Caravelle!" yelled Blanche. "What is going on?"

Thuy lurched to a stop in front of double doors on a corrugated structure. The doors flew open and two men in black charged at the car. They wore baseball caps and masks, but Blanche was pretty certain it was the same bunch who had bedeviled them in Can Tho—and probably Hoi An. "*What the...!*"

"*...hell!*" From the back seat.

Tam Li huddled low to the floor. Thuy didn't say a word, her hands still firmly gripping the wheel. She stared straight ahead as one of the thugs reached for the door of the passenger seat.

"Thuy!" Blanche yelled. She went for the lock. Too late! He grabbed her arm and dragged her out of the car and across the pavement. "Let go of me, you idiot! I'm not going anywhere with you!" The old adrenalin kicked in, the bile of longstanding anger against these tormentors churning. "*No more.*"

The black mask complained hoarsely–mostly in Vietnamese with a shot of French. Blanche dug in while he pulled at her.

His partner worked on the back door. Jean had been quicker than Blanche. The door was locked, but he still fussed with it. Blanche looked up to see Jean's bag fly over the front seat and knock Thuy a good one. She bounced up. Jean hit her again, and she slammed down on the horn.

"You need horn? I'll give you horn," yelled Jean.

Blanche parried with the thug in black. He was short, that was good, but so was she. It was fortunate they'd picked a country to get into trouble in where the people were a near match to her height and weight. She wasn't sure about his prowess, but his eyes told her he was frantic, and that was good, too.

He's frantic, and I'm pissed.

She didn't see any weapons on him, but that didn't mean there weren't any. She scooted around the car, trying to put the fender between him and her. Then, suddenly, it dawned: Haasi and the Kick and Chop. She and Haasi had worked on the maneuver after another misadventure. *Just in case.* Blanche was short on weapons, but she had the one she always carried—readily available when needed—her strength in anger. It flared from spark to full-blown blaze in seconds.

She feinted like she was giving up. She let him get a little closer. She'd gotten out of his grasp, and now he planted himself in front of her, poised to spring at her. It was a bad move for him. He was wide open.

Blanche let him have it in a most vulnerable spot. The element of surprise. He wasn't expecting it. *Oooooh!* He doubled over, both hands on his lower extremity. *Perfect!* She whacked him a good one on the back of the neck and then came up under his chin with her foot. In a split second, he was done for. Kick, kick, chop, chop. And done. *Thank you, Haasi.*

The glass in the back window was smashed in. The horn was still blaring. But the party was over. Blanche looked up to see a uniformed person marching toward them, a baton swinging in his hand. He raised it and cold-conked the black-clad man who was working to get Jean and Tam Li out of the back seat through the window. The uniform was unusually tall. He raised his eyebrows at the thug laid out on the pavement and grabbed the other by the scruff of his neck. A back-up detail, chattering on a radio, was right behind him. One of them pulled Thuy out of the front seat. She'd been knocked out, and now was coming around in a daze. The police shoved them together, all of them with glum looks on their faces.

"Amateurs," said Blanche. She stomped over to Thuy, her hat askew. "You! How could you do this?"

"*Viet kieu,*" Thuy spat at the ground near Jean, a look of scorn on her face. The guard who had hold of her shirt shook the little driver until her hat flew off and rolled away.

"Sorry, madame," he said, addressing Jean. "We see all, not so good."

One of the officials began to impound the car, another noted the facts, including names and passport numbers. "You will need to go to police station. Much paperwork." He handed Blanche a card with an address and time on it. "The police will see you tomorrow, please. And now we will get ride for you." He put his finger to his visor and crisply turned on his heel.

Tam Li climbed out of the back seat and hung onto Jean. Blanche suddenly felt weak with relief. "At least we didn't get Officer Bung-ed," she said.

"No, we've been Thuy-ed," said Jean. "Didn't see that one coming."

———❦———

"That was some kick chop, Blanche. Got the full report," said Stick. He closed one eye and looked her up and down. "Don't know where you store it, but I'd hate to be on your bad side."

"That'll never happen." Blanche laughed. "Those guys—and one untrusty driver—are all locked up. We went over to the station this morning and sealed it."

"Good. You should feel pretty set. Lucky you ran into a bunch of decent po-po, or it would have been over for you. The consulate is going to follow up with the police about this blackmailing and the attacks. That little piece of paper you handed them from the hotel mugging should help identify the guy." Stick leaned back in the leather armchair at the fine Italian dining establishment in the Caravelle. "We have the circle of life. And then we have the circle of scum."

"Do tell, and don't hold back," said Blanche. She tore her baguette into hunks and dipped it in the marinara.

"I know people who know people."

"I know," said Blanche. Jean laughed, and Tam Li looked content and safe. She picked at a pile of risotto with herbs and prawns.

"You know it was Marie. She organized this little crew some time back, kept it on the down-low, and hired the help as the years went along, including, lately, your guide and driver, Thuy. Money talks, I'm afraid. It wasn't hard for Marie to make the connections after she knew you were here looking for Tam Li."

"How did you find out, Stick? I'm sure you didn't just call her up and ask," said Jean.

Stick's loud guffaw filled that corner of the candle-lit restaurant. Two patrons looked their way and went back to their cannoli. "No, not exactly. You led the way, but I guess you could say my connections from Saigon to Hoi An helped."

"Is that where you went?" said Blanche. She was elated to have it all come together. And with Stick's help, once again.

"Yeah, that's where I went. To Hoi An." He drank off half his glass of red. "And it's a bad one…"

"Bad? What happened? Hope you turned in Marie."

"You know the story about cutting off the snake's head? Sometimes it's the only way to get rid of the creature." He forked a large square of lasagna. He chewed contemplatively.

"You didn't kill her, Stick." Blanche had mixed feelings about getting rid of the person who caused a lot of harm and trouble. She didn't want to hear of cold-blooded murder, as if there were any other kind.

"Didn't have to. You'd found her out; she knew it was coming. Probably had a sense about it. She sunk herself," he said. "I done a little detective work, got my, ahem, ducks in a row, so to speak, and went to visit her. My persuasive skills are kinda blunt sometimes: I says to her, lay off, or else. Aside from authorities and wheels that creak slow-like, I says, I got people who will not cotton to your business with Tam Li. Cease and desist."

"So that was it? She agreed to back off?"

"She run off." He downed the last of the chianti. "She had a vehicle at her disposal. Me, I had my crotch rocket. Sorry, my motorcycle. I gave chase. It ended bad. She's dead."

They took in a collective breath. "An accident? And you got out of there? Clean?"

"Clean. No one ever said that 'bout me."

"But you didn't..." Blanche said.

"Miss Blanche, it's done and clean." He got up, once again dispensing with the restaurant tab. "Case closed."

"Stick! Where you going?" Blanche was still half-glass full with a pile of meatballs in front of her.

"You ladies just relax," he said, smiling all around the table. "I got me some business to attend to." He gave Blanche a squeeze on the shoulder, lingered there for a bit, a blank somewhat sad look on his face. And then he was gone.

"Just like that," said Jean, shaking her head.

"Just like that," said Blanche. She couldn't help feeling a spirit had whisked itself out of the dining room. He had come and gone. She knew she'd never see him again.

Thirty-Six

Good to Go

OF COURSE, THE TAB HAD BEEN PAID at the Italian restaurant in the Caravelle. Blanche wasn't surprised, but just once, she would have liked to get ahead of Stick. It wasn't meant to be.

When the three went up to their hotel room, they found a spray of orchids, a set of keys (to Tam Li's car), and a letter from Stick, the handwriting surprisingly florid and careful:

Dear Ladies,

Don't like good-byes, never have. Been too many of them. So, I just write it down here, and that will suffice. Besides, Walter Winchell Dahlkamp's got some writing skills and might as well use them.

We had quite an adventure together. You got your mom, Jean, and Blanche, you got your dad, after a fashion. You done a good job, Blanche, getting after it. You remember that your dad is always with you, no matter you can't see him. But I guess you know that. I feel like I know him, anyways. He's right there looking over your shoulder.

I got to leave now, got a ride to pick up my car. See about Phuong. You take care now and have a good fly-over home.

Maybe I see you over there someday, and when an old dude comes around, one in need of a haircut, dragging a surfboard, a case of brewskis at hand, might be old Stick landing on your doorstep, Blanche, looking to get some cheering up. I got to say, you cheered me up more than you ever know. I'll never forget you.

Stick

Blanche fell back into a chair near the window. She looked out at the street, the sunlight, the flood of bikes. The people passing by, the world spinning. Indeed, the ends were coming together. "Wow, I miss him already," she whispered.

"We'll see him again, Blanche, I know we will," said Jean, squeezing her mother's hand. The "twins" perched on the edge of the fluffy queen-sized bed looked like two regal birds in a nest. "There's something we should talk about, Blanche. Now that we have more or less solved *the problem.*"

Blanche looked up, the letter pressed tightly against her chest. She smiled. "Yes, I know. Bet I can tell what you're gonna say."

"Stick knew. You can kinda tell it from his letter." Jean stood up and hugged Blanche, holding her by her shoulders. "I'm staying, at least for now. Rob will have more paperwork. Mom called him this morning. He's going to help me with the regs to make it happen. I can't leave, Mom, not after all this." Tam Li was smiling, her delicate hands folded in her lap.

Blanche was happy. Stick was helping his friend; Jean was with her mom, and the goons were done. *My father is found!* She was good to go.

———

Blanche sat on her porch at her cabin on Santa Maria Island. The Gulf lapped rhythmically over the white sand; the gulls circled lazily. She wore a black sheath and black wedges—heels were not functional in a cemetery, she'd decided, and she was right about that. She'd managed the spongy grass around her dad's casket just fine, even when her knees almost gave way a couple of times.

It was late afternoon now, and it had been a long day burying Dad. What they'd found of Thomas Fox was now resting in the Pokatoy cemetery next to Rose Murninghan and Gran. Blanche had insisted. He could have gone to Arlington, but Blanche knew Rose and Thomas would want to be together. Blanche was still searching for Thomas Fox's relatives and hadn't found anyone. But she'd keep looking.

Haasi, Liza, Jack, and Cap had been there, and they would all get together later for dinner at Cap's. Now, when the sun was lowering and making its silver path across the Gulf and the wind was down, and the people were retreating for the night, Blanche stood up and went into the living room. She placed what she had of her father—his fruit-can C-rations coffee cup and his Bronze Star—next to Rose's photo on the mantel.

"Hey, Mom," she said.

The decoration had come through, thanks to Hank McMahon's crusade. Specialist Thomas Fox had warned his troop about the explosive device on the tree branch. The record also showed that he'd saved a lieutenant in a knife attack during a VC ambush. Blanche traced her fingers over the shining tip of the star. He never knew, or maybe he did now.

She pushed the cup closer to Rose's photo. The dark green metal had dents and rust. The handle fashioned from the lid turned and beaten into shape with his fingers, a small puncture on its side. It wouldn't be suitable for drinking coffee again, but that wasn't the point. It was perfect for holding memories and dreams.

Acknowledgments

MANY THANKS TO MY GUIDE, Phung Ngoc, and to the hosts and drivers who showed me Hanoi, Hoi An, Ho Chi Minh City (Saigon), and the environs of this beautiful, historic country. Also, thanks to Nhung Bui Langone and U.S. Army Colonel Mike Haas for their personal accounts of Vietnam. The reporting and storytelling of Ly Tran, Bao Ninh, Andrew Pham, Nguyen Phan Que Mai, Kien Nguyen, Frances Fitzgerald, Ken Burns, Karl Marlantes, and Tim O'Brien were invaluable in the writing of this book, as was the military insight of James P. Sullivan, Jr. and Donald "Mick" Sullivan, US Army, and George Reid and James P. Sullivan, III, US Marines.

Thanks go to Judith Anne Horner, my reader and editor. She sees right through Blanche. And many thanks to Elizabeth, Betty, Wally, Jori, and the whole team at Light Messages for their patience and insight.

And, as always, a big hug to Charles for the "writing retreat" and laughs. It never would have happened without that lunch at the Colombia...And his suggestion to visit Vietnam...

A word about the language in *Mission Improbable: Vietnam*— the Vietnamese language is tonal in nature with international influence and many diacritical marks that change the sounds and meanings of the written words. I apologize that the marks are missing in many instances. I'm depending on readers to understand, in the context of usage.

If you ever get a chance to travel on a boat among the "karsts" in the China Sea, talk with the Vietnamese people, eat crunchy red rice at Propaganda, fend off motorbikes in Saigon, visit the city's museums, float out on the Mekong, do it. It's the adventure of a lifetime.

Thank you for reading this latest Blanche Murninghan mystery.

—Nancy Nau Sullivan

About the Author

NANCY NAU SULLIVAN BEGAN WRITING wavy lines at age six, thinking it was the beginning of her first novel. It wasn't. But she didn't stop writing: letters at first, then eight years of newspaper work in high school and college, in editorial posts at New York magazines, and for newspapers throughout the Midwest.

Nancy has a master's in journalism from Marquette University. She grew up outside Chicago but often visited Anna Maria Island, Florida. She returned there with her family and wrote an award-winning memoir *The Last Cadillac* (Walrus 2016) about the years she cared for her father while the kids were still at home, a harrowing adventure of travel, health issues, adolescent angst, with a hurricane thrown in for good measure.

The author returned to that setting to begin the popular *Blanche "Bang" Murninghan Mystery Series* with *Saving Tuna Street*. Having feet of sand, Blanche has ventured into *Trouble Down Mexico Way* to Mexico, now *Mission Improbable: Vietnam*, on to Ireland, and other parts for further mayhem in the series. But she always returns to Santa Maria Island.

Nancy, for the most part, lives in Northwest Indiana.

Follow Nancy:

www.nancynausullivan.com
@NauSullivan.

Other Blanche "Bang" Murninghan Mysteries

Saving Tuna Street

When her dear friend is found murdered in the parking lot of the marina, Blanche Murninghan begins digging into his death. With her friends Liza and Hassi by her side, she stumbles into a pit of greed, murder, drug running, and kidnapping. Blanche has survived her fair share of storms on Santa Maria Island, but this one might just be her last.

Nancy Nau Sullivan

Nancy Nau Sullivan

Trouble Donw Mexico Way

When Blanche Murninghan visits an exhibit of ancient Mayan ruins in Mexico City, she sees that all is not ancient. One of the mummies has a pink hair clip embedded in its hay-like do, and the texture of the skin is not quite right. Blanche, a part-time journalist, starts to dig for some answers and gets tangled in the mystery of the mummy at the Palacio Nacional.